Early Embraces III

Early Embraces III

More true-life stories of women describing their first lesbian experience

Edited by Lindsey Elder

alyson books
los angeles | new york

MANUFACTURED IN THE UNITED STATES OF AMERICA.

THIS TRADE PAPERBACK ORIGINAL IS PUBLISHED BY ALYSON PUBLICATIONS,
P.O. BOX 4371, LOS ANGELES, CALIFORNIA 90078-4371.
DISTRIBUTION IN THE UNITED KINGDOM BY
TURNAROUND PUBLISHER SERVICES LTD.,
UNIT 3, OLYMPIA TRADING ESTATE, COBURG ROAD, WOOD GREEN,
LONDON N22 6TZ ENGLAND.

FIRST EDITION: JUNE 2002

02 03 04 05 06 a 10 9 8 7 6 5 4 3 2 1

ISBN 1-55583-737-9

CREDITS
COVER DESIGN BY LOUIS MANDRAPILIAS.
COVER PHOTOGRAPHY BY SUNNY BAK.

Contents

Introduction

What you're holding in your hands is a diary of female sexual awakening and discovery. It's personal. It's celebratory. It's plain ol' delightful. It's filled with stories of friends who became lovers, adolescents who pushed the boundaries of sexual experimentation, women who discovered their true selves after being "happily" married for years.

When the *Early Embraces* series kicked off with its first volume in 1996, I had no idea that it would become the best-selling phenomenon it has. But now that this third volume is out, it's clear that gay women don't just crave stories of other women's first lesbian experiences—they need them. Our stories are our history, but they can also show us a hope-filled future, and that's the real importance of this book: Amidst all the messages we get that being a lesbian or bisexual is wrong or that it will only lead to a life of loneliness, here we have dozens of women saying, "Being with another woman changed my life—for the better!" (And these brave gals are just a few of the hundreds of women from around the world who submitted stories for this anthology.) These highly personal accounts speak for themselves: They are beautiful affirmations of lesbian sexuality, desire, and love.

If you're reading this book, you've probably already enjoyed your own first lesbian experience, or perhaps you're just beginning to explore the idea of becoming intimate with another woman. If you fall into the first category, more than likely these stories will provide sweet reminders of your own past, and in them you'll no doubt find a treasured part of yourself. If you fall into the latter, may these powerful accounts guide you through your journey with love, laughter, and, above all, courage.

—Lindsey Elder
April 2002

Hairdresser on Fire
Trixi

At first I thought she was a fag. One, she was beautiful the way only young boys are beautiful; two, she was a hairdresser; and three, she wore makeup. You see, this was the early '80s, when only the boys wore makeup. I had to go into Shear Perfection (the best salon in the mall) and find out.

Her voice, unlike her eyeliner, was soft—like a boy trying to hold on to the last threads of femininity. A Bronski Beat fan. She asked me what I'd like done to my hair.

"I'm not sure," I said, hoping to catch some shape under her drab baggy sweater. "What do you think'll look good?"

She stepped back and ran her eyes over my doughy features—the hidden cheekbones, the weak chin. Me—a skinny girl whose only remaining baby fat clung, sadly, to her face.

"Maybe something red because of your coloring. Red and layered just to give your hair shape. What you're doing looks good..."

What I'd been doing was stealing beer from my father's fridge with my best friend Craig then handing him the scissors. Once he nipped the top of my ear. Another time he cut my shirt collar. But my hair always turned out the way I wanted it: chaotic.

Now I was looking at the possibility of taming my shrew: layers.

"I'm not sure about layering," I told her. "I like the way it flies around."

"OK..." she said, probably wondering why I'd come into the salon at all. "Should we just dye it?"

"Sounds good. You pick." I tried to sound casual, friendly. I felt positive she was a girl by the coolness of her fingers and her smooth neck. She smelled like clove cigarettes and Tea Rose perfume.

She trimmed my ends while I stared at her in the mirror. Then she told me her name was Francine. Not *Frank,* but Francine. I finally had the proof I wanted; she was definitely a girl. We chatted about life after high school. She had gone straight to beauty school, and I'd enrolled in community college. We both had hoped it'd be better than this, but at least we got to dress the way we wanted.

I had never actually dated a woman before. My experiences were limited to dark corners in pre-rave clubs to the backbeat of Love and Rockets. A friend of a friend asked me if she could take me home a few months earlier, but I freaked and left the party. She was assertive, with big teeth and combat boots. Angry, aggressive, masculine. I didn't want to be *that* kind of dyke, but part of me worried that it was an inevitability. I'd never met the kind of dyke I'd wanted to date. Or the kind I wanted to be. Only straight experimental friends and scary, angry *womyn.*

"Who's that?" I asked, pointing to a strip of four photo booth pictures hanging on her mirror. Pixie chick with short black hair. Nose ring. Pretty smile. She was wrapped around Francine with her blue beret and six silver earrings.

"That's…that's my ex. Shawna." Snip Snip Snip. "I'm going to do a fire red. Close to one of the colors you already have mixed in here but hotter. Brighter." And she was off to the dye cabinet.

She came back with a white bowl, wooden spoon, and three bottles of color: bronze, purple, and red. "I'll do a test and see if you like it."

"Francine!" a flamboyant hairdresser called out as he entered the salon. He looked me up and down, assumed she and I were friends instead of client and stylist, and chattered on, waving black-polished fingers and batting silver-stained eyelashes. "Franny, girl, you must come down to this party tonight. They're calling it Fire. It will be *the most.* I promise. Warehouse rent party for Michael, Joseph, and the photo boys. Five dollars and you have to paint a part of your body red. Everything's going to be red—the lights, the walls, the boys, the girls. I'm going naked!" He looked into her mixing bowl. "Is that the color you're doing her hair? Oh, then you have to come, too. I'm J.J.," he held out one hand to me while the other one helped itself to a piece of candy from a bowl on Francine's table.

"Trixi."

"Nice name. OK, well, you two come by. It starts at 10 and ends when the sirens wail." And with that he was off to his vanity table on the other side of the store, leaving the two of us sitting in a silent bubble of awkwardness. I certainly didn't want to be invited by default, but she was definitely cute...

"Ah, would you like to come?" Francine asked.

"That's OK. I guess he thought we were friends or something."

"No," she said quickly, "I'd like you to come. Most of my friends have moved away. J.J. always livens up a party, but he never stands still, so I usually end up in a corner smoking cigarettes, wishing I could dance."

It wasn't until later that she confessed to telling me about her ex-girlfriend because she wanted to see my reaction. It wasn't until later that I saw the huge number of friends she had and what a fantastic dancer she was.

"All right," I told her.

A little before 10 P.M. I met Francine back at Shear Perfection. She was closing up, her bright red hands fiddling with the keys.

"I stained my hands a little when I was doing your hair, so I decided to have these be my red item of choice. Your hair looks great, if I do say so."

Francine was wearing motorcycle boots with rolled-up jeans and a flannel shirt. It's too hot in those warehouses for sweaters. All the lights and the people, she told me. "I dig your pants," she said as she touched the fabric. Cotton. Beige plaid, cut off halfway up my calf. Black patent shoes circa 1984. My favorite knee-high socks.

When we were in her car—a yellow Datsun B210 she called "Tweety"—I asked her about Shawna, her ex. "We broke up, but I guess we were really never together," Francine told me. "I wasn't ready for all the emotional drama. I couldn't be as 'open' as she was and that bothered her. She said she might as well be dating a man."

"Lame."

"Yeah," she smiled. "What about you?"

"Uh, I've never been with a girl—"

"I mean, are you dating anyone?"

"Oh...no."

"Why not?"

"I don't like the way guys smell, and I don't know what to do with girls," I confessed.

Francine popped the cigarette lighter and threw in a Bauhaus tape. "Just do with them what you want." I noticed she spoke louder outside the salon. More comfortable.

We parked about four blocks from Fire and followed the music. The streets were covered with angel-wing fags and carrot-top indie girls. Francine grabbed my hand and pushed us through to the door, where she gave J.J. a big hug hello. He kissed my cheeks and let us in for free.

Francine said hi to about three dozen freaks before we made our way to a small wooden-wheel table in the back, far from the speakers and the dancing. We shared a joint I'd brought and some Jack Daniels from her flask and talked about the various people there, where we'd backpack in Europe, and Ayn Rand.

"What do you want to do?" she asked suddenly, shouting over the music.

"What do you mean?"

"Do you want to dance or go for a walk or request a song or smoke or kiss?"

I checked her brown eyes for any hint of humor. None. "Kiss," I said.

Francine put her hands on my hips and kissed me softly. I could taste her peppermint gum. Her thumbs linked in my belt loops as she leaned into me. I put my arms around her waist and kissed her harder.

"Do you know what you want to do with me?" she asked.

"Yeah..." I watched her lips move, feeling confident but naïve.

"Then come with me." She towed me back through the throngs. We walked past the red lights of the dance area and the bathroom to a sheet curtain thrown to cover the mouth of a hallway. NO! was scrawled across it in red lipstick. Francine ignored the command, ducked in, and pulled me with her.

There were four rooms—two on either side—lining the hallway. "The renters," she said. "Friends—they won't care." Then she opened the farthest door and led me inside.

It was pitch-black. She didn't turn the light on. We started kissing again. I felt her hand move under my shirt. Her cool fingers touched my soft nipples, squeezing them with increasing intensity until I moaned.

"Too much?" she whispered.

"I'll tell you if it is."

Her lips moved from my mouth to my neck, sucking hard but low enough not to make any obvious marks. I was wet and anxious. I wanted her to make me come. Francine stepped back, and I suddenly felt her mouth on my stomach, working up to my chest. She pulled on one nipple with her teeth, letting it slide through carefully while she ground the other one with her hand. I reached down to touch myself because I couldn't wait any longer.

"No." Francine's tone suddenly changed. "I'll do that when *I'm* ready."

For a minute I thought that maybe I shouldn't be here.

Maybe this was dangerous. Would I have done this with a man? Well, probably, but *still.*

"OK..." I put my hands on her neck and let them fall across her flannel until they stopped at her surprisingly hard stomach.

Francine continued to play with my nipples, alternating bites and pinches until I was backed against the wall, my hands in her hair, moaning. My nipples burned. My cunt ached. "Please, touch me."

"Soon..." she said, playing with my ass through my pants.

Finally she undid my zipper and slid her thin hand inside. When I was with men I'd feel embarrassed being drenched. But this time I didn't care. I wanted her to touch me, and I didn't care if I was so wet I could feel it on the inside of my thighs.

"I like this," she said, as if she knew I might be uncomfortable.

Selfishly, I made no move to touch her—just leaned back and braced myself. Francine could barely get her fingers inside me, no matter how much I struggled to make room. It was too complicated with both of us standing. Without missing a beat she switched gears and moved straight for my clit, teasing it with small circles and gentle pushes. "Harder."

"No," she said sternly. "Not until I'm ready."

Then we heard the doorknob turning. She didn't stop jerking me off, but we both got very quiet. Two drunk people stumbled in trying to find a place to screw. *The nerve.*

"Here—this one's open. Come on, J.J."

"Christ!" Francine laughed into my ear.

"Just keep going," I pleaded, my ass clenched and my clit hot. I felt every slight movement, my focus entirely resting on my swollen member and her fingers.

J.J. came in with another nearly naked boy. I could barely make out their forms from the dim hallway into our black room. Apparently, they didn't see us either, pushing right past and onto the bed with a thud and a squeak. "Shhh," J.J. giggled.

My breaths were short and struggling. I was so close to coming, but afraid to make any noise. Francine slowed down to a painful pace, knowing I was ready to explode.

"J.J., what have you been hiding in here?" J.J.'s frisky playmate asked.

They moved fast and furious. Fortunately, J.J. was not a quiet lover. He did everything but sing an aria, which gave me a little more room to breathe, literally.

Francine took my nipple in my mouth and bit down hard while she quickened her pace. "Oh!" I cried out. I felt that bite all the way down my stomach and up inside my body. She pressed into me and quickened her pace.

"J.J., you hear something?" his lover asked.

"Don't stop now," J.J. snapped.

I held Francine's wrist tightly outside my pants, begging her to let me come. "When I'm finished, you're going down on your knees," she whispered, just barely above J.J.'s panting and moaning. She moved faster and faster. I was losing my grip on the wall. My legs started shaking. I thought I was going to fall, and then I felt her free arm reach around my waist and hold me tight.

She zoomed in on the extra sensitive spot on the very tip of my wet clit and rubbed it until shivers covered me. I sucked in a mouthful of air, held my breath, and slammed back against the wall.

I came in waves and thought for a moment that I had ejaculated, since my pants and her hand were soaked. She pushed her fingers into me as far as she could to give me a few little spasms at the end.

Meanwhile, J.J. was getting dirty in the background, "Take it, you fucker. Take it all." The bed squeaked a few more times.

"Go down," Francine whispered after I'd caught my breath.

She was so composed, so in control, that I wondered for a moment if she was enjoying this as much as I was. Then, with my back to the wall, I knelt, dropped her pants, and felt her dampness through her panties. I crouched lower, tipped my head back, and sucked the cotton. Francine moaned and leaned her forehead against the wall, forming a tent over me.

I wasn't as patient as she was, so I pulled down her underwear and went right for the goods, taking her puffy clit in my mouth and sucking gently. I felt her tighten up, so I stayed there, sucking for a few more minutes. When I pulled off, the blood rushed into her with a crash. She felt the heat from my tongue ten times more than usual now as she pushed herself into me and bucked against the wall.

I moved my tongue up and down, slowly closing in until I was flicking her center the same way she had just rubbed mine. I was a professional from the moment I started. I was born to do this.

Her scent grew stronger, more musky, and I felt her harden. I sucked in her clit again and worked it around in my mouth until she collapsed forward with a low moan.

"J.J., I know I hear something," the boy said behind us.

"For Christ's sake. If you don't want to do this, then don't. Otherwise, it's rude to talk with your mouth full," J.J. muttered.

"Don't I know it!" Francine laughed while she zipped up, her voice breathy.

"Who's that?"

"Francine!" J.J. shrieked.

"We're going, we're going. Carry on, boys."

She grabbed my hand, and we left the two to their own devices. Francine and I spent the rest of the night dancing, peeing in the alley, smoking pot, and kissing. By the time I got home I was covered with red handprints.

After that night, we dated for five months until I transferred to a university a few hours south. I'd see her on my breaks and get my hair dyed, but the red was never quite the same color of fire.

"Yeah," she told me, "the first dye job is always the hottest, the brightest. It's the one that takes and lasts because your hair's new to it."

Five Summers at Camp

Caitlin S. Curran

When I first met Megan at Girl Scout camp she was 17 years old. I was a not quite worldly 21, dating a guy, as yet mostly clueless about the daily existence of lesbians in my midst. I'd thought about women since high school, but it was in a very abstract, fantasyland sort of way, in which sex was muted and distant. I think I may have been envisioning the Boston marriages of the early 20th century. Spending my summers as a counselor at Girl Scout camp was prepping me, slowly but very surely, to change both my philosophy and my reality about the role of women in my life.

In early June of 1990 I packed my bags and went up to Camp Whispering Pines for my second summer as horseback riding staff. I was full of ideas, ready for another hot, laughter-filled summer working with horses, kids, and fun-loving staff, and thinking wistfully about my boyfriend. He was spending the summer in San Francisco, which seemed very far away from the camp, which itself was nestled into the dry, sage-brush-dotted mountains above Palm Springs, Calif.

I met Megan during staff training, amidst a melee of get-to-know-you games, cookouts, giggles, much singing (Girl Scouts sing a lot), riding sweet camp horses along dusty trails, and swimming nearly every day in the welcoming pool. I don't recall our actual first meeting, which undoubtedly fell somewhere amid the confusion and somewhat controlled chaos of the first day. In a staff of nearly 100, it was easy to know most of your coworkers only marginally. I had a group of friends from the previous summer that I hung out with, partly from genuine liking, partly from a strong fear of being left out. Megan found new friends of her own, other first-timer staff. I can't remember much of Megan from that summer except going on a day off together, with a group of staff, down to Palm Desert, to wander in the blissfully air-conditioned mall and eat "real" food and shop with our meager paychecks. I remember her long dark hair, her wildly infectious belly laugh, her sparkling brown eyes that bespoke fun and a slight zaniness.

My third summer at camp, Megan's second, brought about many changes. She came in as nature director, while I still held my position as mere riding staff. Although older, I felt unaccomplished, held back, unsuccessful. Megan seemed more sophisticated and together this summer, sporting a short haircut and an attitude. I admired her and her let-it-all-hang-out swagger, which was topped with a mischievous smile. I secretly wondered about her sexuality because she never mentioned men. We became friends. The thought of touching Megan in a sensual manner occurred to me on occasion, but of course I never acted on it. I was still struggling to accept my own sexuality. My boyfriend sent me a "Dear Jane" letter that summer, and it allowed me to explore many possibilities and fantasies, although they were all still only in my dreams.

Later in that third summer, I was promoted to horseback riding director when the director abruptly left camp for a family emergency. Filled with a new sense of self-assurance, I must have projected my confidence to Megan, because she suddenly became more interested in me, as I discovered during an evening out in late July. A group of about five or six of us staff had been spending lots of time together, running around camp in a little clique. One of our members had access to a family cabin in the nearby mountain community, and we often went there during time off to drink and relax and giggle like the girls we were. During one of those nights off, we were sitting around the kitchen table, trying to drink one another underneath it and trading war stories. Naturally, the conversation eventually turned to sex.

"Sex," Megan pronounced with all the gravity of one who's extremely tipsy, "is the best thing ever invented."

"Along with chocolate," said someone else, and the table roared with laughter.

"Caitlin knows what I mean. Don't you?" she asked, grinning at me and making my stomach flip-flop oddly. "Sex when it's really great, when it fires you up in your belly. When you come and it whooshes up your body and along your head, like it's going to leave a white streak of lightning across your hair. Know what I mean?"

"Uh-huh," I nodded weakly, pretending a suaveness I did not possess. I smiled along with everyone else, stared furtively at Megan, and again lifted a bottle to my lips without continuing the conversation. Just mentioning sex made me nervous around my friend, although I still wasn't entirely sure why it should make me that way.

Later that night, innocently (or so I assumed) sharing a bed, Megan and I crashed sometime in the early hours of the morning. After I thought she had already gone to sleep, she rolled toward me and stroked my arm and murmured my name. Panicked, I mumbled something about the bathroom and bolted. I didn't return until the soft sound of even breathing from the room convinced me she was truly asleep. I myself barely shut my eyes for the rest of the night, wondering if I should have responded differently, wondering what would have happened if I had. We said nothing about it in the morning, nothing remotely similar happened the rest of the summer, and I returned to college in September wondering if the sound of Megan's voice whispering my name in bed had been a dream.

My fourth summer at camp, Megan was a fast friend and I had conveniently forgotten about the attempted seduction the previous summer. She confided in me that she was having a fling with the pool director. I was suddenly in with the lesbian population of camp, which included a substantial number of the staff. I had secrets, I had secret desires, and I had many opportunities to fulfill those desires—if only I were brave enough to instigate the first steps. Lacking that necessary bravery, I watched Megan and the pool director all summer and was left with lots of questions and undefined fantasies that somehow did not match my expectations. Being surreptitiously attracted to women was becoming a hard thing to do, and I started to wonder if it was really necessary to keep it a secret.

My last summer at camp was a pivotal one in many ways. My job as riding director had reached a peak of accomplishment and satisfaction that comes with having designed a well-run program. I knew the ins and outs of the camp as a longtime staff member. Everyone in the camp knew who I was, and I felt comfortable everywhere I went. Megan and several other people I considered close friends had returned for a final summer themselves. But still something was lacking. I knew precisely what it was, and I decided this was the summer I finally needed to act on my ultimate desire.

Megan had become a certified EMT during the year prior to what would turn out to be our last summer, and she came back to camp as our nurse. She had her very own cabin to stay in all summer, with electricity and running water at her immediate disposal. She was very familiar and comfortable with loving women now. Megan was a force to be reckoned with.

Early in the season, I went up to her cabin late in the evening during my nighttime break. We sat in her room and talked and laughed, and it was very relaxed but charged with something we skirted around yet acknowledged with our eyes. I think I knew then what would happen that night.

"Hey, Caitlin," she said around midnight, "are you going to stay here tonight? We have extra sleeping bags in the cupboard. You can have the bottom bunk." She waved expansively at her bunk bed.

"Sure," I said. My heart was pounding, my mouth was dry, and I was terrified and exhilarated all at once. I knew I wouldn't be in that bottom bunk bed for long.

As I got settled into the bunk I kept sending Megan smoldering yet playful looks. I'm sure it was a very attractive sight, dressed as I was in my calf-length, red-checked nightshirt emblazoned with the camp name and logo, buttoned up to my neck. For her part, Megan kept up a running repartee centered on other camp staff and general world news. I noticed, however, that her dark eyes were much more serious than her words.

Once we were both in our sleeping bags and the lights were out, a tense silence gripped us both. I lay rigid in my bunk for long moments, listening to the crickets chirrupping outside. For all my resolve, my bravado was slowly leaking away.

"Caitlin," she whispered into the darkness, making me jump.

"What?"

"I dare you to come up here." Her voice was saucy yet hesitant.

"Oh, yeah?" I said back, popping out of my bag as if I were a jack-in-the-box. "I'll take that dare."

I was up the ladder and in her bunk in an instant, and as I lay pressed with my back against her we were silent again for so long I could hear my own heartbeat. I was amazed by my own audacity, and I wondered how Megan would respond.

"Caitlin," she whispered finally, and her breath stirred both the hair on my neck and a tightness in my groin. "Turn around."

I turned around and my lips fumbled against hers, our arms reaching around each other and stroking flannel-clad flesh. The softness of her mouth stunned me and made me quiver all over. *This is what it's like to make love to Megan,* I thought somewhere in the back of my buzzing brain. *This is what it's like to make love to a woman.*

She asked me at least four times that night if this was OK for me, was I freaking out, did I need to take it slowly, would I regret it the next day, would I turn my back on her and walk away when the bright morning sun clearly revealed what I had done? She had been burned by straight women before and was loath to get too close to the flame again, despite her interest in me. In answer, I lovingly and passionately kissed her to shut up her worries and focus on our bodies.

I spent time as a counselor at that camp for many years after that fifth summer, although only on weekends and for a few weeks in the summers, volunteering while on vacation from my full-time job. Megan and I remained lovers for the rest of that last summer and were on and off for the next three years. Although we have since slipped away from each other and I hear about her only sporadically from mutual friends, I always thank her in my heart and my memories for being the first to teach me what loving a woman is all about.

LINGERING LIPSTICK

Amy Scott

"Hi. My name's Katie. I'm bisexual and attractive. I live in the city. Do you want to set up a date to talk sometime online?"

That was the answer to my personal ad on the Internet. At the time I was 24 years old and a self-proclaimed lesbian. Proclaimed, but not in practice. I realized in college that I was attracted to women, but my small, conservative college was no place to pick up women. But I was out of college now and was on the prowl. But how? How does one pick up a woman? How does one meet a woman? I'd been fantasizing for at least three years about being with a woman, and I was starved to make my fantasies a reality. But I had no ammunition. No lesbians I knew of in the whole world. No gay people, in general, that I knew of in the whole world. I needed guidance.

Luckily, I met Joey, a friend of a friend. A gay man. Not just proclaimed but in practice. And he led me to the Internet. "Go to chat rooms," he said. "That's what I do." And he did, and he was successful. Here was a way to meet women without going to a bar alone, something I could never do.

I bought a computer almost the next day. I couldn't really afford it, but that didn't matter—I wanted to meet women. So I went on the Internet and into chat rooms. I chatted with lesbians. Real-life lesbians. These people really were out there—I'd just never known how to find them. I was hooked. Every day after work, well into the night, I'd chat with women like me. Every weekend, all day long, I'd chat. But the chatting was only making me more frustrated. Now that I was talking to women, I wanted to meet them face-to-face. Sure, the chatting filled a void, but not completely. I wanted to act, and I was ready to act. It was time to put the theory the test, so I placed an ad on the Web. "Hi. I'm Amy. 24. I'm looking for lesbian or bisexual women to hang out with. Who am I? An avid reader, guitar player, and a working girl who's more comfortable in Levi's and Doc Martens than a dress. If concerned, I'm 5′ 8″, thin, with blue eyes and long brown hair."

I received a couple of responses—mostly couples wanting to add another partner. I didn't want that. I was done with dick, I'd proclaimed to friends and to myself. And then I got her answer. Katie's answer. I quickly replied:"Yes, what time is good for you?"

It was a Thursday night. I ran home from work to set up our date. I instructed my friends to stay the hell away from the phone. No interruptions. I didn't even have time to get out of my work clothes. I just sat there. Typing back and forth with Katie. Smoking cigarette after cigarette. Katie and I talked for hours. About nothing. But at the end of the conversation, I got her phone number.

The next night I called her. Her voice sounded as sweet as I'd expected. I was too excited for words. I was talking to a lesbian! In the conversation, I found out that she was a student. She was 20 years old, 5 foot 6, thin, and had brown eyes and brown hair. We finally decided where and when to meet. Her roommate, to whom she wasn't out, would be out of town for the night. We would go to a movie Saturday night at the Chelsea Theatre.

Saturday I was a mess. I didn't eat. I watched TV most of the day. I showered, dried my hair, and even put on some minor makeup. Then I put on an outfit. Took it off. Put on another outfit. Took it off. This went on for some time until I settled on a sweater, Levi's, and my Doc Martens. I called my friends and told them what I was doing. Their advice: "Be careful. Don't go back to her apartment. You don't know her. She could be a lunatic." I agreed; I'd be careful.

That night I took the train to the Chelsea Theatre. I was early, of course. Crazily overanxious. So I smoked to calm down. I stood outside the theater looking for the woman I had talked to, looking for Katie.

I saw one woman standing against the wall waiting for someone. She fit Katie's description, but she was horrible-looking. I looked at her and told myself that if she was Katie, I could just go to the movie with her and then make a quick escape. I stared at her to see whether she'd notice me looking. She noticed and then would look at me and then look away. I debated whether I should go over to her and ask if she was Katie. But I was too scared. So I just stared, thinking that if she was Katie, she'd get the hint and come over. And then, finally, after moments of torment, a young man came along and scurried her off to the ticket line. I laughed out loud, relieved but thinking that this poor young lady was probably thinking I was a lunatic. I waited a while longer, smoking another cigarette. Katie was late. Maybe she wasn't coming at all. But then a cab pulled up and a young woman jumped out. "Amy?" she yelled across the sidewalk.

"Yes," I answered. "Katie?"

"Yes." She walked over. "I'm late. I'm really sorry."

She was beautiful. Young, pretty, smiling at me. "Don't worry about it," I told her.

Once we got to the ticket line, Katie chose a movie. I agreed, and we went in.

"So how was your day?" I was trying to break the awful silence.

"Good. How about you?"

"OK," I answered.

Then the movie started. We laughed and chatted between scenes. We basically annoyed anyone near us who was interested in the movie. But I didn't care. When we left the movie, I was nervous about what would happen next. Would she like me? Would she want to leave? Would she want to see me again? Had I waited my whole life to be ditched after my first date with a woman? But my questions were answered. "Want to get some coffee?" Katie asked.

"Sure." I was excited. The date was continuing. I had to keep telling myself, *You're on a date with a woman.*

We walked to a diner. I had a cappuccino. I don't even drink coffee. But I would have done anything to continue the date.

"So do you like my new lipstick color? I'm really excited about it," Katie said. The truth? I'd never had lipstick on my lips in my life. I'm more of a lip balm girl.

"It's great," I answered, not knowing what else to say.

When we finished coffee, we walked the streets aimlessly. Or so I thought. "My apartment's not far from here. Want to come over?" Katie asked.

Before I could even remember my friends' warnings, I answered, "Sure."

Intense nervousness set in. I was going to a woman's apartment. I was going to a woman's apartment to hook up. I had never even kissed a woman. And here I was, going to an apartment for the full deal. Did I know what to do? No. My god, what was I doing? And even though these thoughts raced through my head, I followed her along to her place.

We passed her doorman, rode the elevator up, and walked into her apartment. In the living room there were two single futons and a TV. One futon was sitting upright, and the other was down. I was being set up. Hooray, I thought. And then I became even more nervous. We sat and watched *Saturday Night Live.* She'd move closer to me. I'd comment on the show but not make eye contact. We watched *Live at the Apollo.* She'd move closer to me, touch my hand. I didn't know what to do. I talked about the show, about politics, about basically anything that came into my head. I was terrified. I was in the spot I had dreamed of a million times and I was blowing it. I was powerless. Finally, I found myself sitting and facing her. Apparently, she had grown impatient. She moved my face to look at hers.

"Do you know what I'm doing?" Katie asked.

"No," I said.

"I'm waiting for you to kiss me." When she said this, I felt a pang of pleasure hit me from below. I looked at her. I looked into her eyes. I looked at her lips. I imagined my face moving toward her. I tilted my head to the left, looked into her eyes, started to move forward but retreated. I tilted my head to the right, moved closer, saw her looking at me, retreated. I couldn't do it. I wanted to. But I just couldn't do it. It was too weird. I couldn't imagine my lips on hers. I was full of self-doubt. What if she thought I was a bad kisser? It's one thing for a man to think that, but for a woman it's completely different. Much more humiliating. Much more horrific. So I gave up and lowered my head.

After several moments, I finally spoke. "I'm afraid that if you wait for me to kiss you, you might be waiting all night."

"You've never kissed a woman?" she asked.

"No," I admitted, my face still down.

"But you're older. I thought you'd be an expert. I thought you were bisexual."

"I'm not an expert. I just know I'm attracted to women.But I don't know what that means since I haven't put the feeling to the test." I looked up at her.

"I bet one day I'll see you on the streets long from now and you'll be a full-blown lesbian."

"Maybe," I said. "Have you been with women?"

"Yes."

"OK. Why don't you be the brave one then?"

"Do you want me to kiss you?" Katie asked.

I took a deep swallow. I was about to say OK, when I saw it. Her face coming toward mine. It seemed like she was moving in slow motion. Her eyes locked with mine. She moved closer and closer. I closed my eyes. I felt her lips on mine. First a peck. Then she sucked on my bottom lip. Then she put her tongue in my mouth. I returned every motion as if it were a single act. It was odd. No stubble on her cheeks. No pressure. No forcefulness. Just a long, slow, wet, intense kiss. My nervousness left me. In my head I was screaming, *This is a woman! This is a woman! You're kissing a woman!* It was the oddest yet most exciting feeling I had ever experienced.

Katie slowly moved me onto the pulled-out futon. She leaned on her side and continued to kiss me. My lips, my cheek, my neck, my ear. I kissed her back. I rolled over onto her. I lifted my hand and touched her breast. I was uncomfortable, not certain if I should be there. I wasn't entirely sure what to do. I only knew I wanted to touch her. I wasn't sure yet that she wanted to be touched. But then she reached behind her and unsnapped her bra. I slipped my hand under her shirt. I ran my hand over her stomach. Smooth, soft skin. I slid my hand over her breast and placed my fingertips on her nipple. *A breast,* I thought. Small, soft, wonderful. I circled her nipple with my fingers and felt it grow hard. I was still kissing her, but then she left my mouth and sighed. I was doing it right. I was elated and relieved, so I placed my mouth on her neck. And then I took the plunge. The first of the night. I put my mouth on her nipple. I circled her nipple with my tongue and sucked it. She sighed more. And the feeling of her nipple in my mouth—I couldn't believe it. The skin as it puckered and became hard. The taste of warm skin in my mouth.

Katie took my head in her hands and ran her fingers through my hair as I sucked her nipple and caressed her other breast. Then she pulled my head toward her mouth. We locked into a mad kiss. She rolled over on top of me. She stopped kissing me. She pulled at my shirt. "Do you mind if I take this off?" she asked.

"No," I said.

Katie stared into my eyes as she pulled off my shirt. She looked at my bra. At my body. She put her hand on my stomach and raised it to the snap of my bra on the front. She stared me in the eyes and unsnapped it. She didn't kiss me. She just touched and looked at my body. And then she occasionally looked at my face, to see my expression. I'm sure it was one of complete amazement. A face of bewilderment. She touched my breasts. My nipples were already erect. She kissed them. She sucked them. And between each suck, she'd look at me. I was staring down at her in absolute excitement, watching her kiss my breasts. I had never been so aroused in my entire life.

Katie stopped kissing my breasts and looked into my eyes. I looked back at her. She ran her hand down my stomach without breaking her gaze. She unbuttoned my jeans. One button at a time. Then she pushed both sides of my pants apart and looked down at my underwear. I was prepared. I had put on my sexiest French satin bikinis. "These are nice," Katie said as she ran her hand over them. "You're wet." I set my head back on the futon. Her hand slipped into my underwear, and I felt her fingers on my clit. I shook and moaned.

"Is this OK?" Katie smiled.

"Sure," I answered. It was more than OK. It was fantastic. I felt her fingers sliding around me. I was drenching her hand. Then she put her finger inside me. First one. I took a deep breath. Then she added another finger and slid in and out. I met each thrust with my body. I moaned with pleasure, humping her hand. I think Katie sensed how close to orgasm I was. And I don't think she wanted me to climax, not yet. She took her hand out of my pants, and I saw how wet her fingers were. She held them up to her face and stared me in the eyes. Then she put the two that were inside of me in her mouth and sucked them.

"Mmm," she said. Then she put them up to my lips. I opened my lips, and she stuck her fingers in my mouth. I tasted myself. I smelled myself. Her fingers tasted sweet. I tasted sweet. "You taste good, don't you?" Katie said as she held her fingers in my mouth.

I just looked at her. I didn't know what to say. "I guess so."

"Trust me. You taste good." At this point I realized I was

dealing with an expert. Not only had I never been with a woman, but now I realized I was being seduced. Never before had I wanted to be seduced as much as I did then. I was growing braver. I wanted to make Katie feel this way too.

I rolled on top of her. Kissed her. Placed my leg between hers. We rocked together, grinding ourselves into each other's thighs. I kissed her neck and her ear. She started to breathe heavier. I pulled my body down and sucked on her nipples again. As I did, I unzipped her pants. I pushed my hand down under her pants and to her inner thigh. I lightly touched it, ran my fingers up and down. And then I went higher and higher, until my hand was over her underwear. I didn't look at her. I was too scared. I just continued to nuzzle my face into her breasts. Katie was breathing even heavier now. I wasn't sure what to do, but my mind immediately reverted back to what I liked to be done to me. I stroked her clitoris. I put my finger inside her timidly. I had never felt the soft, warm refuge of that place before. I wanted to stay there for a while. To just feel the walls around my finger tense. But when I heard Katie give a high-pitched moan I slid my finger in and out of her. With each moan I heard, I moved faster. Then I went back to her clit. She sighed with relief. I rubbed it. Soft at first and then harder. I could tell she was about to come. But before I could finish, she stopped me. She lifted my head to look into my eyes and we kissed. Not madly as we had before. But slow and softly. Intensely. She rolled on top of me and kissed my ear. And then she whispered, "Now I need more than your beautiful lips." Again I was hit with a pang of pleasure below as she worked her way down my body.

First she kissed my ear. Then my neck. Then my chest. Then she sucked my nipples. One then the other. Methodically. Hypnotically. Then she kissed my stomach. Her tongue ran down my midriff. She kissed my hips. She pulled my pants down and kissed the top of my underwear from one hip to the other. Then she kneeled in front of me and pulled off my jeans.

She pushed my legs apart and laid her body between them. She started at my knee. Kissed my inner thigh. Then the other thigh. I was starving for relief from this torture. I felt her tongue on top of my underwear. Kissing lightly. Then harder. Her tongue flicked against my clit with my underwear between the two. I couldn't take it any longer, so I lifted my hips and slid off my underwear. She dove in. Her tongue circled my clit as two fingers thrust in and out of me. Everything I'd expected when fantasizing about women was coming true. The soft skin. The understanding touching and licking. The thrill of having a woman want to touch me. It was all too much as I felt her inside me. I exploded into an orgasm, thrusting my hips into her face, clenching her fingers inside me.

As my breathing slowed, Katie moved up next to me and ran her hand over my body, sending shivers all over my body.

"Was that OK?" she asked.

"Yes."

"Tell me how it felt."

"It felt like an explosion of pleasure that started at my clit and ran through every nerve in my body," I told her.

"That sounds pretty good," she smiled.

I rolled over on top of her. "I hope it will be for you too," I said, then kissed her. I ran my hands over every part of her body. I couldn't get enough of the soft skin that covered her. I touched her face. I ran my hands over her breasts and stomach and felt the smoothness of her body. It was everything I wanted. And it was here. In my hands, now. I kissed her everywhere, wanting her to feel what I had felt. I pulled off her clothes and put my fingers on her clit. I rubbed her and fingered her. And she gasped and moaned. I put my tongue on her clit. It was an amazing experience. The taste of sweetness on my tongue. The feeling of the wet, smooth skin over it. I licked her up and down. I put my tongue inside her. As far as it would go. I wanted it to go in as far as my fingers had gone. I wanted to drink her in. But she was getting impatient, so I placed my tongue over clit and rubbed it with my tongue. Consistently. Forcefully. Speeding with her breathing. Finally, Katie put her hands on my head. She pulled at my hair and pushed my head toward her as she screamed in orgasm. After the scream, she continued to hold my face to her and bucked during the final seconds of pleasure. My face was wet and sticky. I licked my lips. I was proud beyond belief. I had brought a woman to orgasm. I had made love to a woman. Nothing could stop me now. Immediately, I fell in love with her. At least I thought I did.

I pulled my body up to Katie's and lay across her.

"Thank you," she grinned.

"No, thank you," I insisted. "I needed that as much as you did."

I was ready to hold her and make love to her all night long.

"God, it's late," she said. I looked at the clock on her VCR: It was 4 A.M.

"Yeah."

"I have to get some sleep."

"Should I go?" I asked.

"Yeah, probably. My roommate will be home in the morning, and if she finds you here she'll freak."

"OK." I got up. I was hurt. I wanted to lie there all night with her. I wanted to see her in the morning. I wanted to do this again. I didn't care about her roommate, and I wanted her not to care either. But I got dressed and went into the bathroom. I took a long-awaited pee, then stood in front of the mirror. And then I panicked. I had brown spots all over my face. What were they? Was there something wrong with her? Was she diseased? I hadn't even thought about the possibility of that. Was this punishment for being with a woman? Would I be scarred for life? I wiped at the brown spots maniacally. They smeared across my face. I calmed down. Lipstick, I said to myself. I have lipstick on my face. I looked into the mirror with lipstick streaked across my face and smiled. Evidence. I had been with a woman. Finally.

I came out and kissed Katie goodbye. She promised to call me. I went home. It was 5 in the morning on Sunday, and I was in an empty apartment. I opened a beer and called every friend that would wake up for the call. I told them everything. They were happy for me—but not nearly as happy as I was.

I declared myself a lesbian. This time the theory was proven. Hypothesis tested and deemed a success.

I only saw Katie once more. We went to a movie, and she kissed me goodbye. I realized I wasn't in love with her. Grateful, extremely grateful, but I wanted to be with someone who didn't want to hide me.

Now, years later, I live in the neighborhood where her apartment once was. I'm exactly as she expected I'd be: a full-blown lesbian. Sometimes I wonder where she is now. If she's come out of the closet. Sometimes I even think to look her up. But I never even knew her last name; I only have an E-mail address that no longer exists. But every time I look in the mirror after a friendly kiss on the cheek and see lipstick, I'm reminded of her. Of the excitement of being with a woman for the first time. Of having my fantasies realized. Of having the evidence of a woman's kiss on my face.

Jalapeños Are Not the Ideal First-Date Food

Emily Beller

Meeting Margarita was interesting. She was a blind date, she was my twin brother's girlfriend's cousin, and she was apparently a Latina fireball with a snappy answer for everything. My brother's girlfriend, Elizabeth, described her to me as having single-handedly energized ("terrorized," my brother, Rob, quietly suggested in my ear) her college's student council to ratify a GLBT students of color group; created and edited a newsletter for Latina dykes that in alternate years either won awards and lavish praise or was used as toilet paper by the more creative dumb football players on campus; and started a dating service for queer students of color seeking the same. All this was achieved, of course, before Margarita's junior year. Oh, did I mention that she was also a dean's list honor student headed for graduate school at Yale or Oxford or perhaps, only as a last resort, Harvard?

Being an 18-year-old blond white girl from the 'burbs with little more to my name than having won a school poetry contest when I was 12, I was slightly intimidated at the mere though of a Margarita even existing. Being interested in a woman was not the issue, as I had known I was a lesbian since my junior high years and even had managed to date several women in high school, very discreetly and chastely, of course. My parents, secure in their bastion of a privileged hetero white world, thought I was simply slow to mature, and my brother, with whom I was very close, was the only person to know for years. So the fact that Margarita was a woman was far less daunting than the reality of her overwhelming résumé. But my brother and his girlfriend convinced me to meet Margarita ("She's very sexy, and really, she's looking to expand her horizons, you know, be more *inclusive,*" said Elizabeth), so one August evening before I was to start my first year at college, I primped for an hour in front of the mirror, trying to guess what a sexy Latina fireball would like. The result was that I left my parents' house dressed in jeans, black cowboy boots, a button-down white shirt, and my double-women's-symbol earrings. I set off with my white-tinged blood thundering in my ears and visions of myself being speared by a maniacally laughing olive-skinned woman in front of her friends as she roared "See the *gringa* squeal!"

I know this all sounds very racist, but I want to point out a few things before the jury cries foul. First, I was a really sheltered little girl at the time. Second, did I mention that I was from Simi Valley? This is the place in California where all the white cops like to live because it's, you know, *white.* My particular neighborhood thought it was daring when my brother started to date Elizabeth, whose mother's brother married a woman who had been born in Guatemala. Rob and I were both going to attend a really liberal college in Northern California in the fall, and this was, of course, the mid '90s, but I may need to add slightly more perspective for you: Picture *The Brady Bunch.* Now imagine all those cheerful little white Brady kids growing up on the same street with the even more cheerful and white Cleavers from *Leave It to Beaver.* There you have my childhood.

Onward.

So I drove to the coffeehouse that Margarita had declared to her cousin was a worthy date place. When I pulled up, I immediately knew which car was hers. Did, perhaps, the BOYCOTT GREEN GRAPES! DON'T PARTICIPATE IN DISCRIMINATION TOWARD MIGRANT WORKERS OF COLOR! bumper sticker give it away?

My legs were shaking slightly when I cut the engine, and I had to take several calming breaths. I always felt nervous before a date, wondering if we would kiss at the end or if there would be a follow-up phone call several days later. My dates in high school had been with exactly three different girls, with only one little kiss among them all. While that kiss had been very revealing and exciting, the thought of moving beyond a kiss filled me with impatience and anticipation. Here I was, already 18 years old and still a virgin. My brother often assured me that sex was really cool, and he could only imagine how cool it would be between two *women* (at which point either Elizabeth or I usually smacked him with a book or whatever else was handy at the moment), so I was really curious. But you remember the curiosity fed by wondering about sex for the first time: It is tempered with unadulterated terror.

When I finally managed to get out of the car and try to suavely walk into the café, I was propelling myself with the thought that this date would turn out like the others: nice but unfulfilling. This thought made it all less scary and encouraged me to open the door. The café was typical, filled with black-clad young people intensely reading poetry or gazing soulfully into one another's eyes while they sipped cappuccino and nibbled on biscotti. It struck me as an unusually bland place for a Latina fireball to want to get know a potential paramour, and I began to relax. Perhaps she wasn't a white-girl-eating tiger after all.

"And you must be Emily," a really sultry voice suddenly murmured into my ear, puffing a hot breath across my neck and lifting the little hairs there. I turned around and saw my blind date for the first time.

Margarita was dressed in form-fitting jeans, scuffed black cowboy boots, a button-down white shirt, and double-women's symbol earrings. Her dark curly hair rippled past her shoulders, her mocha-colored eyes were indeed dancing with the fire of the extreme overachiever, and her full lips were opened in a sardonic smile as she surveyed my amazingly similar outfit. I thought that perhaps she might eat me after all, and it was not a pleasant thought at the moment. I surreptitiously checked for a spear.

"Think this might make it into the record books?" she asked, and her voice sounded so much like I thought velvet would sound if it could speak that it was a moment before I opened my mouth.

"Only if we let it get around" was what saucily fell from my lips, and I was amazed that I still had the capacity to flirt.

Margarita smiled, and she looked like a panther about to leap.

"Then let's keep it strictly between ourselves," she said, and she gallantly extended me her arm.

"Listen, *chica,*" she went on as I gingerly took the proffered arm. "This place looks boring to me. I didn't want to scare you, but I can tell you don't scare easily. Would you like to go straight to dinner?"

"Sure thing," I said in a really cheery "Hi, I'm from the Valley and I love to shop" voice that made me cringe, but she didn't notice, or at least ignored it, and we swept out the door.

Margarita drove, assuring me that we would return for my car later, and we rumbled down the street. She yelled to me over the sound of the engine that it was her brother's car and he loved lots of noise. Hopefully I wouldn't let a little thing like noise and what sounded like the muffler hanging off the end and bouncing all over the street deter me from a fun evening?

Of course not.

Margarita drove me to a city I had never been in before, one filled with voices speaking in accented English or no English at all, many confrontational stares from tough-looking boys slowly walking the sidewalks, and pungent smells drifting from homes and the little restaurants that seemed to dot every corner. She pulled up in front of one of those restaurants and hopped out, opening my door before I even had time to undo my seat belt.

"Do you like Mexican?" she asked with that sardonic grin on her face again, and I suddenly thought of the crouching panther again. "I mean *real* Mexican food. South of the border. Spicy like you just can't get in this country."

"I'm game," I said, striving for a less valley-girl tone of voice. What came out sounded apprehensive even to my ears, and Margarita definitely caught it.

"You'll be fine, Emily." My name on her lips sounded inviting, and I felt a twinge of excitement. I was wondering what it might be like to kiss those full lips of Margarita's.

The restaurant was small, intimate in the way of a family-run place. The woman behind the counter greeted Margarita by name and gave her a big hug. When Margarita introduced me, a flurry of Spanish followed, punctuated by laughter and knowing glances slyly directed toward me. Both smiled at me, then the woman led us to a table, muttering another Spanish aside to Margarita as she seated us.

Oh, dear. The *gringa*-roasting visions were back.

"Let me order for you," Margarita said, a devilish glint in those delicious eyes. I let her, of course, since the entire menu was in Spanish. "Do you eat meat, or are you one of those vegetarians?" She dragged out the word so that it sounded almost dirty, and I was relieved that I could shake my head no.

Margarita dominated the conversation. She asked me about my political aspirations (uh, none), my goals for college (uh, unsure), and my stance on lesbians of color and their treatment by the gay and lesbian community (uh, had never thought much about it before this evening). She informed me in no uncertain terms that she was an activist for just about every oppressed group in the world. When she graduated in two years, she planned to go to law school or perhaps enter the Peace Corps for two years. She was also busy filling out a Rhodes Scholar application. This summer she had so far been to Mexico to build much-needed housing for the poor, volunteered as a phone counselor for a Spanish-language rape crisis center, and in three days she would fly to Guatemala to visit her mother's sister and her family for a week before school started. "And, of course, I plan on kissing all the cute women I see wherever I go. And I see a *lot* of cute women. Even white ones." She winked at me, and I took a very long drink of water.

When our food came, it smelled heavenly. I was really hungry by this point. Warring between wanting to look attractive while eating and just wanting to eat, I decided with only one sniff to eat as if my life depended on it. Maybe Latina fireballs would appreciate a healthy appetite.

At this point the evening took a really surreal turn, one I never would have predicted. Margarita was watching me closely as I lowered my fork to my food, and I smiled at her before digging in. She seemed somewhat trustworthy by now.

That first bite just about exploded my head off. Being the little white girl from the 'burbs, I hadn't experienced much ethnic food. Jalapeños were definitely out. Margarita, however, had decided to test my Latina readiness quotient. My food was liberally scattered with jalapeños, thanks to a little finagling with the woman at the counter. The first bite I took must have had at least five or six of the evil little things, and Margarita was leaning forward with a slightly avaricious expression so she could enjoy the show.

My face turned red; I felt it flaming hot and bright. My mouth tasted like gasoline had been poured in and then lit with a match. I started coughing and then gulping water like it was going out of style.

Margarita later apologized, but first she was laughing so hard she couldn't speak. Helpless tears of mirth, all at my expense, ran down her face. I was pounding the table with my fist in agony, and Margarita sat there and laughed. *See the gringa squeal!*

When we finished dinner, all of which was like chalk in my mouth due to my murdered taste buds, Margarita gently put me in the car and drove us back to the coffeehouse, where my car was parked. We were silent on the way, me still nursing a bruised ego, Margarita because she was probably, I thought, plotting another sneak attack. She was, in a way, although it would be a much more pleasurable one.

"Emily," she said when we reached the coffeehouse, still sitting in her car, "I want to apologize for my little trick at the restaurant. And I want to make up for it." Her dark eyes looked directly at me, and I was struck again by how deep and rich they were.

"How?" I demanded rather suspiciously, and she laughed. This time it was a soft laugh, the sort that usually made me melt, and I already felt my knees quivering as we sat there in the half-light of the streetlamps.

"By doing this," she said, and she reached across the seat to me and placed her hands very lightly on my face, then kissed me for a very long time. I was sure I really was melting.

"Will you come to my house, Emily?" Her voice was formal, as if she were asking me to the prom. "I would like to make up even more. My parents aren't there right now, and I could entertain you in style. But everything will be up to you," she said very seriously, her hands still lightly cupping my face, searching my eyes, questioning. "You're a pretty fascinating girl, and I don't want to rush you. But you turn me on," and this plain, quiet statement made me melt even more.

This was going like my favorite dreams, and of course I said yes. How could I refuse a Latina fireball?

Margarita was a tender yet passionate lover, and that evening she taught me much about women and even more about myself. Her full lips lived up to their sultry potential, particularly when they traveled the length of my body and back again, igniting little fires all the way. Her hands were experienced on my virgin skin, and surprisingly gentle, yet also very firm and decisive in how they stroked me and felt every inch of my trembling flesh. The ardent response of my body to her bold use of fingers and tongue and mouth made me blush throughout our lovemaking, even when I was yelling her name as I thrashed in the damp sheets. We must have rolled around in her queen-size bed for half the night. Even now the taste of her skin lingers in my memory as a mixture of spices and sweets, deliciously hot and intoxicating. The discovery that I was a "little vixen" in bed, as Margarita teased me, was a revelation that eventually gave me the courage to explore my world far beyond the little sanctuary that was my childhood.

Margarita and I ended up dating all through my years at college. I decided, mostly because of her, to minor in Spanish, and I spent my junior year abroad in Spain, which was a wonderful and eye-opening experience, even though it was hard to be separated from her. When she graduated, two years ahead of me, she took an entry-level job with a San Francisco law firm to stay near me until I finished school.

Although Margarita and I are no longer lovers, we remain the best of friends, and she is the godmother of my child with my partner Christa. And every year I send Margarita a birthday card with jalapeños on it—just to remind her to be nice to first dates.

Great Expectations

Carrie Larson

Five years ago I was married and had two children—twins. Everyone thought we had the perfect family. My husband, Greg, had been my high school sweetheart, and we had dated all through college. We got married shortly after we both graduated. Greg was a lawyer and brought in a good income, and I stayed at home with the children. We even had a black Lab and a picket fence. Sure, it wasn't white (it was green), but to all appearances, we lived a utopian existence. There was just one problem: I was gay.

I had always thought there was something wrong with our marriage, but I couldn't quite put my finger on it. Sure, I'd had a lot of crushes on girls in high school, but I thought that was normal—you know: "It's just a phase." But whenever I had sex with Greg, I just wasn't turned on. Other women I knew spoke about being really, really attracted to men, but I had never felt that way. I'd recently seen a talk show about women who'd lost their sexual appetites. They talked about going out on "dates" with their husbands and wearing sexy lingerie to rekindle the romance. It had helped them, so I figured, what the heck, I'd try it. Unfortunately, it was a complete disaster. I had bought a two-piece burgundy negligee set from Victoria's Secret, but when I was just about to enter the bedroom and surprise Greg, I lost my nerve. I didn't feel sexy at all; I felt like a caricature of femininity. And on top of that, I realized that sex with Greg was the last thing on Earth I wanted.

When my twin boys entered preschool, things started to change. I had a lot more free time, so I started doing things I'd always wanted to do: I took a tennis class and an art class at the local community college, and I also started going to a book club that met at a local book "superstore." I felt really great; I quickly became a lot more outgoing than usual, and I met a lot of interesting people from all kinds of backgrounds.

The book club was mostly made up of housewives like me (it met at 1 in the afternoon—who else is free at that time?) and retired people. I had been going for a couple of months, and this month we were discussing *Great Expectations,* which I'd read in high school. I was a comparative literature major in college and had really missed discussing books, so I had a lot to say about the novel.

"It's not just a love story," I told the group. "It's a commentary on economic injustice. But it's also about how money can't buy happiness."

Jan, a pretty, dark-haired woman around my age who was the book club facilitator, spoke up. "I think it's all about love—about the *injustice* of love. How it almost always leaves you high and dry by the roadside. But mostly it's just a damn good story. I don't think Dickens really meant much else with the book. This novel was serialized, right? There are lots of cliff-hangers in here to keep the reader wanting more. Maybe that in itself is the metaphor: that love always keeps you wanting more."

When the meeting ended, Jan announced next month's book: *Rubyfruit Jungle* by Rita Mae Brown. I'd heard of that book and knew what it was about, but I sure as hell never read it in high school English class.

The group was starting to disperse, and I was getting my belongings together, when Jan approached me. "I really like what you had to say about *Great Expectations.* In fact, you always have really wonderful insights on the books we read. Our club hasn't been this lively in months."

"Thanks," I said, feeling a bit shy around Jan all of a sudden. Was it because of next month's book?

"Do you have some time? Would you like to grab a cup of coffee with me?"

I looked at my watch: It was only 2:15 and the kids would be in preschool until 4. "All right. I have a little free time."

Jan and I went to Steep's, a little coffee shop around the corner. As I stood in line behind her at the counter, I looked at her body. Now, I wasn't one to go around checking out other women, but I knew right away what was going on here: I was getting turned on. I looked at Jan's behind; it was round and full but not fat. In fact, I don't think she had an ounce of body fat on her. She was wearing a white sleeveless shirt with a collar, and I admired her strong upper arms, wondering why my own arms weren't as toned; I mean, I had carried two babies in my arms for years, had pushed a vacuum cleaner probably 10,000 miles in my life, and swept the floor every day like a woman possessed. How come my arms didn't look like that?

Strangely enough, I didn't freak out when I realized I was attracted to Jan—probably because it felt so right. Is this what all my female friends felt when they talked about being attracted to men? When your entire body feels electrified?

When we sat down, Jan told me about her job: She was a personal trainer at a local gym, where she worked three days a week. "It's great only working part-time," she said. "I make a decent living, plus I get to do a lot of things on those extra two days during the week—like run the book club. Going to work is kind of rough sometimes anyway, since my ex works the front desk at the same gym."

"Really? Wow, I can't imagine having to go through that," I said. "How long did you date him?"

Jan took a big gulp of coffee. "Um, it's not a he…it's a she."

She confirmed what I somehow already knew. But it was nice to hear her say it out loud. I was silent for a long time.

"That doesn't bother you, does it?" Jan asked.

"No, no, not at all," I smiled. "It just makes things more interesting."

After that, Jan and I started going out for coffee a couple of times a week on her days off. When we read *Rubyfruit Jungle* the following month in our book club, it opened me up a little more to the idea that I might be gay. I had thought the retired people in the group would get all up in arms after reading it, but for the most part they were pretty cool. Except for one old man who said, "How can they do it if one of them doesn't have a...you know, member?" When Jan said, "Mail order," the whole group cracked up, and when I looked up at her, she winked at me.

After reading *Rubyfruit Jungle,* I read every lesbian book I could get a hold of: love stories, mysteries, erotica, nonfiction—you name it, I bought it. I was afraid Greg would find the books lying around, so I only bought one at a time, and as soon as I was finished reading it I'd donate it to the local thrift shop.

I also started to realize that my crush on Jan was much more than that: I was falling head over heels in love. She was so smart, so funny, and she had a body to die for. Sometimes she would just look at me and the glimmer in her sapphire eyes would have me fantasizing for days on end. The fantasy would usually start with Jan coming over to dinner while Greg was on a business trip and the kids were at a sleepover. I'd make a gourmet meal—something Mediterranean. We'd get a little silly on red wine, and I'd have classical jazz playing on the stereo. Then I'd say something like, "You know, I've always wondered what it would be like to kiss a woman." And Jan would say "You won't have to wonder for long" and lean in and kiss me. After a few minutes I'd lead her into the bedroom, and we'd make love all night long, her showing me the ropes.

Well, it didn't happen like that at all. I'd known Jan for about six months, and I still loved Greg, but in a platonic way. He was a caring man and a good father, and I didn't want to hurt him. Still, I knew that in order for me to live the life I was meant to live, I'd ultimately have to choose between who I was and who I was pretending to be. It didn't matter, though, because Greg made that decision for me. One night after I'd put the boys in bed, Greg and I were sitting on the couch watching television. He was strangely quiet, but all of a sudden he spoke up. "Carrie," he said, and I could tell from his tone of voice that something was wrong, "I was looking for my old golf hat and I found this in your closet." He pulled out a copy of *Best Lesbian Erotica 1996*. I know, I know, it sounds funny. But imagine yourself in my position, and all of a sudden it probably doesn't anymore.

Right then I knew I could easily come up with some lie: tell him it was just a fantasy of mine, tell him it was our book club selection (yeah, right), tell him it belonged to a friend. But I knew the rest of my life depended on my being honest at this moment, and if it had taken me 31 years to be honest with myself, I owed it to my husband to be honest with him for the few minutes it would take me to "confess."

So I spilled the beans and told Greg everything. I told him about my crushes on girls when I was a teenager; I told him I hadn't been sexually satisfied in a long time (truth be told, I'd *never* been sexually satisfied, but I didn't want to hurt him like that); I told him I was in love with a woman.

Needless to say, Greg was upset. He started yelling and screaming at me, calling me a "fucking dyke" and saying I was going to ruin our children's lives. I was so upset that I ran out of the house with only my purse and the clothes on my back. I got in the car and drove to the nearest pay phone.

"Jan?" I said. "I need your help."

"What's wrong, sweetie?" I'm sure she could tell I was crying. I was an absolute wreck.

"I told Greg I'm gay and he went nuts."

"You told him you're gay? Why would you tell him that?" Jan asked.

"Because I am," I said, and even though I was upset, it felt so good to finally say it, especially to the woman I loved.

Jan told me to come over immediately and that I could spend the night. I drove to her house, shaking the entire time. Did I just screw up my life? Would Jan feel the same way that I felt about her?

As soon as she opened the door, Jan threw her arms around me. "Oh, Carrie, honey, why didn't you tell me any of this before? There's so much I could have helped you with."

She sat me on the couch and got me a glass of wine to calm my nerves. After I had settled down a bit, she took my hand. "How long have you known?" she asked.

"I guess my whole life, really," I told her. "I was just never honest with myself. I've tried so hard all my life to fit in, and I've made a complete mess of my life in the process. At least I have my sons."

"That's not all you have, sweetie," Jan said. "You've got yourself. And look at yourself: You're a beautiful, intelligent, *sexy* woman that any dyke with an ounce of sense would love to have in their life."

"Like you?" I asked.

"Me? I…uh..." Jan stammered, and then looked at the floor.

"Yes, like you..." I said, and then, I don't know where the hell I mustered the courage from, but I leaned in and kissed her. Just a small kiss on the lips, but one that could not be mistaken as a friendly peck.

Jan placed both of her strong hands on my neck and pulled me in for a long, long kiss. Our tongues did a sensual dance that left my entire body feeling on fire. It had never been like this with Greg—or with any guy.

"I love you," I said once we had finished kissing. "And I'm not just saying this because I'm upset. I really love you, Jan."

Jan looked at me with a world of warmth in her eyes. "I love you too. I've been holding my feelings in for all these months because I wasn't sure you felt the same way. I mean, I know we sometimes flirt with each other, but I wasn't sure…you know, it's so hard to tell with straight women sometimes."

"But I'm not straight," I said, and we both keeled over laughing.

"You sure as hell aren't, baby," Jan laughed. "You sure as hell aren't."

The next few months with Greg were difficult, but over time he and I worked things out and he wasn't as upset as he'd been that first night. It turned out that mostly I had bruised his ego, and I found out from a mutual friend that he'd been having an affair with a coworker for the past four months. Greg told me later that he had fallen out of love with me right around the time I had met Jan at the book club. We still cared a lot about each other, so our divorce was pretty amicable, and to this day we share custody of Kyle and Mark.

Jan and I had a torrid affair. Well, it was torrid for all of six months, and then things started to settle down. Turns out that Jan was a lot like Greg—a five-minute wonder in the sack. I even tried out the same burgundy negligee with her, but it was no use. Jan was a "wham, bam, thank you, ma'am" kind of lover. Who knew the lesbian version even existed? When she and I broke up I found it difficult to go to the book club meetings, so I started my own club at a local independent bookstore, where I met my life partner, Renee. She's everything I could ask for in a woman: intelligent, charming, caring, wild in bed, and she's great with my sons. She and I have been together three years now, and I must say that what Jan said at that *Great Expectations* discussion all those years ago is unequivocally wrong: Love *doesn't* always keep you wanting more. Sometimes it's just enough.

Summer's Frisky Kitten
Ellen Tevault

"Do you want to go cruise for guys? Tell your mom you're spending the night with me," Summer said.

Since I was only 16, I had to ask my mother. If my mother had known that Summer's mother wouldn't be home and that she was 20, she wouldn't have agreed.

"OK," I said, not knowing what she had planned for us.

Instead of cruising, she drove us back to her house.

"Let's bake a cake," Summer said, pulling a box of cake mix out of the cabinet. After she had me busy mixing the cake, she said, "I'll be back in a minute."

A while later, I took the cake out of the oven and yelled up the stairs, "It's done."

"Bring us up a piece each."

"You don't want icing?"

"Don't have any. We'll have to eat it plain. Bring up a banana."

I walked up the stairs to her bedroom. She had candles lit throughout and a bed made for us on the floor next to her single bed. At that moment I knew her plans, and I was both scared and excited that my dreams were about to come true.

"I've never been with a girl. I don't know what to do," I told her.

"I know," Summer said, feeding me a bite of cake.

I thought about how she and I had teased her boyfriend that we were going to get him into a threesome. The three of us had flirted during a Halloween party. I was dressed as an old lady, and Summer was dressed as a bunny. I don't remember what he wore because I'd been too busy thinking of sticking my tongue into the holes of her fishnet stockings and grabbing a handful of her cottontail. Looking around her room now, I knew he clearly wasn't invited after all.

Now my wish was before me, and I didn't know what to do. While I ate my cake, Summer sat on the floor across the room from me. Her leather skirt was riding up her thighs. At first I thought it was a shadow until she unzipped the zippers on the side of her skirt and spread her legs farther apart. Then I realized that the darkness was her pussy.

Smiling, I crawled across the floor to her and said, "I don't know what to do."

"I do," she said, grabbing a photo album from a nearby shelf.

When I saw her snapshots of naked women, I smiled. I wanted to pounce on her, but my lack of experience held me back. Finally, she kissed me. Her lips pressed against mine so gently that I wondered if I was dreaming.

When the reality of the kiss set in, I grabbed Summer and kissed her. I probed her mouth with my tongue and explored her clothed body with my hands. I wanted to devour her. My fingers traveled over her curves. I felt her soft breasts through her T-shirt and her round hips through her slick leather skirt. I looked down to her panty hose and mourned the missed opportunity to lick her legs through the fishnet.

"My, you are a frisky little kitten," she said, pushing me away. "Give a girl time. We have all night. My mom won't be home from her date until morning."

I pulled away reluctantly.

"Get ready for bed," Summer said. "I'm going to pee."

Shaking, I took off my clothes and threw them into a heap next to my duffel bag. While I pulled my nightgown over my head, I heard a click. I quickly covered myself up with the gown, then saw Summer standing in the doorway, holding a camera. *Click!*

"Nice body. That'll go great with my other pictures."

"Why'd you do that?" I asked, trying to pull the gown down to cover myself up more.

"What's wrong with you? You have a great body."

"It's not beautiful like yours."

She laughed and shook her head. "No, it's better." She put her camera into her dresser drawer. She walked toward me, and I grabbed her for another kiss. I pressed my whole body against hers. "You are so naughty. Are you always this frisky?" she asked.

I bowed my head and pretended to be ashamed, and she patted my head like a kitten.

"I want you so bad," I said, lifting my head. When I did, her hand slid from the top of my head down the side of my face.

"You're very dominant for a virgin. I'm not used to that. I'm used to having to hold a hand through the whole thing."

"I've wanted this for a long time. I kissed my first girl when I was five," I said, letting her lead me to the bed. I giggled when I realized the time had come. "I've always wanted to eat pussy."

"I don't like that. It tickles."

When she said that, I pouted.

"Don't worry. There's plenty of other things for us to do."

As Summer spoke, she lifted her shirt over her head and unsnapped her bra. At the sight of her small breasts, I swallowed and wondered if I could fit an entire breast into my mouth. When she slid her skirt down her legs, I tugged at it. She shook her head and giggled at my impatience. She stood before me with only her panty hose on.

"Please take those off," I told her.

She slipped off the hose and sniffed the crotch. "You naughty thing, look at what you've done to me," she said.

I smiled, and she held them in front of my nose for me to smell. I buried my nose in them and savored her fragrance. Sighing, I wrapped them around my neck like a scarf. She crawled on top of me and kissed me. I cupped her ass in my hands and pulled her closer to me. Her small breasts pressed against mine, and I wrapped my legs around her hips. While we kissed, I sucked her tongue deeper into my mouth.

When she pulled away, Summer gasped for air and said, "Are you sure you've never done this before?"

"I've been with guys, but not with a girl."

She rose up onto her knees and tugged at my nightgown. With her help I slipped it off. After she threw it across the room, she licked her lips and bent forward. She sucked my nipple into her mouth. When I gasped at the warmth, she bit it. Moaning, I grasped her hair in my hands and pressed her head onto my breast.

While I concentrated on her teasing my breast, she slid a hand between my legs. I jumped when she dipped her finger into my hole. I rose to meet her finger, and she added another. She switched to my other breast while she pumped my pussy.

When I came I felt energized, and my urge to devour her overtook me. I rolled her onto her back and sucked her small, perfect breast. I opened my mouth as wide as I could to take in her whole breast and flicked my tongue over her nipple. I felt cheated that I couldn't fit it all in.

While I savored her breasts, I slipped my hand down her stomach. She tried to stop me, but I persisted. Eventually I planted my hand between her thighs, onto her hot, juicy cunt. When my finger caressed her clit, she jerked and moaned.

"That tickles. Stop."

Obeying her, I moved my hand down to her opening, which radiated heat. I slid in a finger and moved it around in circles, exploring her slick walls. Feeling like there was a world in there that I wanted to explore, I slid in two fingers and tried to reach for the top of her cave. I pumped in and out and added a third finger to reach in as far as possible.

She moaned and pumped against my hand. Every so often I twirled my fingers around to caress her tightening walls. She grabbed my hair and pulled it. Her other hand reached down and pressed my hand into her cunt. She bucked against my hand and screamed as her orgasm flowed through her body.

Breathing heavily, Summer collapsed. "I don't believe you're a virgin. You're too good."

In response, I moaned and slid my hand out of her. I glanced at my lubricated fingers and smiled. I crawled on top of her and sucked her breast.

"You are so frisky," Summer giggled. "How's a girl suppose to recuperate?"

"I want more," I said, nibbling her neck.

"OK, OK." She rolled me onto my back.

Stroking my pussy with her fingers, she kissed me. Our tongues fought for control of the kiss, and I won. She slid two fingers in and pumped against me. I tried to swallow her fingers with my pussy. After a few minutes of intense pumping, she slid her hand out and searched for something.

Hoping she wasn't finished, I closed my eyes and panted. My breaths filled me in short bursts. When I felt her hands between my legs again, I jumped and released the breath I'd sucked in.

"Relax. It's only me."

I opened my eyes and looked into her blue eyes to calm myself. When I relaxed, I tried to glance down to see what she was doing, but she blocked my view. I felt something slide into my hot hole and gasped at the cold intrusion. She inserted it and pumped it in and out of me. I moaned and thrust against it. When I clamped my walls around it and pushed my juices out, it collapsed under the pressure. I screamed as I came.

When I recovered from my release, Summer pulled the object out and said, "Look at what you've done to my banana. I'll have to get another."

I giggle, and she kissed me.

We went at it all night long. When her mother came home in the morning, Summer shushed me as I moaned with another orgasm. Eventually we showered and she took me home. After that night we saw each other a couple of times to chase guys, but we grew apart. She ended up marrying a man, and I came out of the closet as a lesbian.

Summer left me wanting more. I had to wait four more years before a woman let me taste her on my lips. To this day, I still crave fishnet stockings.

My True First

Ashley Waters

My *actual* first was with a man, as it is with so many other fellow lesbians. I guess I should be honest and say a string of men, or maybe a short piece of yarn of men. I was trying to find one that worked the way I wanted, but I never did. Looking back, I was just trying to hide behind the undeniable: I loved women. I loved looking at them, I loved thinking about them, and I loved dreaming about them and touching them. When I decided it was time to sow those oats, I did. With two women in a two-year span. They both were young, beautiful, caring, and the experience was wonderful with each of them. This is what I wanted. Then I met my *true* first.

I work in a factory as a tradesperson. One day I was asked to watch over a woman, Lisa, who was entering the extensive training program and try to make sure she didn't experience any of the sexist crap I had gone through. I reluctantly agreed.

There were two people at work, Paul and PJ, that I felt worthy enough of knowing that I liked women and that I secretly wanted to peek at the same dirty magazines that men try and hide behind the pages of *Sports Illustrated.*

Lisa was assigned to my area so that it would be easier for me to do that "watching" I had agreed to. Her first day on the floor, the three of us—Paul, PJ, and I—watched her, all right. She was beautiful. Workers from other areas even popped up to see the "new girl." No matter what people tell you, men gossip more than women, and their words travel *fast.* Both Paul and PJ commented on how hot Lisa was and joked about how they were going to "get" her. Without hesitation, I said, "No, *I'm* going to get her." But I wasn't joking. I knew I'd have her no matter what her situation. No, that's not true. I wish I'd had that kind of confidence. All I did was hope that someday I'd be the one.

I introduced myself, or maybe she introduced herself. I'm not sure; I was just enamored with her. An introduction was made nonetheless. And eye contact. The most beautiful green eyes I had ever seen were looking right at mine. Well, not actually *at* mine, but *through* mine, through my soul, searing everything along the way. As if that weren't enough, she had the most enchanting smile, with a set of dimples that could light up a room and melt a heart. She also had the cutest round butt that jutted out against her work pants and threw me into a state of confusion as to whether to stare at the front of her or reposition myself to get an eyeful of the back. All I knew was that I wanted it all.

Lisa and I started having lunch upstairs in the quiet, rarely used learning center. I'd arrive early sometimes and stretch my arms across our table in the back corner to measure how far apart we were and how I could get in an innocent touch here or there. She wore one of the newly designed work shirts, a button-down men's shirt with vertical blue-and-gray stripes. There was wave to her stripes, though, as they passed over her perfectly sized breasts. She had the first two buttons undone everyday. If I sat at just the right angle, which I always managed to finagle my way into, I could see the outlines of her lacy-edged bra and just a teasing hint of cleavage. Lisa and I would talk about, well, everything—including her problems with her husband and my continuing struggle to keep the peace with someone I used to be close to.

One day we agreed to meet outside of work for lunch on a Saturday afternoon. That Friday I had given Lisa a copy of a short story I was writing that contained an explicit lesbian lovemaking scene. I guess I wanted to see how she'd react. I figured that if she was appalled by it, I'd know where I stood. And if not, then it was worth a shot. At that lunch, to my wonderful surprise, Lisa confided in me that not only had she enjoyed the story, but when she read it at work she contemplated going into the women's restroom and masturbating from the feelings it had stirred in her that hadn't been…"stirable" for a while. This was good news.

They say time flies when you're having fun. Case in point: Lisa and I arrived at that restaurant shortly after they opened for lunch, and the next thing we knew the lights were being dimmed for the dinner crowd! Somehow or other it had come out that I had indeed been with women, and she had *so* many questions, all of which I was happy to answer to the best of my ability. Lisa was aglow with this influx of knowledge, and I was aglow somewhere else.

Things escalated from there. I wanted nothing more than to be near Lisa and help her realize what else was out there, how it could be so different and better. I called her and talked to her for hours on end, saw her every day, wrote letters to her at all hours of the night, but it was never enough. I was falling in love with her. Lisa had turned my world inside out, sent me into an inner turmoil that both excited and frustrated me. I consulted with my first woman lover, Jen, on what to do. I told her I just wanted to see Lisa happy—I wanted Lisa to experience what it was like to be with a woman, and deep down I wanted it to be me. I asked Jen how I could offer myself to be the one Lisa could try it with, without getting hurt myself because I already had strong feelings for her. Jen said there was no easy way to approach this—either go for it all the way and hope Lisa wanted me back, or don't go there at all.

By this time, Lisa had separated from her husband, and we were spending as much time together as possible. During one of our talks she expressed that she wasn't sure what lesbians do in bed except for the image I had planted in her mind from my short story. So one afternoon I rented every film I could think of that contained a lesbian love scene. I wanted her to see how many different ways there were and how each experience was just as beautiful as the next. Lisa sat on one end of the couch and I sat on the other. As I popped each movie in, she sat with her legs up, her fist up at her mouth with her thumbnail lodged between her teeth, and her eyes glued to the screen. I watched her every expression. I couldn't tell whether it was horror, curiosity, excitement, or fear on her face. I think it may have been a combination of all of them.

In the middle of the short stack of movies, Lisa asked to pause to use the bathroom. (She had been drinking wine coolers to relax—I think I should have been the one drinking them!) I stood outside in the hall, waiting. I didn't hear any retching noises—a good sign.

Lisa came out (of the bathroom, I mean!). We made eye contact. I asked her if she was OK, if she wanted to stop watching them. She said no. I asked her what she was thinking, what she was feeling. I could tell she wasn't sure how to answer. Uh-oh.

Her back was against the wall in my hallway. I was facing her, standing very close. I thought of a particularly awkward moment in my story, and this moment paralleled it perfectly. I'm shy by nature, but I couldn't take it any longer. So I softly grabbed her hand, moved it back behind her, grabbed the other, and with the same hand held them both against the small of her back. I held these two incredibly soft and warm hands, and I moved in closer. I asked with my eyes if it was OK to kiss her. My heart felt a "yes" come back. So I did. I kissed the most indescribably soft lips I have ever known. It was a fairly long kiss for a first, and her tongue licked my lips and gently pushed through to meet my own eager tongue. We continued to kiss in a controlled but passionate way. These lips were not meant for forcefulness; they were meant to be savored—sampled over and over. I felt goose bumps travel down the back of my neck and spine. This wasn't a kiss, this was a revelation. All the letters I'd written her, all the conversations we'd had in which I explained how unique and wonderful it is to kiss a woman, were, to be honest, crap. Words could not describe what I felt inside. Everybody I'd ever been with and everything I'd ever experienced with them put together paled in comparison to this kiss.

Suddenly every corny cliché I'd ever seen or heard in every movie, TV show, or book, made sense. Yes, I felt like I could fly, it was time to exhale, I felt born again, the earth moved, and all of that. *Please, God, let Lisa feel the same way too,* I begged as I pulled away in slow motion. I slowly opened my eyes to see hers were just opening as well. *Now what?* was the only thing on my mind at that point, and I think maybe on hers too. Well, we'd done it; we couldn't go back now. Was this cheating? She was still married on paper, although the marriage had ended in her heart. *God, forgive me if this is cheating, but I can't help myself. I love this woman,* I thought.

Lisa and I talked about the kiss and what we felt while sitting on the couch—no movie playing; no need for that anymore. I touched those hands, those tiny milky-white hands. We kissed some more, and I touched her face, her hairline, her dimples, which were all as soft as those hands. Each kiss was as enticing as the first. But it had to end there. The last thing I wanted was to move too quickly. This woman sitting before me was a vision, an angelic presence sent from above to teach me about love, compassion, and trust—all the things I thought *I* would teach *her*.

For the next two months Lisa and I spent a lot of time together kissing, touching, holding, and caressing each other. Now it was time to take it further. We were on her king-size bed, and we undressed each other slowly. I had no doubt that this would be it. There was candlelight in the background, and the flicker of the flames highlighted her reddish hair. The soft music playing relaxed me as I once again was overwhelmed by the chiseled perfection lying beside me. Our naked bodies fit together like a jigsaw puzzle. The closeness brought on a barrage of passionate, heartfelt kisses. I paused to breathe her in, and I let the hot breath out onto her. I progressed down her body, kissing and licking every inch of her. The subtle moans coming from above as I lightly tugged on Lisa's nipple ring with my tongue excited me to no end. Her areola grew hard, and I felt the same growth under my fingertips as I caressed the other breast simultaneously. I intermittently grabbed the entire breast and kneaded it like a pile of dough.

I continued down Lisa's body, touching, caressing, grabbing, sucking, and battling my animalistic urges to devour her whole but cradle and protect her as well. I'd come back up and kiss her sides, her breasts, her neck—oh, that luscious neck! I was on fire inside, and I exhaled hot breath into her ear until I felt her pelvis grind into mine. A thin coat of sweat covered me, helping me glide my way back down that magnificent body passionately and feverishly. I kissed her belly, licking around her belly ring. I'd done all this many times before, but this was different. I felt her hands run through my hair as I inched down even farther. I brushed my lips over the smooth skin where hair had once been until I had watched her shave it off just days before. I stopped and pulled my lips and tongue away just as I arrived at the opening of her engorged lips.

Again Lisa moaned. I kissed and softly touched her calves, knees, and ended at her thighs. Against my cheek I felt heat radiating, an energy pulsating from this, the very center of her being.

The love I felt for Lisa at that moment made me want to break down and weep. Flushed with what I can only call the true miracle that this great love has allowed me to experience, it changed my every action. I slowed right down. I was going to experience the single most treasured thing she could share with me—her very being, her love, her soul.

I positioned myself with one hand lightly massaging her left breast and the other under her right buttock. There was a puddle of come under her, so my hand slipped under her cheek easily. As I felt the dampness, my only regret was that I wasn't there sooner to catch it all in my mouth. But I was there now. Strangely, I felt scared. I'd done this many times before with those two other women. In fact, I'd had plenty of practice, because I wasn't usually accustomed to allowing myself to be touched or "performed" on. In the past, I'd been perfectly content to please a lover without worrying whether I was going to get it as well. But as I said, this was different. I wanted her to feel every pulsing throb that was going through my own body. I wanted her to feel—to know—the love that I felt for her at this moment.

I kissed her swollen bright-pink outer lips. I traced them with my tongue and slipped it between them until I found what I'd waited so long for. Lisa's breathing was heavy as I ran the tip of my tongue over her swollen center a few times. "Is this OK? Is what I'm doing OK?" I asked her. Lisa groaned and nodded. I took that as a yes. I proceeded to lick, kiss, and suck her clitoris and the surrounding area. It was warm, wet, and slippery, and I took in as much as I could. At one point I actually heard some of her juices squirt out against my chin as I buried my face between the folds that welcomed me. When I felt her clitoris flutter, I'd stop and move to another area. I didn't want her to climax, not yet. I wanted to relish the sweetness of this pure act.

With all of my "playing," however, her clit was swelling and beating, so I took the hint and grabbed onto both butt cheeks, squeezed them, and fluttered my tongue as fast as I could. I felt Lisa's body thrust wildly, bucking like a rodeo horse. I gladly held on for the ride, trying all the while to keep my rhythm. I think it became too much, because as she let out deep groans, she sat up, grabbed my head, and pulled it up toward hers and kissed my face, which was coated with her sweet juices. I was exhausted—not from the performance of this beautiful act, but I too had a feeling tear through me that I can only conclude was the remnants of my own urgent release.

As we lay there and became aware of our surroundings again, we laughed as we realized that somehow we had ended up sideways on the bed—a perfect 90-degree flip. Contemplating what had transpired between us, I realized another first was at hand: This wasn't just sex—I had made love for the first time. And the strangest thing was that I had wanted *her* to touch *me*—I needed her to. I'd never before had this urge, this desire to complete the act by having my own orgasm rip through me, as I had so desperately wanted her to feel.

Two years later, we are still together. When her marriage had legally ended, finally, all restraints against our love were gone. We live together with our cats in a happy, loving home. To this day, when we make love, it's blissful and beautiful and perfect, and maybe most importantly, it's equal. I love and crave her touch just as much as I love to touch her.

When I told a few friends that I was writing a story about my "first," they asked me if Lisa had inspired me to put pen to paper. I told them no. I needed no inspiration to write this. Each and every day this story writes itself with love and joy and a beauty that continues to touch and awe me in so many ways. Don't get me wrong, Lisa inspires me with every word, every touch, every searing look—every day. But the inspiration to write this story came from wanting and yearning to live a life of love, happiness, patience, compassion, trust, and honesty—all the things that she taught me first.

Lesbian Singles Party

Hilary Watson

Every woman in the house—and trust me, when I say every woman, I mean *every woman*—was wearing a blazer. A few had the sleeves rolled up. Some wore wifebeater tees underneath. But they all wore blazers. And they were all old. We're talking *way old*.

I had on an outfit I felt sexy in—a sleeveless blue velvet top with black stretch pants and heels that brought me up to about 5 foot 5. I stood in the entryway at the back end of a long line of excitedly bobbing mullets, still holding the hip little flyer that had been handed to me by a very cute chick on the campus of the University of Texas. "Hundreds of Hot Lesbian Singles!!!" it read. "Prizes, Tarot Readings, Dancing."

Where was that cute chick? Was she just part of an advertising ploy? The old bait and switch? She was probably out right now at the really hip Austin lesbo party. A party where 20-somethings like myself could mingle and compare tattoos.

A 40-ish woman, wearing a bright red blazer and a face like my mother's, sat behind a table. One by one she greeted and registered the guests, and guest by guest the space between us shortened. When I finally reached her, she raised a graying eyebrow at me.

"Name?"

"Hilary."

"Two *l*'s in Hilary?" she asked, filling out my name tag.

"Whatever you think's best," I said, and began to cry.

Not that I didn't totally have the best reason. I was 21 and my best friend, Trudy, who also happened to be the love of my life, had just told me she was in love with my other best friend, Rachel—who happened to be the love of her life. Trudy and I used to take ecstasy and make out all the time and it was always so perfect; we just never went any further because neither of us knew what to do. OK, we *knew* what to do.

We just hadn't done it before. And I guess neither of us was willing to look like a dork.

"What's the matter, honey?" asked the woman. Bless her for her kind tone, because I was full-on losing it.

"I'm only 21—this isn't the way it's s-s-upposed to h-h-happen."

"Don't worry, sweetheart. There's a whole house full of beeyootiful wimmin here to cheer you up." With that happy phrase, she handed me the two items she'd dished out to every poor single lesbo who registered at her post that night: a daisy and a name tag. Both would have looked great in the lapel of my blazer—if only I'd worn one. Oh, well.

Once in the hallway, clutching my daisy, I wiped my eyes and tried to locate a good place to chuck my name tag. Suddenly, a woman with brown hair and bad posture sidled up to me. She was wearing a tan linen blazer, but at least the cut was semi-stylish, and that alone made her sort of attractive. Juxtaposition is sometimes everything. She grabbed my arm and pulled me into a corner. "Hi, I'm Mary. If you say you're my date, we'll get a prize."

My eyes dried out. I tucked the daisy in my hair and tossed my name tag into a ficus-tree pot. I let Mary walk me back to where the red-blazered mother figure was manning the party admittance desk.

"You again!" the woman laughed.

"We just met! And we have a date next Friday!" announced Mary. She seemed quite proud.

"Wow, that was fast." With an exaggerated flourish the woman extended a lime-green slip of paper, which Mary snatched and held to her nose like she was inspecting a counterfeit bill.

"All right! A weekend at Nocona Hot Springs! " Mary howled.

"And a free massage for two, " the red-blazer woman piped in, wriggling her salt-and-pepper brows.

Queasily, I followed Mary off into the living room, where she continued to peer at the paper. Eventually she remembered my presence, or at least she got tired of inspecting the paper, and when she looked up, there I was. She squeezed and rubbed my arm, which felt a little bruised. "Hey, thanks," Mary said. "Great prize, huh? Excuse me, I gotta go to the bathroom."

She moved off to the bathroom, and I moved toward the patio, where I hoped to find a younger crowd or at least some kind of strong drink. Just before I stepped across the threshold, I overheard Mary introducing herself to someone. "Hi, I'm Mary. If you say you have a date with me, we can get a prize."

Once safely on the patio, what did I see?

More blazers.

Damn, this party sucks!

But at the far end of the yard was a bar, and at that bar was a beautiful spiky-haired blonde in a cobalt-blue minidress. She was easily more than six feet tall, and as she accepted a glass of wine sweetly by the stem, she looked up and out over everyone. When she saw me, she stopped looking, and then she smiled. And then she drank.

I thought, *Wow! Is it the wine or me you're drinking?*

It's you—now get over here. Her eyes were blue, like those of a timber wolf. Soon we were sharing a bottle of merlot. "Are you some kind of gymnast?" she asked. "You remind me of a gymnast. Your arms are so muscular, but your body language is so soft."

"I'm a dancer," I told her.

"A dancer! Well, what kind of dance do you do?"

I bit my tongue about erotic dancing at the Peppermint Unicorn to supplement my X habit. Instead I told her I did modern and that I had choreographed and performed a solo and had been chosen to perform it at a national competition in Washington, D.C. I told her I had a videotape of it back at my apartment. Which was true.

Then I told her that I liked her lips and her cheekbones and her shoulders. Which was also true.

"Your eyes are like nothing I've ever seen before," she said. "They're so amazing. They're spaced so far apart." She moved her finger back and forth from my left eye to my right, to the left to the right. "So wide apart," she repeated, then, "Oh, Jesus. I'm drunk."

"You don't seem drunk to me," I lied.

"Well, I am," she said. "I'm very drunk and you're very young and you've never even been with a woman before."

I drove her back to my apartment, which was just a mile or so away, ogling out of the corner of my eye how her skirt hiked up on her thighs and the dark shadowy zone between her legs.

My place has a lot of cool stuff to look at, props to make me look artistic and sexually sophisticated. She wandered around looking at my collection of erotic photography books, and I went out on the back porch for a smoke. After a while she shouted at me from inside, "Hey, what are you doing with this?" It was a book by Anne Rice—writing as A.N. Roquelaure. She held the book in her hand and smirked. "What are you doing with *Beauty's Punishment*?"

I told her I loved that book.

"So, a little perv, are you?"

"Yes."

"This could turn out to be a fun evening."

"Yes."

She dove back into my things while I finished my cigarette. She dug through my CDs and pulled out *The Hits* by Prince and, smiling, came up to me with it.

"You like Prince?"

I blew smoke up at the stars. "No, I *love* Prince. I love love love love love Prince."

"I'm becoming kind of bored by Prince—but I do like that one song 'Erotic City.' "

I took the CD out of her hands and told her I wanted to go back to the party.

When we got back, the crowd had thinned and everyone had taken off their blazers, so there was something newly sexy in the air. I put "Erotic City" on the CD player, walked myself to the middle of the living room, and closed my eyes. When I finished dancing, I looked over at her and she just stood and stared. Then we went back to my place.

The first thing she did was to kiss me while pushing my body into all these poses, and I just went with it. "Your spine is so flexible. Your body just goes whatever direction I ask it to." She kissed me and put her hand in the small of my back, and I let my back fold over and she bent with me. She used her hands to move me everywhere. She took my shirt off and pulled the edge of my bra aside to reveal my nipple. Her face flushed red as she looked at it. "So tight and brown," she said. Then she kissed it with a sweet, soft brush of her lips. The door to the patio was open, and the night air blew in across my skin. "Feels good," I said, shivering some.

"Are you cold, honey?"

"No. I love it," I told her.

"Good," she said, and took my nipple in her teeth. As the sharp pain went steadily through me, she turned me in her hands like a toy.

My eyes rolled back in my head, and for a while I didn't even know where I was.

When she stopped, we were on our knees facing each other. I reached under her short dress and lifted it over her shoulders to expose her black bra and ripe curved breasts—two perfect spheres, lifting and falling with her breath. And I saw her soft, flat stomach and her cheap black nylons with a run down the inside of one thigh. I threaded my fingers into that run and, when her blue eyes widened, ripped for all I was worth. I tore those crappy supermarket stockings right off her as she fell back and laughed and helped by kicking her legs.

Together we snatched up scraps of ripped nylon and threw them all over the room.

She was naked except for her bra.

She reached both hands behind her back and popped the clasp. Then she stretched her arms out in front of her, and the bra slipped down to her elbows. I gasped when I saw her breasts. Greedily I dragged the bra down her arms the rest of the way and flung it to the wall. Then I stared. She had perfect, large, beautiful breasts; tight, clay-colored nipples; and a glossy look in her eyes that made the room spin. I lowered my head, and her hand came behind it as she twined her fingers deep into my hair.

I bit down on her nipple, then tried to bite again, but she pulled my hair so I couldn't, and I moaned. We shared a smile. "Bite harder," she said. And so she teased me like that for a while, urged me to bite harder, suck harder, forced my face into her breast, forced me to stuff my mouth with it. Ordered me to lick lightly, held my hair so I had to lick lightly. She squeezed her breasts together so the nipples were kissing each other. I put both of them in my mouth, tonguing and gnawing.

The moan she let out—I still hear it at the strangest times of the day.

Then we were kissing again. Soft, perfect kisses. Her hands moved confidently over my body. She brushed the crotch of my panties with her fingers.

"Oh, you're damp. I can feel how damp you are—you're soaked."

That's when I got stage fright. This wasn't some choreographed performance or some sordidly structured lap dance. This was real. She really meant to fuck me. I freaked inwardly as her hand slipped inside the waistband of my panties.

I whispered, "I don't like penetration."

"You don't?" She paused.

"I've never even let a boy do it."

"Why, baby?"

"I don't know..." (And I really didn't; something had always just stopped me.)

She looked at me quizzically, trying to digest this new information. But then she smiled. "You're scared, that's all...but you *are* getting fucked tonight." And it was said in such a way that I felt fine. Our tongues danced together like old lovers, her taking the lead.

Her soft mouth wandered down my stomach; my belly-button ring clicked against her teeth. Then, with an exquisite hovering tease of lip, tongue, saliva, teeth, she was on my clit. Her finger entered me, then held still, then it was just that tease again, that teasing mouth. It was just her finger, but I felt terrified. I didn't know what I was going to feel. But then I just felt...amazing.

"Oh, my god," I said. "What are you doing?" I felt so innocent. And I had been afraid of feeling that way. Through the haze of sex, I realized I had created this artificial girl, this vampy, sophisticated sexpot who read erotica and danced at a sex club but climaxed alone with her vibrator every night. I didn't want to be that person anymore.

Now, innocent felt perfect with this big, safe amazon fucking me and soothing me at the same time. She had her hand on my ass and rocked my pelvis for me, rocked me over and around her finger, rocked me into and across her mouth. She lifted my legs over my head, then held them—straight-armed, one hand cupping my heels, and her mouth staying with me, her finger staying with me, one finger and her mouth staying with me.

I came hard. So hard. Hard on her mouth—and that one finger.

That was the start of everything, of letting go.

Later that night she had me fuck her with my hand. She made me fuck her hard, and I was scared I was going to hurt her, but she told me not to be afraid, and it was like she was teaching me not to be afraid of things down there, least of all a woman's hand or fingers. She showed me what a pussy can really take.

"I don't want to bruise you," I said.

"That's OK. I'd like to know you were there. I'd like to feel it driving home to L.A. tomorrow morning. It'll keep me from falling asleep at the wheel."

The next morning was a little awkward. She woke up shocked about how young I was. I felt somehow guilty that she had no panty hose left and had to borrow a pair of my boxers (which she never returned, thank you very much). I got a postcard from her sent from some shit town in Arizona where she'd crashed at a motel for a night. It said she'd stopped and had peach ice cream at the place I told her to and it was as good as I said it would be. That was all I needed to know.

The Busgirl
C.J. Evans

It was 1989, and I had just come out to my college roommates. I'd known I was bisexual since I was 15 or 16, but I'd never had the courage to act on my desires for women. My entire freshman year I was attracted to my English TA, but she was straight (and kind of mean), and my crush was obsessive and futile. When my sophomore year rolled around and I was going to be moving into an apartment with three friends, I took them each aside separately and came out to them. Living as a closeted bisexual in the dorms my freshman year had been manageable, but I knew it would be rough to try and keep the secret from my new roommates. Fortunately, my friends were all open-minded (I wouldn't have told them if they weren't), and they were all cool when I came out to them. One of them, Kate, even checked out a book of lesbian erotica from the library and read it out loud with me. We were cracking up the entire time—a lot of it was so hackneyed and terribly written.

A few weeks later I saw an ad in the school paper about a dance that was being held by the Ten Percent Club, the campus gay and lesbian group, that Friday night. I asked Kate if she would go with me, since I was nervous about going alone and didn't know any other gay people at school. Kate was straight, but as I said, my roommates were all pretty liberal, and she agreed to go with me.

"I'll split if any hot chicks hit on you," Kate smiled.

"Yeah, right. Like that's going to happen," I laughed.

The next day, Thursday, the day before the dance, I was running for the bus headed for campus, frantically trying to wave it down. I had a 7:50 A.M. anthropology class that I was chronically late for. Plus, it was raining outside and I had a huge anthro project in my satchel. I finally caught up the bus at a red light and climbed inside. I was a complete wreck, trying to maneuver my way through the crowded bus with a cup of coffee, my umbrella, and my overflowing satchel. All of a sudden this grizzly guy turned around and jabbed me with his elbow, causing my entire project to spill out of my bag.

"Oh, sorry, lady," he said.

"Whatever," I snarled.

"Here, let me help you with that." I looked up and saw the prettiest blue eyes I'd ever seen, on the sexiest woman I'd ever seen. She had short blond hair and a crooked smile and porcelain skin. A little on the butch side but slightly feminine. A tomboy, which to me is the sexiest kind of woman on earth.

"Thanks. Thanks a lot," I managed, as she got my papers together and handed them to me.

"No problem. No problem at all." We were making some serious eye contact, but then she suddenly looked out the window and said, "Oh, it's my stop. See ya around...I hope."

Now, to this day I'm really bad at recognizing when someone's hitting on me. Usually if I'm at a bar and some cute girl is staring at me, I think, *What? Do I have chili on my face or something?* But on this autumn day in 1989 I had actually been *checked out* by a girl. Man, did I ever hope I'd see her around again.

All day long I thought about her, so much so that I was practically glowing. When I got home from class later that afternoon, I told Kate what had happened.

"See, you don't even need me," she said. "You can get all the girls you want by yourself."

"I need you for moral support!" I laughed. "Besides, what if she shows up at the dance tomorrow night?"

"How do you even know she's gay?"

"Oh, I know. Believe me, I know."

The next night I was so nervous I thought I was going to pee in my pants. But I didn't, of course. I got all dolled up in my best jeans, a black T-shirt, and my nicest pair of Doc

Martens. I ran some gel through my shoulder-length brown hair, put on a little lipstick, and was ready to go.

"Meow!" Kate said as we headed out the door toward the student union where the dance was being held. "Hello-o-o, Kitty!"

I cracked up and threw my arm around her, glad I had such a good pal.

When we got to the second floor of the student union, we paid our $2 cover and went inside. My eyes totally bugged out at the sight of so many gay people gathered together. The first thing I noticed was two gay men dressed in leather in the corner, one with his arm slung over the shoulders of the other. At one table, a bunch of middle-aged butch women sat around totally cracking up and pointing at their clumsy friend trying to bust a move on the dance floor. Dozens of pink and white helium-filled balloons clung to the ceiling. The mood in the place was definitely celebratory, which put me in high spirits, even though I was nervous, since I was attending my first official gay and lesbian event. Plus, I was hoping I'd see the blond girl from the bus, so my adrenaline was pumping full force.

After going up to the bar and getting a couple of bottles of water, Kate and I found a table near the dance floor and sat down and watched the scene before our eyes. The sound system was pounding out Sister Sledge.

"She's cute. What about her?" Kate asked, pointing to a girl on the dance floor.

"Too short," I said. "I wouldn't like being the 'big' one."

"What about that redhead in the corner?"

"Too pretentious-looking. I can't go out with anyone whose earrings weigh more than she does."

"You're too picky," Kate said.

"Yeah, well, I have a right to be picky. I'm a freakin' sex kitten! Meow!" I keeled over laughing, which cracked Kate up too. In fact, we were laughing so hard, everyone around us must have been staring at us. And then the impossible happened: Right when I looked up, tears streaming out of my eyes, who was standing over me but the blond girl from the bus.

"I didn't know I was that funny-looking," she said, grinning from ear to ear.

"Oh...uh...hi," I said, trying to compose myself. "Kate, this is...um...I'm sorry, I didn't get your name."

"I'm Joanna." She reached to shake Kate's hand.

"I'm Carolyn," I told her.

I guess Kate could tell right away that this was the girl I'd told her about. It was probably pretty obvious by the way I was acting—like a huge dork. Plus, I'd described Joanna physically in detail to Kate at least five times the previous day! Well, being such a good friend (or tormentor), Kate immediately excused herself, saying she had to use the restroom. But I made some "I can't believe you're doing this to me" eye contact with Kate before she left.

"Um...do you want to sit down?" I asked Joanna.

"Sure," she said, and she did. "Is this your first time at one of these dances?"

Man, were her eyes blue. I must have looked like I was freakin' hypnotized, the way I was just zoning out into them. Still, I had enough sense to answer her. "Is it that obvious?" I laughed.

"No, no, I didn't mean that," she grinned. "I just meant that I've never seen you here before."

"This is the campus Jews for Jesus dance, isn't it?"

Joanna and I busted up laughing, which was just the icebreaker we needed. I looked out onto the dance floor for a moment and saw Kate doing the funky chicken with two gay gays, which cracked me up even more. It looked like she was having fun, and now I had a little time to get to know Joanna better.

Joanna and I sat there talking for nearly an hour and a half—and Kate danced the entire time! All the dancing gay guys thought she was the belle of the ball, screaming "Go, girl!

Go, girl!" over and over as she undulated and shimmied across the dance floor.

I learned that Joanna was also a sophomore, that she was treasurer of the Ten Percent Club, and that she loved old movies and board games, just like me. In fact, we had a lot in common: We were both only children, daughters of preachers (why are so many preachers' kids gay anyway?), and both rode green ten-speed Schwinns around campus! She also told me she had just declared her major: art history. I told her I was still deciding between English and anthropology but that I'd probably eventually do a double major, which would keep me in school for at least five years.

"You can't finish in four?" she asked.

"I'm kind of slow," I laughed.

"I hope you're not slow with everything." Just then Joanna smiled and gave me a quick kiss on the cheek. A kiss so sweet and tender that I probably should have gone straight to hell for what it did to my loins: Immediately I was wet.

"No, not everything," I grinned.

Just then Kate ambled up to the table. She was sweaty but had a big smile on her face. "Hey, I'm going to this party at this guy Geoffrey's house," she said. "You guys wanna come? It's just down the street from our place on Wilson. He's really cool." She pointed to a cute blond guy on the dance floor grooving out to "Dancing Queen."

"Sounds good," Joanna said.

"Yeah, let's get out of here," I smiled.

So Joanna, Kate, and I headed out and walked the 15 minutes to Geoffrey's place, which, it turned out, was only two doors down from my apartment. I had a gay neighbor and didn't even know it! We went inside the upstairs apartment (it was a duplex), and the place was *packed* with gay men and lesbians, mostly college students but also a few older people.

"You guys friends of Geoffrey's?" a stunning, tall brunette asked us as we came in.

"Sorta," I said.

"Hi, I'm Sena, his roommate. He'll be here in a little bit. Grab a beer. The keg's in the corner."

We all grabbed a beer, then Kate—gay social butterfly that she now was—went over and started chatting up a couple of guys who looked like they might be straight. Maybe she'd get a date tonight too.

The place was so packed we could hardly move, so Joanna and I went out onto the balcony in the back, which was, for some strange reason, empty. We looked out into the starry sky.

"So...you're really cute," Joanna said. "I noticed you right away on the bus. In fact, I noticed you when you were *running* for the bus."

"Oh, man, did you see *that*?" I laughed.

"Yeah, it was pretty funny."

"You're not just cute," I told her. "You're beautiful. And 'cute' doesn't get dates. *Sexy* does." My whole life I'd been plagued by people calling me cute. It was always "Oh, Carolyn, you're so *cute,*" never "gorgeous" or "sexy" or any of that. I guess *cute* is better than hideous, but it gets old after a while.

"I think you're absolutely breathtaking," Joanna said, and then she put down her beer and leaned in and kissed me—on the mouth this time. If there were a hundred stars in the sky that night, I wouldn't know it, because I saw thousands of them in front of my eyes once she pulled away. So *this* was kissing a girl. Right then I knew I'd never need to be with a guy again. This was it. Fuck bisexuality! I was a full-on *dyke*!

"That was nice," I said, fumbling for words, so instead of saying anything else, I kissed her back. This time it was more serious. Our tongues intertwined passionately; my entire body was aching for this. And *this* wouldn't do. I needed to sleep with this woman ASAP.

"Hey," I said, breaking the kiss, "I live two doors down. Wanna blow this place?"

"Good plan," Joanna said, grabbing my hand.

On our way out of the party I waved to Kate, who was engrossed in conversation with a jocky-looking guy. She just winked as Joanna and I left and made the short walk to my apartment. Luckily, my other two roommates, Angela and Holly, were out for the evening, so we had the place to ourselves. I grabbed two sodas from the fridge, and Joanna and I got comfortable on the couch.

"So you wanna finish where we left off?" I smiled.

I didn't even have to wait for an answer. Joanna pulled me to her and kissed me passionately. I put my hands on the back of her head; her short hair was fuzzy and tickled my fingers. I searched out her mouth with my tongue then nudged it playfully against her two front teeth, which had a small space between them. I bit her lower lip gently. Joanna trailed kisses down my face to my neck.

"Mind if I take this off?" She tugged at my T-shirt.

"Let's go into my room first," I said. "What if one of my roommates walks in?"

Joanna agreed, and we went into my room and shut the door behind us. She pressed me up against the door and kissed me again, this time a little more forcefully. "Let's take this off *now,*" she said, and pulled my shirt over my head. I undid my black lacy bra and let it fall to the floor.

I turned on a small lamp by my bed and shut off the overhead light. We both got comfortable on my futon, me on my back and Joanna straddling me.

"Oh, baby, you are so beautiful," she said, kneading my breasts, and I was so glad to hear those words, especially coming from someone as hot as Joanna. My crotch was so wet I thought I'd soak the futon.

Joanna scooched down and started sucking and biting my breasts, slurping on my nipples like they were candy, circling over and over with her tongue. She made her way down my torso with her warm, wet mouth until she got to my belt.

In a couple of swift motions she undid the buckle. Her quickness and agility were turning me on more and more by the second. After I helped her take off my jeans, she went in for the kill, sucking my red-hot clit through my damp cotton panties. The sensation was exquisite but pure torture: I wanted that tongue right on my clit. So I pulled down my panties and let her have it.

Now, I'd had guys perform oral sex on me many times, but they never knew what the hell they were doing. I was always like, "Um, excuse me, are you going to be done soon? Your head is blocking *Nightline*." When Ted Koppel is more interesting than having your clit sucked, you know something's amiss. But with Joanna it was completely different. She knew just how to please me, sucking my entire clitoris into her full lips, tonguing under the hood, flicking fiercely then gently, then teasing it with little licks. When she put two fingers inside me and continued to eat me out like crazy, I thought I was going to burst. My pussy was sopping wet with slippery come.

"You taste so good," Joanna said, and she pulled her fingers out and brought them to my mouth. "Here, taste."

She was right. But I'd bet my entire checking account *she* tasted better.

Joanna put her fingers back inside and added a third, thrusting me full force. She went back to tonguing my engorged clit, licking my entire vulva with her masterful tongue, around and around and around. My entire body shook as she brought me to the edge; chills flooded my skin as I cried out in release and ecstasy.

"That's it," I laughed. "Tomorrow I'm buying a monthly bus pass."

Joanna just laughed as she covered my face with kisses. We made love several times that night. And even though it was my first time with a woman, I knew how to please her—and brought her to orgasm several times—since I just did what I thought would make her feel good. And, as the saying goes, who knows a woman's body like another woman, right?

Joanna and I dated for the rest of our sophomore year, but then she transferred to a college with a better art history program. The program at our school had lost a lot of its best faculty members in the past few years, and their funding had been drastically reduced. (I was sure it was because of the new football stadium the college was building.) We tried to maintain a long-distance relationship, but we were now 900 miles apart, which took its toll on both of us, so we eventually broke up. But 13 years later we're still friends and even E-mail each other several times a week, updating each other on our love lives (we're both chronically single). Still, Joanna was one of the hottest lovers—and definitely the most caring—I've ever had in my life. And to this day, I'm mostly attracted to tomboyish blond women. Wonder why?

Oh, and by the way, my friend Kate ended up dating a tall, dark, and handsome lacrosse player she met at the party that night. They became "college sweethearts" (that phrase totally makes me cringe) and will have been married eight years this fall. Every chance I get, I remind her how my taking her out for a night of gay fun and frolic led to a lifetime of happiness for her!

Does It Count?

Kate Dominic

Does it count as a lesbian experience if it was only in my head?

It happened at a queer writers conference. My reasons for being there are a different story. But that day I fell ass over heels for two women. That's right, not one, but two. I tried to convince myself it was because I have such terrible gaydar that this was the first time I'd realized I was with women who liked women—or maybe I should say who *also* like women? Whichever, the women I met suddenly seemed to be in a whole new category: *available.*

Which I am not.

I live het. Married het, kids het, pets het. I'm happy—content, even. I was *not* expecting the sudden mini orgasms that swept through my cunt at the sound of the one woman's voice. At the living honey of her words, running thick and sweet and viscous over my skin as she talked about her sex, her sexy stories. Or the warm, clear, hazel-eyed stare of the woman across from me in the audience. She looked at me in a way I'd only recognized in men before. And just like that, in the space of a heartbeat, my whole world turned upside down.

I wanted her. Wanted her back. Wanted her desperately. I smiled, inept as a teenager, afraid, unsure what to do, hesitant—except my body wasn't hesitating. It was stunned at my reaction and her...offer? I watched her full cinnamon lips twitch upward, her beautiful eyes go green and sparkle. The flash of pink tongue as she parted her lips, ever so slightly, and licked.

I came so hard my face flushed.

Her voice. Her smile. Her, her, her. My mind upended and flooded with memories of the only girls I'd ever kissed. So long ago. In junior high, at slumber parties, where we had contests to see who was the best kisser. We wore panty hose over our faces so we couldn't see who we were kissing. Until that night I'd never known lips could be so soft, that a kiss could be wet and hot and arousing, even through nylon. At that age, I barely understood arousal, and my Roman Catholic sex education hadn't mentioned anything at all about *wanting* to do the unmentionable things we weren't supposed to do, though we'd been told not to do them with boys. Kissing girls wasn't explicitly on the list, though I imagine the nuns never imagined the types of kisses we were sharing.

Then again, maybe they did. Maybe they just didn't want to taint that one exquisite sliver of our awakening sexuality in the name of a patriarchal clergy. Maybe they kissed each other that way.

Maybe not. I remembered the texture of nylon on my lips as I watched the honeyed woman on the podium. Her long, golden curls flowed around her shoulders as she spoke in her slow, thick Southern drawl. I was in the second row, seated on the end, allowed to stare by virtue of being in her audience. She wore a thinly knit beige sweater. I imagined it was cashmere, which makes me sneeze and itch, but this was my fantasy, and cashmere is so soft. The sweater clung to her breasts like a second skin, rising and falling as she spoke, the soft flesh jiggling, her nipples perking up ever so slightly when she laughed. When I closed my eyes—but I didn't want to close them—I could see my hands reaching to cup the soft, full swells of her breasts.

Even in the daydream, even when in my mind I walked quietly up and stood before her, she didn't see me. There was just enough room for me to stand between the podium and her. She continued speaking, looking at the crowd, though in my ears her breath hitched slightly when I reached up and my thumbs stroked her nipples. A little shiver ran down her body as the tips rose up to meet me, tips full and elongated, like she'd nursed a baby at some time in her life. I slid my hands over her shoulders, ran my palms up and down her arms, raising tiny shocks of static electricity as I wakened her skin to my touch. The hair at her wrists stood up, soft and fluffed as the sweater threads. My own skin rose in wonder at the feel of her. I traced the outlines of her hands, leaned down and nuzzled my face in the valley between her breasts, slid my hands under the bottom of her sweater, up between the soft weave of the cashmere and the silk of her warm, living skin. Unclasped the hook hidden in the heat between her mounds.

Her breasts fell forward, full and heavy against my waiting cheeks. I nuzzled more, inhaling the scents hidden in the sweater—yarn dust, her soap, a hint of something light and floral that was uniquely hers. She breathed deeply, a quick shiver stretching her shoulders as my lips traced the slope of her breast. Her nipple was hard, poking up against my cheek. I nuzzled like a baby questing for sustenance, my hands sliding around her back to hold her to me. And when I was hungry enough, when I wanted her so badly, when I felt her body heat in the rock-hard point, even through the sweater, I opened my mouth and latched on, pulling the swollen tip into my mouth.

She shivered as I blew, hot and wet, through the fabric, the weave of the sweater rubbing me, rubbing her, like moist silk, like hot cashmere, as I licked and sucked and worked her nipple. My cunt got wetter and wetter the more I sucked, the harder I sucked. She licked her lips, moistening them, wetting them until they glistened like liquid spice, bit softly on her lower lip as she paused and fidgeted behind the podium. Inside my mind I groaned, imagining her naked areolas were that same exotic color, imagining them growing wet and deeper red as I sucked them awake. Occasionally she gasped, closing her eyes as I nursed sensation from her. I wondered whether maybe she was as surprised at the unexpected waking female wet dream as I was at the two large wet circles growing dark brown in my mind on the front of her sweater.

I wondered if anyone else saw.

I slowly kissed my way down, kneeling in front of her, tonguing her belly button through the soft cashmere as I unbuttoned her jeans and carefully worked the zipper down, pushed her jeans down over her hips, down to her knees, her ankles. The patch of lacy silk covering her crotch drew me like a bee to nectar. I nuzzled again, inhaling her sweet, musky scent, urging her thighs apart, even as mine clenched tightly, straining for friction. I inhaled long and deep and raggedly as my hands slid in back of her and I caressed her bottom, the firm, muscular, rounded, female—damn it!—*female* curve of her hips.

She shivered when I stroked my face lightly over her mons. My nose pressed against her labia, pressing the already damp silk lightly in. She moaned softly and went very still as I breathed in her scent, over and over again, imprinting the smell of sex-wet panties and horny female vulva into my brain. I held her tightly and looked up, watched the wet, aroused buds of her breasts move naturally against the cashmere as she inhaled deeply.

I licked the silk in her crevice. She gasped, stopped talking, and closed her eyes. I imagined she saw me in that second, saw my head between her legs, my tongue flicking over the outlines of delicately embroidered magnolias, my lips kissing the tiny silk butterflies, my wet red hungry tongue lapping at her cunt through the sopping lace. Imagined she saw—and smiled.

I licked her for all I was worth, licked and sucked until my tongue was raw on the silk and her panties were drenched with my saliva and her melted honey. Tasting, always tasting, I sucked the mingled juices from the silk, then tongued them back inside her. Her voice was thick and her hips swayed toward me, undulating as I rubbed her swollen clit with my sore tongue. I held her hips tightly, snaked my tongue under the edge of her pantied crotch.

She gasped and arched toward me. And as she moved,

my tongue pushed her panties aside and slid into the slippery, tangy heat between her labia.

She gasped as the heat of her inner pussy closed around the tip of my wiggling tongue. Her juices ran down into my waiting mouth. She tasted so good. Like the sweet tang on my finger when I'm masturbating—not the thick cream of a climax, but the slipperiness of arousal just before an orgasm.

She opened her legs as far as her pants allowed, bracing herself. I reached up and yanked her panties down to join her jeans. Spread her thighs and carefully parted the glistening, slippery, softly furred lips. Pressed my face to her and inhaled again, this time more deeply, drawing her molecules in to dance in my nostrils, learning the smell of woman, woman, woman. Stuck out my tongue and licked slowly up her drenched slit, licked deep in the liquid heat inside her, through the valley of her lips, teasing, learning the pleasure nub by heart as it trembled against my raw, sensitive, quivering tongue. Licked again and smiled with pure pleasure as she sank her hands into my hair and trembled above me. I shivered. My tongue felt so much more than my fingertip on my pussy ever could. I wiggled her engorged nub, flicked it with my tongue, licked and sucked and worked the prepuce over it, then held the cover back even farther and flicked my tongue, fast and furiously, mercilessly, over her fully exposed clit.

As the rhythm of her words vibrated in my ears, my whole world became the valley between her thighs. I wanted her climax, needed it to release the pressure building in such unbearable waves inside me. She cried out softly, shaking, to my ears alone. I held the prepuce back, took the swollen, quivering, dark red nub between the insides of my lips and sucked it tenderly into my mouth. Sucked it lovingly and ruthlessly against my mercilessly flailing tongue. She screamed, threw back her head, her body stiff as she gripped my head to her, and she started to shake violently. I sank two fingers into her, pressed up hard and firm against the bump deep inside her pussy. She screamed again and her juices gushed onto my chin and she shook against me, my nose buried so deeply in her crotch I could hardly breathe. The waves rolled over me and my cunt convulsed and my face flushed and my own panties got wet, wet, wet again.

I held her until she stopped shaking. She smiled, breathing softly and deeply as I kissed her clit, as I tenderly kissed my way down her vulva and gently lapped up her juices until she was clean. I pulled up her panties, kissed her clit again through the already drying silk, and tugged up her jeans. I reached under her sweater and closed her bra, carefully pulling the sweater back into place. I hugged her to me, my arms wrapped around her waist, inhaling one last time as I let her warmth flow over me.

Then I quietly stood up and tiptoed off the stage. She was still speaking, still turning the pages of her notes. I sat back down, surprised to open my eyes and find my seat still warm and my clenched hands tingling and my legs pressed tightly together, and the faces around me all glued to the mesmerizing lover on the podium—as though my world hadn't just changed so profoundly.

I barely saw the other woman move. She was sitting to my left, almost directly across from me in the U of seats, yet when I closed my eyes again, she was standing in front of me. She was short, the way so many dykes are short, with light brown hair in an easy butch cut. Her beautiful hazel eyes sparkled deep-green with lush brown whorls, and her lips, her full, strong lips that looked like they would be soft, so soft, when they kissed, curved in a firm, commanding smile. She stood with her feet wide apart, her weight on both legs—a dyke stance. And she was wearing no-nonsense brown corduroys and a light gold sweater, maybe cashmere. Her breasts were firmer than the speaker's, yet this woman's breasts moved naturally. This was not a woman who wore a bra. She didn't say a word, just snapped her fingers and pointed for me to slide down in the chair.

I did. Slid down until my head rested on the jacket draped over the back of my chair. She yanked open my vest, tugged apart the buttons on my tailored blouse, and with one flick of her wrist opened my bra. My breasts fell forward, against my chest, into her hands. Wordlessly, she stroked the sides of the naked curves, the speaker's voice fading to a hum in the background. The hazel-eyed woman cupped my breasts in her hands and rubbed until my nipples rose stiff and exposed into her palms. Then her fingers closed around me and she tugged, hard and imperiously, gradually pulling the areolas out into her fingertips, sliding, milking, snapping, until each tug echoed all the way deep into my cunt and I was panting in the chair. She stepped between my legs, laughing silently as I looked down, shocked, and realized I'd opened my legs for her. I opened my mouth to speak, but she shook her head sharply, her fingers never stopping their tugging, milking torture as I arched my chest toward her and my panties grew wetter and wetter.

She slipped a hand quickly into her pocket. I gasped as nipple clamps snapped onto my engorged tips. They hurt, pain hurt—swollen, pressure, pleasure pain hurt. She tugged gently on the chain between the clamps and nodded, smiling at my moan, her eyes glittering, boring into mine, like she knew exactly how each tug transmitted waves of sensation deep into my cunt. Like that was exactly what she wanted to do.

As I lay there gasping, she dropped the chain and yanked up my skirt and slip, bunched them together and stuffed the hems into my waistband. I watched, stunned, as she drew a knife from her pocket and slit the sides of my panties, yanked them unceremoniously out from under me, and tucked the thin pink nylon in her pocket like a trophy. She roughly grabbed my legs and knelt between them, slid her hands around my hips, and pulled my ass forward to the edge of the chair. She picked up the nipple clamp chain and tugged it, hard enough to leave me gasping, and as I shook beneath her, she buried her face between my legs.

The air around me was almost too thick to breathe. Her tongue was hot—erotic, liquid-sandpaper hot. She swiped her way up my slit, ignoring my cries as she tongued the juice from my hole, pulled my prepuce back from my clit and worked the naked nub until I was shaking. And she used her teeth. I thought I'd die from it. She bit, and I shook with a climax that didn't quite reach my core, just intense enough to leave me wanting to scream for more as I arched against her. The vibration of her silent laugh hummed against my vulva as she licked the running juices from my hole. She knew just where to touch, how often to tug on the nipple chain, how much abrasion and pain my poor, desperate clit and labia could stand—without letting me come.

I bit back a scream as a clamp snapped onto my clit. Watched in desperate, fascinated horror as she attached that chain to the other one. Her tongue worked down my slit again as each tug on the chains—each painful tug on my clit and nipples—sent jolts deep into my belly. My juices ran out toward her as I rocked with the waves of pleasure pain. I heard the snap of a glove, looked down to see her gloved hand gathering my juices, gathering them as she tugged mercilessly on the chains. Then her hand slid lower, and her slippery fingers slicked up firmly against my ass lips. They kissed her back, involuntarily. Kissing in rhythm to the painful pleasure tugs. I moaned as one slick finger pressed imperiously in, pushing past the gate; cried out as her finger slid all the way in and started stretching, slicking and stretching and fucking my ass with her strong, gloved, feminine hand. Clamping and punishing and awakening my nipples and clit until they screamed for the release of an orgasm.

"I want you," I whispered, the words shimmering around me as they fought their way past my lips. She smiled, her hazel eyes twinkling, and bent to kiss my vulva.

"This is for tongues," she answered, softly, her voice vibrating through my skin and spine. She slid her tongue into my cunt, fucking my pussy with her tongue, fucking my ass with her finger, squeezing the orgasm out of my clit and my nipples and from somewhere that shattered like glass deep inside me. Squeezing and fucking and licking as my body imploded as it convulsed and the waves surged out of me, consuming me with their fire, with the heat of her tongue. And the passion of wanting her with my soul.

Then she released the lower clamp. My head echoed in my screams as the blood rushed back in and met the orgasm surging outward. She held me close as the final tremors took me and I collapsed against her, crying, clutching my hands in the softness of her hair and holding on to the incredible, sexy strength of her wonderful, living female body.

When I quieted, she kissed my labia, smiling as she licked my juices from my still-trembling clit. I moaned with contentment as she withdrew her fingers and patted my satisfied asshole. Whimpered as she peeled off the glove and knelt back up and I followed the determined look in her eyes, watched her fingers moved deliberately to the nipple clamps, cried out as she released the first one and roughly worked the feeling into the tip. She smiled as my cunt clenched in another small orgasm. Smiled again, as she released the other side and I shook again. She palmed my breasts, briefly, comforting my sore and tender nipples. Cupped my pussy and comforted it, my well-used and tender clit and my unhappily empty but still tingling pussy. Then she winked at me, stood up, pressed my legs back together, tossed the inside-out glove in the trash, and walked purposefully back to her seat.

My eyes opened to thunderous applause. I looked around quickly, disoriented, trying to get my bearings. The speaker was nodding to the crowd, accepting their accolades as she thanked them, smiling as she walked back to her chair and carefully sat down.

I looked around. No one was looking at me. No one was noticing me, noticing the profound thing that had happened to me—noticing the change in my life. I had desired another woman, not just once, but twice. Wanted them so badly, I'd climaxed just from hearing their voices, just from seeing them.

Does that count? Does that count as having sex with a woman? Does it count if that's all it can ever be, at least in this life?

And what on earth do I do about it now?

First Love, True Love

Deborah Dukes-Pierce

I kept very still and had my eyes on the clock: It was almost midnight. I was hoping my husband would fall asleep quickly so I could sneak out of bed and tiptoe down the hall to my office. I patiently waited until his breathing grew heavy, and then I slipped out of bed. I went into the office and sat on the chair. I hit the mute button and signed on. I held my breath and prayed that she'd still be online. "She" was Debbie, a young woman I'd been corresponding with online. We had innocently met in a chat room, and even though I was a married woman living in Pennsylvania and she was a single girl living at home in Oklahoma, we both fell desperately in love. We had joked about meeting each other, but because I was married and we lived some 1,200 miles apart, it didn't seem realistic. It was only a fantasy. As time went by, however, we realized that meeting each other was a must. We both had to know if what we felt for each other was real, if it would carry over physically. It seemed a natural progression.

Debbie and I had started out just chatting online, then progressed to talking on the telephone, then flirting online, and then having phone sex. I wanted to touch her so badly that I promised her I'd do everything possible to make our union happen. Early on we had confessed to each other our attraction to women and the fear we both had of coming out. We soon grew very close, and she was the only person in whom I could confide. Even though I was married and had never met her in person, I wanted nothing more than to make love to her.

I logged on and was grateful to see her screen name.

"Hi there," I typed.

"I've missed you," she replied.

I wanted so badly to touch her, to smell her, to whisper

in her ear. I could hardly contain my emotions.

"Listen, I'm planning a trip to Nashville in a few weeks," I wrote. "Would you like to meet me?"

Debbie hesitated a few moments then wrote, "I'd love to."

My heart raced. We both quickly signed off and talked on the phone until the sun came up, discussing our rendezvous. The plan was for me to tell my husband that I was going to Nashville for a few days to visit some friends. I'd then rent a car and drive to Oklahoma to meet Debbie. She'd tell her parents that she was visiting an old friend. They had no idea that all this was happening, and they had no idea she was in love with a woman. Out of fear of rejection, she had never discussed her homosexuality with them. We both knew that this trip was risky, but it was too important to let others stand in our way.

I bought my plane tickets and anxiously counted the days. Neither of us had been with a woman before, so we were both nervous and incredibly excited about meeting. I wanted everything to be perfect, so I asked Debbie what she wanted me to wear and how she wanted my hair to look. I knew she liked long hair, and mine was very curly, so I was sure she wanted me to wear it down. She told me that when she first saw me she wanted me to have wet hair and wear a men's white dress shirt, tight jeans, and a certain cologne.

I got excited just thinking about our first encounter and knew that if we were to meet in public, I wouldn't be able to contain my excitement. So I decided that meeting in a hotel room would be the best thing. I promised her that if she felt uncomfortable in any way when she got there, she could call it off. Debbie agreed that she wanted to meet me and told me to make all the arrangements. I phoned the hotel the next day and, being optimistic, booked a room for two nights.

Several weeks later I boarded a plane in Baltimore and daydreamed of our encounter. When I arrived in Nashville, I called Debbie and told her that I'd rent a car and make the drive to Tulsa. She couldn't believe it was really happening, and neither could I. I asked her if she wanted to back out of it, and she said no. She was getting ready to leave and make the two-hour drive to her friend's house. I told her that when I arrived at the hotel I'd call her again.

The next day I checked into the hotel in Tulsa and called Debbie's cell phone. She answered and told me she'd be there in an hour. My heart pounding, I set up the room so that everything would be perfect. I placed scented candles on the bedside table, turned on some slow music, and pulled the curtains shut. I took a shower, put on my best white dress shirt, jeans, and the requested cologne. Then I waited. Suddenly the phone rang. It was Debbie. "I'm in the elevator," she said. "I can't wait to see you."

I couldn't believe I was about to meet her. I stood at the door with the phone next to my ear. Then I heard the elevator door open.

"I can hear you," I whispered. I looked down and saw a shadow at the door. "Is that you?" Debbie said yes, and we both laughed. I told her I was going to hang up now and asked her if she was ready. She said she was.

I put the phone down, held my breath, and opened the door. I'll never forget what I saw. There she was, looking ravishing. She had told me she was tall, but I had no idea she was almost six feet. She took my breath away. She was much more gorgeous than she looked in the picture she had sent me a few weeks before. She was wearing a tight green button-down shirt, blue jeans, and open-toed shoes. Her makeup was perfect, and she had beautiful full lips, with a small mole I hadn't noticed in her photo. I wanted to grab her and kiss her hard, but I knew I should take it slow. She had her head down, and I could tell she was very nervous.

"Come in. Let me take your things," I said.

Debbie walked in without saying a word. I wondered if perhaps she was disappointed with how I looked. I had sent her a picture, but it had been an old photo and I had changed slightly. My hair was darker, and I was older. She was considerably younger than I was, so I thought maybe I looked too old. I searched her face for an answer but couldn't read what she was thinking. I led her to the edge of the bed, and we both sat down.

"Are you nervous?" I asked.

"A little," Debbie whispered.

I took her hand and held it. I told her she was beautiful and that I was glad she had trusted me enough to see me.

"I can't believe it's you," she said softly.

"It's me. It's me. I'm the person you fell in love with," I reassured her.

I hoped she couldn't hear how loud my heart was pounding. I didn't want her to think I was nervous. I had brought her a present, and I thought now would be the best time to give it to her. I leaned back and reached for a small, neatly wrapped box. "Here, this is for you. It was my grandmother's before she died, and I want you to have it," I told her.

Debbie opened the box and saw the gold heart pendant on a gold chain. She smiled and thanked me. I asked her if I could put it on her, and she said yes. I opened the clasp and put my arms around her to fasten it. As I pulled my head back, I gently kissed her neck. I couldn't resist kissing her tenderly. She just smiled and didn't say a word, but by the way she tightly squeezed my hand, I knew she liked what I did. I looked her in the eye and asked, "May I kiss you?" Debbie didn't reply, so I wasn't sure she had heard me. Maybe I'd whispered it too quietly or maybe I'd imagined I'd said it. I waited a few minutes and again asked, "May I kiss you?" This time she looked me in the eye and said yes. I started to tremble. We both slowly leaned toward each other and gently kissed. I couldn't believe I was finally kissing the woman I had fallen in love with a few weeks before. She firmly grabbed my shoulders and pulled me down on the bed.

"I've been wanting to kiss you for such a long time," she whispered.

"Me too," I panted.

We kissed again, this time our hands exploring each other's bodies. I couldn't believe how *perfect* it felt, how right and comfortable. We both had tears of joy in our eyes and held each other tight. I was on top of her and pushed myself up on my hands. She unbuttoned my shirt. I wasn't wearing a bra, so my breasts fell out, lightly grazing her lips. Debbie started sucking my nipples, and I felt my excitement rise. I kissed her hard again and told her I loved her. She told me she loved me too, and we kissed again.

We quickly tore each other's clothes off then made love for the next several hours. It was new to both of us, and we laughed and cried with each new experience. I couldn't get enough of her skin. When I tasted her for the first time, I couldn't believe how wonderful it was. When she tasted me, I couldn't believe the ecstasy I felt. Debbie and I both agreed that all the times we had been with men, it was only sex. This was the first time we had ever truly made love. For the next two days we stayed in bed, laughing, kissing, holding each other, and not wanting our fantasy weekend to end.

On Sunday morning, after a few hours of sleep, Debbie and I were both sad about leaving each other. We had known this time would come, but after what we had shared together, the separation seemed unbearable. We made small talk and tried to make each other laugh. But every kiss felt like it would be our last, and every time I touched her skin I felt myself ache. When I told her I'd decided to divorce my husband and "marry" her, Debbie stared at me in disbelief. We both cried and hugged each other tightly. I promised her I'd make the separation and be by her side before the end of the year. We only had to wait a few months to be together forever. She just smiled and whispered, "I love you."

Despite our newfound joy, however, Debbie and I

walked to our cars with a sense of dread. When we reached my rental car, I asked her to sit next to me for a few minutes. We sat there holding hands and looking into each other's eyes. I wanted so badly to stay with her, but I knew I had to go. She leaned over and kissed me passionately and let out an incredibly sexy moan. I told her to be strong and wait for me. She just cried and nodded. Then Debbie got out of the car and walked away. I slowly pulled out of the parking lot and looked in my rearview mirror for one more glimpse. I wanted to have her face in my mind forever.

They say not every story has a happy ending. Well, I'm proud to say that this one does. I did leave my husband of nine years and eventually moved to Oklahoma. Debbie and I have been together for more than two years, and we've spent both anniversaries—and plan to spend every one to come—in the same hotel room, in the same bed, doing the same wonderful things over and over and over again.

Seventeen
Alison Dubois

It was during my junior year of high school that we met. She looked so much like Jaclyn Smith that she could have passed for her twin. In fact, the first time I saw her, I did a double take. She was the epitome of what I, at age 17, found attractive in a woman, with dark hair, dark brown eyes, big breasts, and full hips. It didn't matter that she was 15 years older than I was, nearly twice my age. I fancied the idea of an older woman enlighten me to the world of lesbian love and lust. She was perfect.

Our introduction, however, was not. I'd just ditched PE class, as I'd done many times, and was slowly walking home. Not too fast, because I didn't want my folks to know I'd cut class. Then I spotted her.

It was June, right at the end of the school year, and it was a warm day. She was stretched across a lounge chair, sunbathing in a skimpy two-piece swimsuit. Trying to steal glances without being too obvious, I stole one glance too many and collided with one of her shrubs. Scrambling to my feet, I saw her grinning, her shades pulled down. She knew *exactly* what had happened. My cheeks burned with embarrassment.

"Are you all right?" she asked in the sexiest voice I'd ever heard. Imagining what else that voice could do gave me chills.

"Yeah. Sorry about your bush," I said, blushing all over again from the double entendre.

At first I thought she was going to laugh, but she just pushed her shades back up. "Well, it seems to be intact. What's your name?"

"Alison."

"Nice to meet you. I'm Vivian," she said. "Would you...?" She held out a bottle of suntan lotion. How presumptuous! Nonetheless, I felt strangely compelled to oblige her.

Feeling my heart in my throat, I took the bottle. Up close she was even more breathtaking. She leaned forward as I squirted a puddle into my palm and slowly massaged it into her bronze skin. It was so soft; it made me tingle all over. I'd never touched an adult woman's bare back before. It made me shudder and wonder what it would be like to touch her in other places.

"It's so hard to get one's back, you know what I mean?" she asked, but I could scarcely hear her. My focus had shifted to the smooth curve of her ass, which her skimpy lime-green suit barely covered. "What is that marvelous scent you're wearing?" she asked, and inhaled deeply. "It smells like jasmine—my favorite. Do you mind if I call you that? It's such a pretty name."

"Um...sure, that's fine." I stammered, returning the lotion. She took it, then squeezed my hand while looking deep into my eyes. That squeeze made a direct line to my crotch. Who was this brazen woman?

"Drop by again, Jasmine," she said casually, getting comfortable again. I was speechless. She was dismissing me! How dare she!

Inasmuch as I was swearing her off on my way home, I knew I'd return. Who could resist? She was a Godiva bonbon to a chocolate aficionado.

Over the summer I stole away from my house every chance I got and went to Vivian's, and we became fast friends. In fact, I gave up many nights of sleep just to be with her. We went on shopping sprees, dined out, and danced until the wee hours of the morning at clubs only she could get me into. Initially, Vivian was hung up on my age. I stopped trying to convince her I was 18 just about the time she started calling me precocious.

She introduced me to ballet, classical music, friends, and the whole stealthy world of the gay community that I hardly knew existed up to that point in my life. She gave me my first taste of *our* culture. It was wonderful. I felt more alive than ever.

One night while nursing a club soda amidst the glitz of Largo's, I thought I caught a glimpse of something else in her eyes, beyond the role of mentor, teacher, or even seductress: It was in the way she held my gaze. Her stylish sassiness was somewhat more subdued, as if it had been softened somehow by something intangible. There was a distant wistfulness in her eyes that shone through the flashing red, blue, and yellow glitter of the strobe lights. Was it love? But suddenly Vivian became aware of my scrutiny, and in that moment it was gone. It was as though she revealed a secret she had wanted or needed to keep hidden.

"What are you thinking?" I asked her.

"That it's late and we should go. After all, you've got class tomorrow, schoolgirl." Her voice trailed as she rose from the table.

If she had been thinking about my age, I'd never know, for she didn't say and I never saw that look again, even though I would think of that moment many times. I'd contemplate how a seemingly perfect evening of dancing, dining, and wonderful flirtatious exchanges could so abruptly be spoiled.

By now I'd pretty much figured nothing was going to happen between Vivian and me, since nothing had after all this time. Foolishly, I equated her to the baby dykes at high school who just talked a good game.

"You're still jailbait. I could get my ass in the sling, you know?" she said one evening in her half-caustic, half-smug way. I shrugged it off, knowing she couldn't be all that alarmed, because she was the one who continued to invite me over and went out and about with me all summer. Still, her show of conscience did surprise me.

Suddenly the tone shifted. She was mixing herself a screwdriver, and against previous declarations that she wasn't going to give me any booze (and "contribute to the delinquency of a minor," as she put it), she handed me a glass, half full. I looked at her.

"Oh, what the hell. Live dangerously!" She clinked our glasses. "Here's to reckless adventures and wild nights, hmm?"

"Why not?" I said in a low voice. She smiled at me in that familiar way of hers, making me wonder if I'd again blown some unspoken rule of "lesbian etiquette." Sometimes, in my insecurity and naïveté, I wondered if she was secretly laughing at me.

"Jasmine...how is it that you've always known you were gay?" she asked while refreshing our drinks.

The alcohol was making me feel loose. I let the taste of it roll on my tongue before each swallow to really absorb the taste of it. "Hell, I don't know. When I was little I just knew I liked little girls, and as I got older, big girls and now...women...all kinds of women," I said, feeling cocky, but Vivian wasn't impressed. Instead she looked a bit miffed.

"You don't know how lucky you are," she said, more serious than I'd heard her all summer. I'd been tempted to say something witty, but her expression made me think better of it. Clearly this wasn't the time for levity.

"What do you mean?" I inquired softly.

"I mean, you didn't have to survive a disastrous marriage and your family disowning you just because you were different." She left her glass on the table, and her words wedged between us as she went to the double glass doors, where she stopped, silent.

I knew my family hadn't been thrilled with me, but obviously things had been rougher for her. It intrigued me; I wanted to know what she meant. This was a side of Vivian I was totally unfamiliar with—worlds apart from the suave, elusive woman I had come to know. A part of me wanted to hold her, this broken doll, so apparently wounded and hurting.

"I'm sorry," I said.

"What have *you* got to be sorry about?" She was unexpectedly curt. I felt the sting like a slap. Setting my glass next to hers, I decided it was time to leave. I brushed by her, but she caught my hand and pulled me into her. "I didn't mean that."

Our eyes met. She knew I was pissed and wanted to leave, but she needed me to stay. She brought her hand to my face and caressed my cheek lightly. Then she traced a finger over my lips.

"Jasmine...such a pretty name," she said, almost as a whisper, as she breathed into my ear. It gave me a rush; excitement was quickly replacing my anger. I felt her kiss my earlobes, felt her nuzzle her cheek against mine. "What a beautiful girl you are, Jasmine." She took my face in her hands. "And you want to be a woman so badly, don't you?" Her eyes were searching mine. I couldn't answer, so my heart answered for me with its furious percussion. How could she not hear it?

Without music, we were dancing. Waltzing across the floor, hip to hip, thigh to thigh, cheek to cheek. Lovers doing a mating ritual. Her eyes locked into mine. Making me aware of nothing but her—her eyes, her face, her body. We seductively glided around the room.

"Vivian," I heard myself say in a husky but vulnerable whisper—this time there was no nuance of flirtation, only genuine desire talking—"make me your woman."

We stopped dancing. Fear and wantonness pulsed through my body with each beat of my heart. Slowly, Vivian took my hand and led me to her bedroom—a room I'd visited only once and quite innocently, only to bring her iced tea on a hot day. Fearing she was suffering from heatstroke, I'd been more than willing to play nurse.

I looked at the familiar double bed with the forest-green comforter that she took me to and stopped. A gentle breeze roused the blue-green curtains, tickled the chimes outside. For a second I flashed back to our other evenings, sitting on her porch looking at the stars and hearing those same chimes serenading us. But the touch of her fingertips on my cheek brought me back to the present.

"Scared?" she asked.

"No," I lied, then felt a flush of embarrassment. Suddenly I no longer felt so cocky. Just 17. A teenager at the doorway of womanhood.

"It's OK, Jasmine," Vivian said in a reassuring way that made me aware she knew how terribly frightened and unsure I really was.

It started with a kiss, so light I hardly felt it. Slowly she guided me with soft kisses, gentle caresses. Suddenly my fervor to have her kicked in, and I returned her kisses with a fiery passion. My fingers and hands freely groped the body I'd desired for so long.

But then she pushed me away. I stood there, bewildered, still breathing hard. What did I do? "What's wrong?" I asked.

"Slow down, baby," Vivian smiled. "I'm not going anywhere. I'm all yours." She learned forward. "We've got all night."

Suddenly it sank in. I stood attentive as she unbuttoned my shirt, tucked her hands under the open shirt to ease it off. I watched it fall to the floor. I swallowed the lump in my throat, but another replaced it almost immediately as Vivian reached around to undo my bra. As she took it off, I felt exposed and excited, wondering if she found me attractive.

I just stood there, feeling a heated rush course through me. She looked deep into my eyes as her hands grazed the fullness of my breasts. She bent to kiss them, then drew on one nipple and twisted the other between two fingers. I couldn't help gasping; my whole body was trembling. I'd pushed my fear to the back of my mind. I needed her to take me; nothing else mattered.

Vivian reached to undo my faded Levi's, but I surprised her by pulling her lacy tee over her head. I had to see her. All those months of anticipation were suddenly being realized. I unfastened her bra, pulled it off slowly, revealing her firm, full breasts in increments. It gave me goose bumps; she was gorgeous.

We came together. The newness of it was exquisite, like no sensation I'd ever experienced. Beyond feeling my own breasts, it was unfathomable to appreciate the duality of such softness, such perfect form. I let my fingers explore the silky skin of the plane of her back, midriff, and shoulders. I tried to imitate the fabulous way she'd made me feel with her kisses by planting a series of delicate pecks over her shoulders—as though I were covering her with an invisible shawl—and across her clavicle and along her neck. When she sighed, I figured I must be doing something right.

"Vivian..." I breathed into her ear.

"Hmm?" she asked, but I couldn't respond. I was filled with too much emotion.

She gently pushed me onto the bed and unbuttoned my pants. I lifted my hips as she tugged them free. My heart was pounding so hard I thought I was going to faint, but somehow I managed not to. Instead I raised myself slightly as she slid my panties down. Even though my whole body was on fire, I felt terribly awkward. This was virgin territory. Now I felt scared, perhaps afraid of being inadequate.

Vivian caressed the inside of my thighs with her knuckles. I heard myself groan. With both hands she opened my legs wide. I shivered, feeling very vulnerable.

"Relax," she whispered in a kiss at the edge of my hairline. I felt myself grow more light-headed as she trailed kisses and caresses across my navel and along my hips. She positioned herself between my legs and kissed and licked the folds of my pussy, but then she moved back. "You're beautiful," she said as she climbed on top of me. "I want you inside me. I want to ride the bone of your hips and feel your fingers thrust into me. Will you do that for me, sweet baby?" she taunted, knowing I would have done anything to please her.

She straddled my hips and guided my fingers inside her. I felt embarrassed at my inexperience and yet jubilant to finally know her so intimately. She was divinely wet, and my hand easily slid in and out of her slippery, inviting cunt. With each thrust of her hips against my hand, against my flesh, she shook more and more, her sighs growing louder and louder. Suddenly she reached down, closed my hand into a ball, and shoved hard against my fist. She jerked and cried out. Her cunt had completely swallowed my hand—I felt close to climaxing just from the sensation.

"Jas-mine..." her voice faded into a raspy moan. "Baby, give it to me now, as hard as you can, as deep as you can."

I obliged, pumping her pussy with all the strength of my 17 years of being raised on a farm doing hard chores. I went in as deep as I could, against the pain of my fingers and arm, then slid almost out—over and over—which made her groan loudly each time. Finally, her vaginal walls clamped my hand so tightly I thought my fingers would go numb. I felt a gush of juice, heard a primal grunt, and felt her body convulse above me for a few moments.

Vivian collapsed against me, and I cradled her with my free arm. I was surprised to feel how sweaty she was, not realizing at first that I was just as sweaty. She panted in my ear softly. "My Jasmine," she cooed.

I started to ease my hand out, but she gently stopped me. "Not yet. Just a little longer. I want to feel you inside me." She kissed me tenderly. "I won't keep you waiting much longer."

Of that I had no doubt, but my immediate concern was how snugly my hand fit inside her. I was worried about getting it out, how I could do it without hurting her. But hers was the voice of experience, so I deferred to her request.

Then, in a gingerly fashion, she started to rock back and forth. My fingers felt tingly all over as her slick cavern massaged them back and forth. She growled as she kissed me again. This time I knew she meant business.

"Go, baby," I coaxed her, and she did, arching up and throwing her head back. Her bountiful breasts collided against each other and bobbed loosely. The mere sight of her made me feel heady. The faster she bucked, the harder I thrust, until in one cataclysmic force she screamed, pulled up impetuously, and released my hand. Then she flopped beside me, gasping.

"You suck the air right out of me," she said between breaths.

"Oh, yeah?" I said coquettishly.

She shot me a devilish grin. "Just begging for it, aren't you?" she said playfully before climbing on top of me. She gave my right nipple a yank, which sent a jolt to my clit.

"Oh!" I cried. She snickered, proud of herself. Then she pinched my other nipple and I jerked. All at once she was kissing me so intently I could hardly breathe. Her fingers were freewheeling agents working me into a frenzy. Just as I thought I'd go insane from wanting her so badly, she stopped kissing me and worked her way down to my throbbing clit. Her lips were scorching my skin every inch of the way. She nestled herself before the gate of my heaven. I held my breath in anticipation as she opened my lips with her tongue and then darted in and out of me. There were no words to describe the delicious way she was making me feel, building me up more and more (as if I needed it). I was more than ready to release, but she was in control, pacing me.

"Vivian..." I whimpered, needing her to take me to utopia.

She lifted her head momentarily, then flicked just the tip of her tongue over my clit. With each lick, my clit responded with a start. She was deliberately driving me crazy.

"Oh god, oh god, Vivian!" I begged.

Then she gave it, and I felt it, like honey rolling from my

soul and just as sweet. Her lips pinched my clit as her tongue continued to assault the tip. In a flash I was coming in waves, my body feeling almost ethereal. She rode those waves like a surfer during high tide.

After a while she crawled into my arms. She kissed me, giving me a taste of myself on her lips. It was a peculiar mix of salt and earth and woman.

I wanted to tell her I loved her. I wanted to tell her how much she meant to me, what this night had meant, but it all seemed trite, so I didn't. And she didn't. We didn't remain together, but for that night it was enough to just lie in the twilight with the faintest tinkling of her chimes lulling us to sleep. It was the first night in a very long time that I slept so soundly.

Flea Market Find

Jenn Hwang

Last year I was working a booth at a flea market in Los Angeles, something I do every few weeks to bring in some extra cash. I go to thrift stores just outside of L.A., where I can buy collectibles and vintage clothing for next to nothing, load them into my mint 1965 Ford pickup, then haul them back to La La Land, where I can totally jack up the price and sell them to unsuspecting "antiquers." It sounds cruel, I know, but I'm a record store manager struggling to make ends meet. Plus, it's hard work driving around for hours and hours looking for cheap finds and rooting around in dozens of crappy thrift stores. So I figure I deserve the cash I bring in from my merchandise—which is always high-quality.

Just two months before, I'd split up with my boyfriend of three years, Brian. Mostly it was because the sex was bad and not nearly as frequent as I would have liked. I'm pretty much a sexual animal and like sex to be down 'n' dirty but not quick—the latter of which was Brian's M.O. He was in and out so fast you'd think I was a Taco Bell. And I was probably too aggressive for him. One time I ordered a strap-on dildo online, and when I got it in the mail I suggested I screw him with it that night. He was into it at first, or so he said, but right before I was about to enter him, he backed out, saying it was too weird for him, it would make him a fag, etc. If you can't stand the heat, get out of the kitchen, I always say. So I didn't miss him that much. But I did miss having sex.

It was a hot summer Saturday afternoon, nearing 3 P.M., and business was slow, so I started packing up my stuff. I'd already brought in 325 bucks that day, so I was ready to split and head for the beach to catch a few waves. (I've been an avid surfer since high school.) Just as I was packing up the last few things, two striking women approached my table.

"Hey, how much for this cool '50s lampshade?" one of them asked. She was almost six feet tall and had silky brown hair past her shoulders. Her black T-shirt read MOTHER in silver lettering.

"I'll give it to you for 30," I said.

"Thirty bucks? You're kidding," her friend, a gorgeous petite brunette, said. "I could get this at Goodwill for a dollar."

"Then drive out to the Goodwill in Chino and see if they have one for a dollar," I told her. "That's what I paid." I laughed, since I was just teasing them. I'd actually bought the shade on eBay for $12 (plus shipping).

"Well, I never!" the tall one said, laughing. "OK, how about 20?"

"Twenty-two and you've got a deal."

She pulled out a 20 and two ones and handed them to me, but as she did, she squeezed my hand meaningfully. "I like your style," she said. Then she turned to her friend and added, "This one's a keeper."

"And I like your shirt," I told her. "Are you really a mom?"

She turned around and showed me the back. More silver letters spelled out FUCKER. This time the joke was on me.

"Now I really like it!" I said.

Even though I'd only ever dated men, lately I'd been increasingly interested in the possibility of sexual exploration with another woman. Maybe it was from finally getting out of my half-baked relationship with Brian; maybe it was from living in L.A., where pretty much anything goes; maybe it was from watching too many episodes of *Jerry Springer;* or maybe it was just because I'm a horny bitch willing to try anything once. One thing was certain, though: This tall chick was H-O-T. Her frame was thick but not fat, she had curves in all the right places, and she had sort of an "alternative" edge about her; she looked like your typical rock 'n' roll L.A. *guy,* but with a lot more class, and the silkiest, shiniest hair I'd ever seen in my life outside of shampoo commercials. She was a rock 'n' roll amazon to die for.

I packed her lampshade into a box with some tissue paper (I always treat my customers well), but when she wasn't looking I took one of my business cards and brazenly scrawled on the back, "Call me. I promise I won't disappoint." Now, I never would have done this if I'd had the slightest inkling that this girl was straight. But both of these chicks were sending out major dyke vibes, so I figured I had her pegged as a lesbian—or at the very least bisexual, especially since half the women I knew in Los Angeles had slept with a woman at some point or another.

"Thanks for the great deal," the tall one said. "I'll have to come back when all your stuff's not packed up."

"You do that," I smiled. "I promise I won't disappoint."

A few days passed, and I was at work at the record store checking my voice-mail on my lunch break. Message 1: "Jenn, it's Mom. Your dad's trying to fix the vacuum cleaner again. He's got dirt and lint all over my linoleum! Call me!" Message 2: This is The Gas Company (the gas company in L.A. is *actually* called "The Gas Company"—how original). Please call us to make payment arrangements." (Like I'm going to waste a check to send them $6 a month, which is the usual amount of my bill. I prefer to let it build up for a while, then send them the payment. Please.) Message 3: Hi...um...this is May, the woman who bought the retro lampshade from you on Saturday? I got your note. If you wanna go out Saturday night, I'm game." And then she left her number.

Yeah, I was game, all right. I played it cool, though, and waited until I got home from work to call her back.

"Yeah, May, this is Jenn...from the flea market," I said when she answered the phone.

"Hey, thanks for calling me back."

"So you wanna go out Saturday?"

"Sure," she said. "I'd love to. By the way, that shade looks great on my lamp."

"Another satisfied customer of Jenn Hwang," I laughed.

"So do you want to go to a movie or something?" Her voice was much more timid than it had been Saturday afternoon.

"A movie?" I asked, and then I took a much more serious and direct tone. "Listen, let's just cut to the chase. I know what I want. Do you know what you want? Why don't you just come over to my place around 8 on Saturday night? I live in Silver Lake, near the reservoir. Know where that is?"

She said she did, and then I gave her directions to my place. She told me she lived in West Hollywood, which is gay central in Los Angeles. Figured. "This is kind of crazy," she said. "I mean, you could be a serial killer or something."

"A serial killer who sells bad velvet paintings and wind-up toys?"

May laughed. "All right, all right. I'll be there at 8. But only because you're fucking hot."

Now, *this* was the woman I'd met at the flea market. "And wear that MOTHER/FUCKER T-shirt," I told her, "so I can see if there's any truth in advertising."

Over the next few days all I could think about was Saturday night. In my head I kept replaying various sexual scenarios that I'd hopefully engage in with May: We'd do it on my kitchen floor, in my bathtub, up against the wall, etc. I even went to the mall to buy something sexy to wear: black leather pants and a tight black Lycra sleeveless tee. Saturday afternoon I went to the grocery store and bought the best merlot I could find, a dozen white roses, and some lube. I'll get to that part later!

It was nearing 8 o'clock that night, and I was psyched, waiting for May to arrive. Just then I heard the buzz of the intercom. I pressed the ANSWER button and said hello.

"It's May. I hope you're ready not to disappoint me."

I chuckled softly and buzzed her in. When I opened the door, May was wearing a long black leather coat, which was strange, considering it was the middle of August. I saw she had on her MOTHER/FUCKER T-shirt underneath.

"I see you've done as told," I said, pointing to the shirt. She came into my apartment and closed the door behind her.

"Yeah, well, I hope you don't mind a little artistic license," she said, opening the coat to reveal that she was *only* wearing the T-shirt underneath—as well as a pair of black high heels. Damn!

"Great minds think alike," I told her, and she was raring to go, because just then she pressed me up against the living room wall, mashing her full lips into mine. Her tongue was like an agile snake exploring the wild. Ten seconds of this and I didn't care if I *ever* saw Brian again. What had I been thinking?

May pulled off her shirt and I took off mine. Since I don't usually wear a bra, we were breast against breast, hot skin against hot skin. "Oh, baby, you're so sexy," she said. "I wanted you from the moment I saw you."

"You just wanted my lampshade," I laughed, but not for long, because May's hot mouth quickly shut me up. Then she grabbed my crotch and moved her hand up and down, kneading my cunt. "I'm going to make you so wet you're going to soak through this leather," she said. She slid her hand down my pants and felt how wet I already was. "Jesus," she whispered in my ear. "It's like Raging Waters down there." (That's a cheesy water park in L.A. I know, I know, it doesn't sound sexy, but I like a gal with a sense of humor.)

May slid her hand out, and then she helped me take off my pants and underwear. We were still standing against my living room wall. Then she got on her knees and buried her face in my pussy, lapping me up like cream. I squatted slightly over her while she sucked and slurped me into ecstasy. "I swear," she said, pulling a way for a moment, "if I'm ever on death row and they ask me what I want for my last meal, I'm going to tell them 'pussy.' " Again I cracked up, but when May started tongue-fucking my hot hole, I shut my trap.

"Oh, you're fucking good," I told her. "You are a motherfucking artist."

Just when I thought I couldn't stand it anymore, May brought me to the edge and I came in huge waves, my engorged clit feeling like it was going to explode. After the first time I came, she went back in for more. "Come for me, baby," she said. "Come on, let's make you come again." And I did...two more times.

But I was ready to please her now. "OK, you didn't disappoint," I laughed, "so now I won't. Stay here. I'll be back in a second."

I went into my bedroom, got the dildo I'd never gotten to use on Brian, put one of his condoms on it, grabbed the lube I'd just bought, and came back into the living room with my hands behind my back. May was sitting on the couch, legs spread wide. "Like what you see?" she asked.

Jesus Christ, she was gorgeous. "Fuck yeah!" I said. "Do you?" I held out the eight-inch strap-on.

May's eyes bugged out at the sight of the mammoth cock, then a huge grin spread across her face. She helped me put it on, then asked, "How do you want to do this?"

"From behind," I told her, and she turned around, propping herself on the couch cushion with her hands. I lubed up the cock, gently placed my hands on her plump ass cheeks, then entered her pussy from behind, letting her take it in slowly.

"Oh, fuck yeah," she said, even though I'd hardly begun.

I built up speed, not thrusting full force yet, but getting there. As I did, I slapped her ass gently. May moved in time with me, meeting each thrust with her hot, juicy pussy, her beautiful ass meeting occasionally with the leather harness I was wearing. "Come on, baby...harder, harder," she cried. "Faster." I was pounding this hottie full force now, and eventually she screamed out in pleasure and rode a huge orgasmic wave.

May and I fucked many times that night, in between

glasses of merlot and several cigarette and snack breaks. I lay on the couch and had May sit on my face as I ate her out; we had sex in the shower and on the living room floor; she fucked me hard and fast with the dildo, as I'd done with her. You name it, we tried it. By 4 A.M. we were wiped out and fell fast asleep.

I woke up with her tongue in my ear. "Hey, sleepyhead," she whispered, "it's almost 11. Wanna get some breakfast?"

"Yeah!" I said, then slid down and buried my head between her legs.

May erupted in laughter. As I said, I like a girl with a sense of humor.

May and I still sleep together semi-regularly, but we're not monogamous, and I've mostly been dating women. Sometimes we have three-ways with one of her more-than-willing female friends. She never fails to surprise me. I occasionally date guys, but I *refuse* to let them go down on me anymore. You can't switch to Spam once you've had caviar.

When I told May later that she was my first female lover, she was incredulous, wondering how I could have known exactly what to do. I just said that I had promised her I wouldn't disappoint and that customer service is always my priority!

THE TROPHY BRIDE

Lynne Antonio

My Uncle Kyle was finally coming home from the Army after 12 years. My mother's baby brother, he left when I was only five, and the few memories I had of him were vague, blurry images of a pimply-faced teenager with a penchant for playing the blues harp in my grandparent's backyard or sitting alone in a corner draped in moody silence.

Now he was returning at last, and the entire family was buzzing with excitement, not so much because they'd missed him terribly but because he wasn't returning alone. Kyle had recently married, and all anyone knew of his wife was that she was a good deal younger than him and she was an above-the-knee amputee. Everyone was more than just a little curious about his youthful bride.

Everyone, that is, except me.

I was wrapped up in my own world, struggling to make it through high school, tuning out to the Doors 13 years after Morrison's death and praying that sandalwood incense would mask the scent of pot that was the dominating aroma in my bedroom. I couldn't have cared less about the homecoming of my long-lost uncle and his new wife. I was 18 and busy. I dressed mostly in black, wrote gloomy prose poems about suicide, and smoked clove cigarettes. I was *intense*.

Normally, getting out of family events had been a breeze. I'd simply explain to my mom that, no, I wouldn't be attending Aunt Debbie's birthday party because—and here I would pause dramatically—I had a date. It worked almost every time.

This trick worked so well, of course, because Mom was beginning to secretly suspect something unspeakable about her eldest daughter. Why, for example, was I always clipping pictures of Martina Navratilova out of the newspaper and tacking them to my bedroom wall? And exactly why did

I have a battered paperback called *Rubyfruit Jungle* stashed under all the white cotton panties in the top drawer of my dresser? And who the hell was this Mariel Hemingway person, anyway?

So, although the disgusted bursts of accusations were still more than a year away from passing Mom's lips, tiny seeds of suspicion were beginning to take root in the rich, dark soil of her dubious mind, which was why she was always so tickled by my dates with boys.

But on occasion, even the I-have-a-hot-date-with-a-raging-hormones-jock-you'd-be-so-happy-with excuse just didn't cut it for her. When it came to Uncle Kyle, I was going and that was that.

And so I went.

The shindig was held at my grandparents' home on a Sunday afternoon. Kyle and his wife were living there temporarily until they both could find jobs and another place to live. For their sake, I hoped it wouldn't take them long to do either.

My grandfather was a big tough Texan infamous for long-winded stories of growing up "on the prairie" and carrying around a spittoon that he wasn't bashful about using in front of anyone. My grandmother was a typical stand-by-your-man, boys-are-more-valuable-than-girls woman of her generation. They were both sweet enough in their own peculiar ways, but I wouldn't be going out on a limb if I said they could easily drive a person insane if not taken in small doses.

When I entered their kitchen that day, I was relieved to see there weren't a whole lot of people milling about; apparently only a dozen or so had showed up, including my parents, my younger sister, and myself. My mother's two sisters were both chopping vegetables at the counter by the sink, and we all greeted each other with brisk cheek pecks. I turned around to see a pretty stranger with short dark-blond hair seated at the table with my grandmother, peeling potatoes and laughing.

My mom moved forward, bent over, and gave the young

woman a prolonged hug, saying, "You must be Paige! I'm so glad to finally meet you!"

Introductions were made all around, but I wasn't able to get out more than "Hi" when I was shuffled off to meet Kyle, who was in the living room where all the men were watching TV and waiting for the little ladies to finish preparing their meal.

When he stood up from the sofa, I was stunned by how tall he was, but I didn't have time to ponder it much because in the next second I was lifted off my feet and crushed in his arms. "Damn, girl, you sure have grown up!" he said, squeezing with what I suspected was all his strength. "I sure have missed you!" I could only grunt into his chest before I was plunked down and able to breathe again. He looked down at me with a huge white grin before turning to my sister and putting her through the same rigmarole. There were a few minutes of uncomfortable small talk, and then my grandmother came and dragged me off to set the dining room table.

Throughout dinner I remained quiet, just listening and observing. I noticed right away that Kyle did most of the talking. He had a story for nearly any subject anyone broached, and he told his tales without ever letting his fixed grin slip a single notch. I also noticed that he talked about Paige as if she weren't sitting right there beside him, and he never referred to her by name. It was always "my wife."

Paige seemed nice, if extremely nervous. She had the bluest eyes I'd ever seen in my life, and I watched them dart around the table as if she were a mouse surrounded by feral cats that hadn't yet noticed her. I didn't blame her. I felt the same way sometimes—and I knew everyone there.

After dinner, when I was certain I wouldn't be missed, I managed to grab my jacket and slink outside to sneak a cigarette. I went into the backyard and hid behind the rambling old oak tree that still wore the tire swing that two generations of children had played on. It was early spring, and a soft misty rain was falling from a sky the color of oysters. I gave the tire a little kick just to watch it spin, feeling a little sad because I knew even then that I wouldn't have any children of my own to stand behind and push, the way my mom did for me and her mom did for her.

I was studying the frayed rope when I heard someone softly say, "Hey, you."

Peering around the tree while simultaneously flicking away the butt, I saw Paige making her way across the lawn toward me. I noticed then how drastic her limp was. "Hey, yourself."

"What are you doing out here, huh, missy?" she asked, feigning suspicion.

Giving the swing another tap with my foot, I said, "Nothing. Just enjoying the quiet, I guess."

Paige stopped beside me and nodded. "Your family can be overwhelming."

"That's an understatement," I laughed.

She pulled a pack of Kools from the pocket of her red nylon jacket and said, "I needed some air. This is so weird, meeting everyone at once."

"I can imagine."

"I'm just scared I'll call someone by the wrong name or something and everyone will think I'm a moron."

I tried to smile reassuringly as I watched her light a cigarette. She had beautiful, strong-looking hands, with perfectly shaped nails she kept trimmed and unpolished. "I wouldn't worry about it," I told her, dragging my eyes away from her gorgeous hands and back to her face. "Nobody is too much of an asshole or anything."

She laughed lightly, like a drowsy brook traveling over gleaming stones. "That's comforting."

We stood without speaking for a moment, listening to the ping of water droplets striking the leaves above our heads.

The ethereal sound of laughter floated to us from inside the house, barely audible, as if we were hearing the otherworldly echo of long-forgotten ghosts.

Paige looked up and seemed to be contemplating the intricate network of the branches overhead. She blew out a cloud of smoke and, without looking at me, said, "Look at this tree. I sure wish I could climb this big old lady."

My gaze followed hers, and though I said nothing, I felt myself smile.

"I know I'm supposed to be a grown-up now and all," she said. "But to tell you the truth, I'm a hell of a lot more comfortable with you kids."

I thought about this for a second, then asked, "How old are you, anyway?"

She finally stopped looking up at the tree and looked at me. "I'm *old*!" She laughed. "Twenty-four!"

"Wow, you *are* old!" I teased. "You might even be older than this tree!"

"Shut up!" She giggled and swatted at me playfully. "You're not supposed to be a wiseass!"

"Oh, I'm not? Who told you that lie?"

Paige jerked a thumb at the house. "They said you were *the serious one*." She said the last three words in a sarcastic bass.

"Ah," I nodded. "Well, don't believe everything you hear. Just because I wear black and don't kiss ass doesn't mean I'm Wednesday Addams."

"Too bad, I really like Wednesday Addams."

I cracked up. "So do I! She's my favorite character on that show!"

We talked for a while longer and were amazed to discover all the odd little things we had in common, such as sharing the same middle name and birthdays one day apart.

Eventually we both grew uncomfortably damp and decided to return to the house and the family within. Soon after that, my father announced that it was time to go home.

Saying goodbye to all my relatives, I surprised myself by offering a hug to Paige just before we left. Hugging virtual strangers wasn't something I was normally in the custom of doing, and though I didn't see her again for several weeks, she returned to my mind often as someone I was definitely curious about and wanted to know better.

When Kyle got a job at a shipyard working the 4-to-midnight shift, he and Paige were finally able to move out from under my grandparents' roof and get a place of their own. Kyle had decided that he wasn't particularly keen on the idea of Paige working right away, so she was stuck alone in their two-room apartment most nights. It wasn't long before she began calling family members to come over and keep her company. We were the only people she knew in the entire state, so her options were somewhat limited.

At first both my sister and I would visit Paige once or twice a week. We'd take a bus over and hang out with her, watching TV, eating popcorn, shooting the shit. I came to believe that Paige was the coolest semi-adult I knew, never asking me about school or plans for college or jobs or any of the other things teenagers get nagged about so much they'd rather hammer nails into their eyes than answer those questions again.

Instead Paige talked about music and movies, books and art. She told us about growing up in Wisconsin, the harsh winters she'd endured there and the family she'd left behind to move to New England to be with her new husband.

It wasn't long before my sister grew bored with hanging out in Paige's shoe-box apartment and I began to make the journey alone. The first few times that it was only Paige and myself, we acted as we always had, but I was secretly happy to no longer be sharing her company, and I suspected she felt the same way.

One Friday night in late May, I got up the courage to show up on her doorstep with a notebook under my arm, finally daring to read my poems aloud to someone I hoped would give criticism honestly but gently.

When Paige greeted me, dressed in a summery white blouse and denim cutoffs, it was the first time I'd ever actually seen her prosthetic leg, and I surprised myself by barely giving it a momentary glance. It was her smile that caught my attention more than anything, the crooked smile and the prolonged eye contact that accompanied it.

Sitting in the center of the floor reading, I often looked up at her across from me on the couch, a shabby coffee table between us, trying to gauge her reaction to the dark, bitter confusions of my thoughts and feelings. She sat placidly, paying close attention while nursing a beer and smoking her ever-present Kools. When I finished, Paige smiled with what I thought might be pride. "Those are beautiful, Lynne," she said. "I mean it. I really think you could be a great poet someday, if you wanted to."

I blushed and mumbled, "Thanks." I was stunned she had used the word "beautiful." On the few previous occasions that I'd read to my mother something I'd written, she had always sniffed disapprovingly and muttered words such as "depressing" and "sullen." No amount of explaining on my part could ever get her to acknowledge that beauty can sometimes be found in darkness as well as light.This seemed to be something Paige understood instinctively.

"Come here," she said, patting the cushion beside her. Once I was sitting next to her, close but not touching, she said, "I used to write poetry myself. A long time ago. I was younger than you, even."

I nodded but remained silent.

"I'm starting to think maybe I should get back into it," she continued. "Maybe it would help out with this loneliness, you know? It sure as hell couldn't hurt." She dragged deeply on her cigarette and then mashed it out in a glass ashtray on the end table nearest her. "I don't know how much longer I'm supposed to stay locked up in this shithole. I think when it comes right down to it, Kyle just wants to keep me like a pet or something. The pretty little trophy he saved from the slums of Milwaukee, the cripple who needed a sweet prince with a heart of gold."

I couldn't believe what I was hearing. "But...I thought you guys were happy. Kyle always tells my mom that—"

"Oh, god," she groaned, waving a dismissive hand. "Forget what he says. The only reason we moved back here at all is because he wanted to come home a hero. He wanted to show his whole family that he wasn't a loser anymore. 'Look, Mom and Dad and everyone! I married a girl with one leg! Doesn't that make me a super-swell guy? Doesn't that just prove I'm a saint? Who the fuck else would want her? She's damaged goods!' "

Sunset-red blotches of anger burned in her cheeks while her eyes hardened into tiny ponds reflecting a frozen blue winter sky.

"You're not damaged goods," I offered quietly, unsure how to react to this side of her that I had never seen before.

She let out a sour laugh, drained the rest of her beer, and placed the empty can beside the ashtray. "He won't even touch it, you know," she said, rapping her knuckles against the flesh-colored socket of the prosthetic limb, just beneath where her thigh ended. "Fuck, he doesn't even like to look at it. He doesn't say anything, but I can tell. Whenever I take it off, like at bedtime, he always looks away real fast, like it's the grossest thing in the world. Yeah, he's my savior, all right."

After lighting another cigarette, she looked at me and suddenly smiled apologetically. "I'm sorry, Lynne. I shouldn't be talking to you about this, Kyle being your uncle and all."

I shrugged. "I don't really know the guy. Actually, I know *you* better than I know him."

Paige nodded thoughtfully and seemed to be debating something in her head. Several minutes tiptoed by while I nervously toyed with the wire rings of the notebook in my lap, unsure what to say or even if I should say anything at all.

Finally, she spoke. At first her voice was tinged with the frayed remnants of anger, but as time passed and the room grew dim around us, the anger passed with it, leaving in its wake only a hurt and sad resignation.

She told me about the car accident that had stolen her leg only two years before, when she was 22, not quite a year before she'd met Kyle. She spoke of the horror she felt when she regained consciousness in a hospital room and learned that she was no longer a whole human being. As she described the pain, both real and phantom, that she'd had to learn to endure and overcome, her face became obscured by shadows that grew out of the increasing gloom of the darkening apartment until she became a black silhouette and a disembodied voice.

Without thinking about it, I helped myself to one of her cigarettes and sat, rapt, as she went on with her story, telling me of the humiliation and struggle of learning to walk with a prosthesis, called "gait training," and the occupational therapist she believed saved her life.

By the time I'd finished the cigarette, Paige had also finished her tale, and silence once again descended upon us. Without a word she leaned forward, and I watched her shadowy figure as she pulled off the prosthetic leg and leaned it against the coffee table.

"That's better," she sighed, sitting back again. "It's like taking off a shoe, you know?" There was a brief pause, and then she suggested I turn on the TV across the room and, while I was up, why not grab us each a Bud from the kitchen?

I did as she asked, feeling somewhat awkward and shy, though I couldn't pinpoint the reason for my sudden timidity.

Back on the sofa, I cracked open my beer and drank deeply, grateful to have something to do. When the can was half empty, I set it down and glanced at Paige, whose face was now visible in the meager light thrown by the old black-and-white television. I was surprised to see that she was smiling at me.

"You seem nervous all of a sudden," she said. "Is something wrong?"

"No, I'm fine," I lied, feeling like an idiot. "Why?"

"Does it bother you that I took that off?" She used her chin to point at the prosthetic.

"No, why should it?" I wondered if she was giving me some kind of test.

She shrugged, and we both turned our attention to the TV. An old Katharine Hepburn movie was on, the one where she and Cary Grant are chasing a leopard all over Connecticut and getting into all kinds of crazy trouble.

I was beginning to relax, drinking the rest of my beer and laughing at the movie when Paige spoke again, her tone very casual. "It might make you feel a little less weird if you touched it, you know."

Surprised, I looked at her and considered asking if *she* would feel a little less weird if I touched it, but instead I simply said "OK," placed the beer can on the table, and turned my body so I was sitting sideways on the sofa, facing her. I bent forward and reached over her lap, my fingertips grazing the stump of her left leg, tentatively at first, as if I were afraid of hurting her, and eventually with genuine interest and curiosity.

Out of the corner of my eye, I saw Paige smiling again, her face mere inches from mine. "Soft, isn't it?"

"Uh-huh," I nodded. It *was* soft—soft and delicate, like baby skin.

"So, now you know that I may be the Bride of Frankenstein, but I'm not—"

"Oh, *shut up*!" I laughed. "No one thinks that! You're such an assho—"

She stopped my teasing with a kiss, her lips pressing against mine for the briefest of moments and then pausing, lingering, unsure. Without hesitation, I kissed her back: tender, feathery kisses unlike anything I'd ever experienced.

Too soon she pulled away from me and, grinning, asked, "I'm a *what*? What were you about to call me?"

"An asshole," I blurted, laughing again, despite my fear and hammering heart.

Eyebrows raised, Paige said, "Oh, an asshole, huh? We'll see if you really think I'm an asshole." And then she was kissing me again, slowly, with the relaxed ease of someone completely confident in her talent, her technique, and her power to seduce.

Without a twinge of guilt, I gave myself to her. Allowing her tongue to gently explore my lips, I realized how badly I'd wanted this all along, since that first day behind the tree in my grandparents' yard, when I'd first noticed her crystal-blue eyes and her flawless, graceful hands.

I heard myself moan softly as I leaned toward her, grasping her arms and daring to let the tip of my own tongue meet hers with careful, nervous probes.

Impatient with my shyness, Paige had no difficulty taking the lead and boldly proceeded to wrap her tongue around mine with hard, tangling strokes that caused time and place to fall, spinning, to the bottom of the universe.

We kissed forever it seemed, long enough to be aware that the movie had ended and another had begun.

Lost in her full, supple lips, I gasped in surprise when at last I felt her hand on my breast, gently cupping it and rolling my stiff nipple between her thumb and forefinger.

"Is this OK?" she whispered, her mouth now brushing against my earlobe.

Burying my face in her neck, I could only murmur a hushed sound of approval. With no earthly idea what I was doing, I was perfectly happy to let her be the aggressor, a role she played with astonishing adeptness.

As if to prove my point, Paige eased her hand up under my T-shirt, reached around to my back, and unfastened my bra with a skill that would have impressed Houdini. A few more swift, smooth moves on her part, and we were both naked from the waist up. She stared unabashedly at my bare breasts, her mouth curved up in a tiny smile, before bending her head to lap lightly at first one nipple and then the other.

Gripping my left hand in her right, she quickly guided me to her breast, apparently knowing I would never have had the courage to be so brazen myself.

Touching her as if I feared she might break, I became aware of my own ragged breath, sounding so desperate and raw that it was unrecognizable to my own ears. "Please," I whimpered deliriously.

Paige raised her head, her eyes wide with concern, until she understood that it wasn't fright or pain on my face but an unmistakable, fiery desire. She pulled me against her and lay back on the sofa, taking me with her, positioning me so that I straddled her, one foot on the floor for balance.

Looking up at me, she asked, "Have you ever done this before?"

Unable to speak, I shook my head.

"Never? Not even with a boy?"

She seemed pleased when I shook my head again, and reached for me, drawing my mouth to hers and sneaking her hand up between my legs, rubbing my sopping pussy through my jeans.

I thought I would explode with the need to be touched and instantly began pushing myself hard against the heel of her hand, my entire body trembling violently.

Almost at once, Paige stopped what she was doing and asked, "May I?"

I nodded frantically, biting my lower lip for fear that I might scream.

Moments that seemed like centuries later, she unzipped my jeans and slid her hand inside, her fingers gliding expertly over and into my impossibly slippery cunt.

"Oh, my god," she whispered, "you are *so wet*..."

As she softly stroked my swollen clit, I groaned loudly, shuddering uncontrollably and, an instant later, erupted violently into my first shared orgasm. I remained braced above her for who knows how long, waiting for the volcanic waves to subside, and when they finally did, I collapsed on top of her, panting as she slipped out of both me and my jeans.

Neither of us spoke. Paige stroked my back, her strong, beautiful fingers tripping down the rungs of my spine until I grew drowsy and closed my eyes, my head on her chest, listening to the calm, steady rhythm of her heartbeat.

At some point she said my name and I sat up, alarmed.

Smiling, she said, "You're gonna miss your bus, baby. It's almost midnight."

"Oh, shit!" I exclaimed. I looked down at her helplessly. "But I didn't...I mean, you didn't..."

"There'll be other times," she said, rising into a sitting position beside me. "Things happen when they happen."

I tried to protest, but she swiftly shut me up with another long, tender kiss. I didn't want to leave her, but I knew Kyle would be home soon, in addition to the very real possibility that I could miss the bus if I didn't get going.

Reluctantly I gathered up my notebook and snatched a Kool for the road. She went back to reclining on the sofa, smoking her own cigarette and watching me with lazy interest. I remember exactly how she looked, lying there, naked but for those faded cutoffs, one leg tapering down to a deliciously feminine foot, while the other leg ended just above where her knee once was. I thought she looked beautifully sublime, and I knew there would be no end to the poems I would write about her, every one of them trying to capture her extraordinary essence and never quite getting there.

Despite what she said, there never were any other times for us; though we weren't related by blood, she *was* married to a blood relative, even if he was a stranger to me, and I think as a result neither of us was comfortable with pursuing anything further.

In the end, I graduated from high school and moved far away, occasionally seeing Paige at holiday gatherings, but only occasionally. We never did speak of that one night we spent together in the flickering blue glow of an old television, but the poems *were* written, and the words, like memories, live always.

Hang-ups

CeCe Ross

It was my first time in a lesbian bar. When I returned later that evening it was my second time in a lesbian bar. I made a beeline for the same cherry-red barstool only to find myself welcomed by the same frizzy-haired 40-something bartender.

"Hey, CeCe, you made it back! Couldn't stay away, huh? What'll it be? The same?"

"That's cool," I said.

"CeCe, this is Andi...Andi, CeCe...CeCe, Andi."

"Hi," I said, and Andi, a tall, tomboyish white girl, stretched out her hand. Short dark hair, no makeup; she sat slouched on the barstool in a pair of red hip-hop pants and a black wifebeater. She had long, toned, olive-skinned arms. I wanted to let her know immediately that I was straight, that I was only there to do "research," but instead I just sat there like a dope.

"I knew you'd be back." The bartender pulled out a glass and dumped in a scoop of ice cubes. "Not that I'm implying anything. No ma'am, not me. But here you are." Crinkled curlicues of badly permed hair hid her expression as she placed my glass of mineral water on the bar and dropped in a wedge of lime to make the whole works fizz.

I sipped with my hand wrapped tightly around the cold glass. *I can hang with this,* I told myself. *Sure I can.* I checked myself out in the mirror: a fit, sleek, pecan-colored sister with a hip cropped natural. My power suit had been lifted right off the pages of that month's *Essence*—from a spread on female entrepreneurs. (To be an entrepreneur, one has to look like an entrepreneur.) In my short-short business skirt, with my long-strapped little black purse, I was everything that my parents, Oprah, and my sorority wanted me to be—including straight.

I tried not to look at the reflection of the woman sitting next to me, attempted not to notice her cruising me with those warm brown eyes, that dimpled smile.

"This," the bartender announced, jolting me off my stool, "is CeCe's second time ever in a lesbian bar."

"Really?" Andi beamed my way. "Hey, congratulations."

"Her first time was just under five hours ago."

"Well, you've become quite the regular." Andi leaned back with one foot hooked on the bottom of the barstool, tossed a look out into the bar, then one at me. "So, how do you like it?"

I stared out across the bar to where a lone wispy blond danced around in a middy T-shirt and bell-bottoms. Her split ends whipped through the smoky air.

"It's cool, it's cool. I'm comfortable with it."

But, of course, I wasn't comfortable—at all. A month earlier, Pam, my best friend and sorority sister at Howard, had blown my mind by coming out to me. I had flown up north to San Francisco to visit her and her new ecologist girlfriend—a sloppily dressed woman with a pierced septum. Saturday night they had taken me out to this lesbian club called Skirts. At the club my limbs turned to wood and I couldn't breathe or swallow. When I spoke ("Get me...out...of here."), it seemed like I was listening to someone else—instead of myself.

Pam assumed I was "disgusted." We sat on her couch talking until 2 A.M. while the ecologist snored in the next room.

"It's not like that...I'm not disgusted. It's just weird," I'd told her.

"Weird?"

"No, not weird—I just need some time to get used to this. You know, this stuff just never occurred to me."

"You need to come to grips with all your hang-ups, girl. Otherwise, our friendship *might* be in jeopardy."

"What hang-ups?" I said. "Please, don't be pissed off."

"You're damn right I'm pissed off."

Once I got back to Los Angeles, I took a late Saturday afternoon drive to "gay town"—Santa Monica Boulevard in West Hollywood—and walked into the Palms to "interview" the bartender. She was very friendly and didn't seem to think "my research project" was anything out of the ordinary. That evening I strolled along the boulevard going in and out of various shops, cafés, and taverns. I thumbed through *Rubyfruit Jungle* at A Different Light Bookstore. I investigated a store full of pornographic greeting cards and inspected the piles of condoms and sex-toy displays. By then it was almost 9, and that's when I went back to the Palms. The bartender had told me there'd be some more action by then—but there was just Andi and a few other women, and that dancing hippie.

Since the place was dead, Andi offered to take me to Girl Bar, a dance club a few blocks away. I was tentative but curious, so I accepted.

The street was dark and hot. Shops closed. Buff boys in spandex T-shirts milled about the sidewalk as the robotic nasal crooning of Cher's *Do you believe in life after love?* pumped its way out of every bar on the street. My volunteer tour guide for the night bopped cutely down the sidewalk, red pants scissoring along. "You are some friend," she told me. "No, really; I mean it. You came here all by yourself, into this neighborhood, forced yourself to meet some gay people and go out dancing with me—all so you'll be more comfortable around your friend."

"It's no big deal," I shrugged. Andi seemed to be mocking me slightly, but there was no way to prove it, so I simply kept following her.

Soon we crossed Robertson and came to a tall staircase. At the foot of that staircase stood a very hairy man in a leather vest—no shirt.

"Hey, Bruno, what's the cover?" asked Andi.

"Fifteen bucks. There's a singer later."

"Oh, yeah? Who?"

"Beryl Mope. She's a rock star from Canada. Very hot."

Andi and I climbed the steps. In a smoky booth an unsmiling female Elvis impersonator sat behind a thrashed-looking cashbox. That old Gloria Gaynor song blasted inside.

First I was afraid. I was petrified.

"My friend here," Andi shouted, gesturing toward me as I pretended to check out a poster for some folk singer, "this is her very first time ever in an all-women dance club. I've brought her here on a mission in the service of lesbian cultural education. Can't we get some kind of discount for that?"

Elvis smiled. It practically killed her. "OK, ten bucks covers both of you."

I spent so many nights just feeling sorry for myself.

Andi bounced across the dance floor through the tangle of rockin' babes, then stopped dead center to bust her groove. I joined her, still pretending to be cool about my surroundings. *Not bad for a white girl,* I thought, checking out the way she moved. *What if I were gay? Would I find her attractive? Would she find me attractive?*

"Hey!" I had to shout over the music, and Andi moved in close, put her ear right next to my mouth. She smelled like sandalwood soap and lemons. "Which of these women are your type?"

"My type?"

"Yeah!"

"Take a guess."

I pointed to the hippie girl we'd seen dancing earlier at the Palms.

"No way."

"Why not?"

Andi shrugged.

I failed with a couple more choices.

"Know something?" she said.

"No, what?"

"You keep picking white girls!"

"Huh?"

"White girls—you keep picking white girls! Why's that?"

"Oh, you like *the sisters*!" *So that's why she wanted to be my tour guide,* I thought, more than ready to be offended.

"Not necessarily, I just don't rule them out. How about you, CeCe, do you rule anybody out?"

"I like men," I replied. "And as far as color goes...black is mine."

Now, wasn't I sure of myself?

Andi stopped dancing, grabbed my hand, and led me off the floor and up some steps that led to an elevated section where women and a few men lounged around scoping the floor. "Here's where you get the bird's-eye view—hey! Now, she's cute!" A tall, dark-haired woman wearing a tight mint-green miniskirt had just stepped out on the floor.

"You're drooling," I observed. "Go ask her to dance."

"No way! I'm too shy."

"Are you kidding? You're not shy."

Andi hesitated. "No, but *she* makes me shy."

I squatted down, reaching under a rail to tap the miniskirt girl on the shoulder. "Hi," I said. "What's your name?"

"Kelly." The girl turned back around again.

"Her name's Kelly," I said.

"Nice." Andi seemed stiff and awkward all of a sudden.

I squatted to tap Kelly on the shoulder again. "Kelly, where are you from?"

"San Diego."

"Kelly, where are you staying?"

"At a hotel in Venice."

"Hey, Kelly, do you want to dance?"

"That depends on who's asking," said Kelly. "If it's your

friend there, the answer's yes." Kelly looked at Andi and gave an inviting jerk of her head. Andi leaped over the rail. Suddenly I felt as if the whole world had turned completely upside down. So I did what any proud black heterosexual woman in shock would do: I fled to the bathroom. There, I sat on the toilet coming to terms with a shocking reality: I felt jealous.

When I came out, I couldn't find Andi anywhere and the crowd had thinned out to a few stragglers listening to some tired singer crooning a bitter tune about drugs and unrequited love. I scanned the place for Andi one more time, then went outside. I looked at my watch: It was 3:30 A.M.! The air was cool and crisp. Someone was smoking pot. I looked around, and that's when I saw Andi on the other side of the street. She was sharing a joint—and some very intimate space—with the woman in the green miniskirt.

I hurried off along the littered sidewalk. Though it was only two blocks to my silver Passat, the walk felt long and confused. I fumbled inside my little purse to find the remote and click off the alarm. When I reached the car door, I hastened to open it, as if somebody was chasing me. *Ah...comfort,* I thought, sinking into the gray leather seat. *Finally, I can relax. But what am I so worked up about?* Then it hit me what Pam had said about me getting over my hang-ups. I thought about my life. I was a vegan who didn't drink, smoke, or do caffeine. I wasn't sure if I believed in God, but I said prayers on my knees every night before falling asleep. I never even once consciously entertained the possibility that I was attracted to women. Yet here I was, my chest heaving and a decidedly damp feeling between my legs. Now I knew why I'd had a panic attack at the lesbian club in San Francisco—I was feeling attracted to the women there and I'd felt too exposed.

The purple night was easing into morning. I reached over to the backseat for my black briefcase, springing its gold snaps and extracting a yellow legal pad. I tried hard, for once, not to think about things—just drove around the block on autopilot and slowed when I came up to where Andi and Kelly stared dreamily into each other's eyes. The gray light of the street lamps revealed their tired faces as each took a turn at the little sliver of a joint.

I stuck my head out the window, shouted "Hey!" and flashed my sexiest gap-toothed smile. "Here's my number." I extended the folded yellow paper, my hand offering a perfect square.

Andi and I were together for only six months before my struggles with homophobia grew too much for her. Hang-ups don't just go away overnight, but mine have sure gotten better over the last three years: I am now out to my family and colleagues. And I even have a little cappuccino now and then—decaf, of course.

To Andi, who saw past my cool facade, this sister will always owe you one.

Tomboys Forever

Kate O'Neill

I met Casey when we both 12 years old. She was the resident tomboy on my block in a suburb of Chicago, and I was the tomboy wanna-be who inevitably cried buckets every time I fell off my bike or skinned my knees when I fell playing handball with the other kids. No one ever made fun of me, though, probably because my mother was the principal at the junior high school. I had inherited special status and therefore got away with a lot.

Casey also had special status, because she was the toughest kid around and a natural athlete. Even older boys respected her and let her be the leader when we played games. She was always the captain of any team at school as well as on the block in the late-evening twilight of summer and the short winter days on the weekends. I think I must have worshiped her then, although I didn't realize it until years later. We weren't close when we were young; Casey was one of the most popular kids both at school and on my street, and I was part of a peripheral little gang that tried to be cool and usually miserably failed, perhaps because none of us was a real tomboy.

All the kids in my town went to different middle schools and one of two junior highs, then everyone was somehow crammed into one little high school that had dignity and history but not a lot of space. When we got to high school, Casey was an instant success. Even the teachers were tolerant of her antics, although I could never figure out how a grown-up could be fooled by a kid who was so see-through and blunt.

"Cassandra Elizabeth Michaels, you will please stop tormenting Daniel and give him back his lunch?" one of them would say.

"Miss Grant," Casey would respond, cool as a cucumber, "I like to be called Casey, and I was just looking at Daniel's lunch bag because it's so interesting. Look, ma'am, it's been drawn all over and even painted on. I think Daniel's a closet artist, and he's really good," and while the class giggled at poor Daniel, the teacher would get up to examine his lunch bag, exclaim that Casey was right, and ask Daniel if he was in art class. Daniel became one of Casey's special pets, and no one dared pick on him again for being a closeted anything.

I somehow drifted through my freshman and sophomore years being mostly unnoticed. Still having dreams of being a bona fide tomboy one day, I tried out for the softball team my sophomore year, and to my amazement, I made it. Casey, of course, was the captain.

The summer before my junior year I spent a lot of time practicing catch with my mother and little brother in the backyard. They were both thrilled that I was on a genuine sports team ("Wow, Kate, you're, like, all athletic now," my brother complimented me) and were determined to help me in any way possible. One day my ultra-helpful mother suggested I call Casey Michaels and ask her to coach me a bit through the summer.

"Katie, she's your captain. Surely she wants a good team next year? Don't you have practice this summer with the team anyway?" The no-nonsense voice was out. Uh-oh.

"Not till August," I mumbled, burrowing deeper into the couch and staring at the TV, willing my practical mother to vanish.

"Well, it's only June now. I'm sure she'd love to help you."

With a long-suffering sigh, I called Casey at home and managed to ask for softball help. To my surprise, she agreed to my mother's harebrained scheme. Because she was in summer school due to having almost failed geometry, we agreed to meet on Saturdays at the park. We met early in the morning so we'd have room before the weekend crowds appeared.

That summer was definitely the best one of my life so far. Casey and I met not only on Saturdays for practice, but we soon started to meet on weekday afternoons after her summer school class after she discovered I was a reluctant math whiz.

"Good grief, Kate, you're like a genius or something. Are you going to go to MIT or Caltech or one of those nerdy schools?" she'd ask, and I'd shriek and throw ice chips from our sodas at her, and soon an all-out war would ensue, which only ended when her father pointedly stuck his head in her bedroom and pretended to turn down a volume dial.

At the start of our junior year I was a much better softball player, and I was suddenly part of the in crowd, being Casey's new best friend. I rode high on a crest of popularity and inclusiveness, and it was glorious. Casey, as it turned out, was also destined to have a glorious year, because something remarkable happened: She became beautiful overnight. Her light brown hair turned golden-red and wavy, even though it was short; her muddy blue eyes were suddenly like aquamarine pools; and her teeth were straight and white after years of braces. I hadn't really noticed it, spending virtually every day with her over the summer, but when we went back to school, people were stunned to see tomboy Casey Michaels suddenly rivaling the prettiest girls in our class. Her popularity soared even more overnight due to the shallowness of the American culture we all lived with. Not that she still wasn't a tomboy of the first order.

"Kate, I swear, any of those geeky boys asks me out and I'll deck him right in the hallway. Just you wait."

She never got her chance, probably because any time one of the boys got near her she practically bared her fangs and hissed at him. And they all knew that tomboy Casey could still wipe the floor with them. The boys, and eventually the girls, treated Casey the same as ever, although there was a new look in their eyes every time they saw her. Being pretty opened up even more doors than being tough, I discovered.

Something changed between Casey and me, however. It happened slowly, creeping up on us without warning. I know

I didn't notice it till junior year was almost over and we were celebrating a triumphant softball year. After a victory party at Casey's house one night, we were all tipsy from the single glass of champagne Casey's parents had allowed each of us, and we were acting silly. I noticed Casey kept giving me funny looks all night, but I thought it was the champagne. Around midnight we said goodbye, as the last of team straggled out the door into waiting parents' cars. I was spending the night, as had become common.

"Kate," she said as we tried to navigate the stairs to her room, "I can't walk! Someone took away my feet! Hold on to me." She gasped and giggled, and I had to laugh at the sight of the great Casey fumbling up the stairs. So I helped her up to her room, trying to be quiet in deference to her parents, who had turned in only minutes before. They undoubtedly heard us crashing around, and they were nice enough not to come out and mock our uneven movements. Her parents were pretty cool.

When we managed to get to Casey's bedroom, I sort of dropped her onto her bed, and she lay snorting with laughter, trying to cover her mouth with her hands. I gently pried off her shoes, then collapsed next to her to keep my head from whirling more.

"Kate," she whispered after a while. Her giggles were gone.

"Yeah?"

"This is weird."

"Huh?" I said, confused.

"I was looking at you all night," she said, and she turned her head to mine where it rested inches from hers on the bedspread. "And I had this really weird thought."

"What was it?"

"I wanted to kiss you," she said simply, sounding a bit puzzled but not taking her eyes from mine. My heart thumped and I stared at her. Kissing Casey wasn't something I had thought about, but the idea didn't frighten me at all. After all, this was my best friend. I trusted her. And it made sense, since neither of us had ever displayed a remote interest in boys except as sports (and math) rivals.

"Really?" I whispered. She nodded.

"Well," I said, "go on. Kiss me."

"Uh," she mumbled, but then she closed her eyes and pushed her face closer to mine, and suddenly our lips were touching. Our tongues met, and I could taste champagne and Cool Ranch–flavored Doritos, and I could taste Casey. Suddenly the thought of kissing her filled me, and I didn't want it to stop. I had never kissed anyone before now, and neither had Casey. The thought of virgin flesh meeting for the first time excited and startled me.

We must have spent half the night kissing and touching. I played with her breasts beneath her T-shirt, then daringly stole my hands under the cloth to feel her hot skin, to gently twirl the nipples in my fingers until they hardened and she moaned, pressing against me. She in turn kissed and sucked on my neck, leaving hickeys that I wouldn't notice until late the next day, when my brother caught sight of them. Casey also kissed my bare arms from shoulders to palms and back again. I had never known my arms could be so sensuous.

We eventually fell asleep tumbled together on the bed. We snapped awake in the morning when Casey's mother cheerfully yodeled "Good morning" from outside the door and told us that breakfast would be ready soon. Fuzzy-headed from the night, mouth tasting of cotton and, still, of Casey, I turned to her. Again we looked in each other's eyes, and we were both fearful.

"Kate—" she said, and at the same moment I said "Casey," and we both smiled and relaxed.

"Kate," she tried again, "I've been feeling close to you all year, you know? I mean, we're friends and all, but there was something else, and I just couldn't figure it out. But I think I get it now."

"I know exactly what you mean," I assured her, and with a mischievous grin she planted a little kiss on top of my nose.

Casey and I dated in secret the rest of the spring and all summer before we told anyone. In the fall we went to the homecoming dance together, with Casey dressed in a tux and me in a dress—my tomboy wanna-be status still dogging me. The fact that we went to the dance together wasn't that big of a deal, since there were two gay couples who went also. It was the late '90s, after all, and this was Chicago. Both sets of our parents were really cool about it, and we didn't really surprise anyone at school, since tomboys are somehow branded as lesbians anyway.

This spring, Casey and I are graduating from college. We're still together, she is still the sexiest tomboy I know, and I've given up softball in favor of computers. But I finally found something I can beat Casey at every time: I play a wicked game of pool. I am very proud of being a tomboy forever.

FUMBLING

Alicia Bramm

I was a student in the theater department at a state college. My friend Nicki and I had worked on several plays together, mostly backstage. We'd had a stagecraft class together and also a technical theater class, but we'd originally been introduced by my friend Rachel, who had gone to high school with Nicki. My entire freshman year I'd had a crush on Rachel; I'd met her in an acting class and immediately fell head over heels for her: She had golden-brown hair, blue eyes, high cheekbones, and a sweet smile. But Rachel was primarily straight, even though she was questioning her sexuality. When I told her I had a crush on her, she flat-out rejected me—but kindly. She also told me that Nicki had a crush on her too.

The following year Rachel transferred to a college with a better acting program, and I was pretty despondent. I'd kissed a few girls, but I'd never had sex with a woman—even though I knew I was gay—and I had hoped and hoped that my feelings for Rachel would be reciprocated. Nicki and I always joked around a lot, but I never really saw her in a sexual light; she was kind of nerdy—she always wore striped button-down shirts tucked into corduroys, she had a goofy haircut, and she was a biology major, even though she worked on a lot of plays in the theater department. She kind of looked like the AV Club guys in high school, and she was totally into *Star Trek* and sci-fi movies. I mean, I'm into science fiction too, but not to the extent she was. And I draw the line at *Star Trek*.

As I said, Nicki and I would joke around a lot, and I'd even make salacious remarks to her sometimes, mostly to see if I could rile her up or get a reaction out of her. One night after a tech rehearsal for *The Merry Wives of Windsor,* a few of us had gone out for some beers at a bar where a lot of theater people hung out. Nicki and I had gotten pretty buzzed that night, and we were walking home together, since we lived near each other.

"There weren't any cute gay girls in the whole bar," Nicki whined.

"Except for me...and you," I said.

Nicki looked down at the ground, a little embarrassed. "I never know when you're joking."

"Well, why don't we find out?" I said. I guess the beer had gone straight to my libido.

"You mean right now?" she asked.

"Your apartment's just two blocks away," I smiled.

So even though we'd never talked about being attracted to each other, Nicki and I went to her apartment. She got a couple of beers out of the refrigerator and put Jane's Addiction on the stereo. We sat on the floor, with the lights dimmed, and she lit up a cigarette.

"You shouldn't smoke," I said. "It's bad for you." (It's funny—tragic, really—how I was so anti-smoking back then, and now I smoke a pack a day. I started just a year after I'd scolded Nicki for smoking, when I was acting in a play and the character was a smoker. My mom still doesn't believe me when I tell her how I started smoking.)

"Yeah, well, a lot of things I do are bad for me," she laughed. "Like being here with you tonight."

"We haven't even done anything yet," I said, and I could tell we were both nervous. I wasn't that attracted to Nicki, but I thought she was cute in kind of a dorky way, and she was smart and funny and nice, so I forged ahead; I really wanted to have sex with a woman, even if she didn't make my knees buckle like other woman had. Maybe beautiful women were overrated. "So why don't we start now?" I said. (Yeah, yeah, I know—it was a pretty pitiful way to begin.)

Nicki put out her cigarette and took a swig of beer, and we both leaned in and started kissing. Then she put her hands on either side of my head. We started out tentatively, but then built up momentum until we were kissing passionately, our tongues intertwined. Just when she nipped at my lower lip, her big furry white cat jumped in my lap. I remember it had some kind of occult name, but I can't recall exactly what. It fit, though, because that cat was evil.

"Jesus!" I said, and pushed the cat off my lap. I've never been a cat person. In fact, I'm often *afraid* of cats, probably because when I was little a neighborhood cat killed my pet rabbit we kept in a cage in the backyard. "Now, where were we?" I asked Nicki, still keeping my eyes peeled for another surprise feline attack.

Nicki lived in a studio apartment, so her bed was in her living room. She led me by the hand to the bed. We sat facing each other, and she helped me take off my T-shirt and bra. She moved her head down to my breast and sucked my nipple. I couldn't believe I was actually having sex with a woman. I'd had sex with guys a couple of times in my life and didn't enjoy it at all. I liked how Nicki was taking her time with me, and I didn't have to worry about whether she'd be able to "get it up." She was tender and slow. All the guys I'd been with had just had *their* pleasure in mind. Not Nicki. She wanted me to feel good—and she did just that.

Nicki had told me before that she'd never had sex with a woman, even though she was also a lesbian, and looking back on that night, it was pretty obvious that we were fumbling through it. But we did the best we could and played it by ear—by "hand," really—mostly trying to get each other off manually. I really wanted her to go down on me, but I could tell that wasn't going to happen that night. We were both too nervous to try it so soon—and when we finally did a few weeks later, it was fairly halfhearted. The funniest part of the whole night was me trying to fend off her cat and trying to kiss her with cat hair in my mouth. It's pretty bad when the clearest memory you have about the first time you had sex with a woman is that of her evil, shedding cat.

Nicki and I had sex several times over the next few weeks, but I wasn't in love with her, and I knew I never would be. While it was fun and exciting to finally have sex with a woman, the passion just wasn't there—on my side, at least. So I told her we should just be friends. I received a letter from her in my mailbox the next day; she wanted us to keep seeing each other, saying we'd have fun, it wasn't anything serious, etc. I only 20 and I was new at this, so I went along with it. I thought maybe my feelings for her would grow into something more.

I remember working backstage with her during the run of *The Merry Wives of Windsor;* it was a cabaret show, and they served beverages—including beer—during intermission. The tech crew would always get free beer, and Nicki and I would have a couple of beers with the guys before the show—and during. Sometimes we'd get a little sloshed, and during almost every show, while we weren't needed (we were in charge of props), we'd sneak behind this big black curtain and make out—which was pretty thrilling, because we'd never know if we'd get caught or not.

But the thrill of having sex with a woman for the first time wore off for me, and I was pretty lame about breaking up with Nicki. I'd never had to break up with anyone before; I'd always been the dumped one. So whenever she'd ask me if I wanted to come over, I'd make some half-baked excuse like I wasn't feeling well or I had to get up early the next morning. She got the message after I did this a few times.

To this day I regret how I treated her at the end, especially since she was so kind and funny. But there was one consolation: Almost as soon as I "broke up" with Nicki (which I never officially did), she found a girlfriend, someone she'd known since high school who had recently moved to town. From a mutual friend I heard they're still together—after 11 years. I guess the bad karma I created has been following me around since then, because I'm perpetually single. Regardless, Nicki, if you ever read this, thanks a lot for the few weeks of fumbling but terribly sweet sex. You helped break me in! Wherever you are, I hope you're happy and in love.

PFLAG: Your One-Stop Dating Shop

Natasha Metcalf

Two years ago I was 17 and had just come out to my mom and dad. It wasn't easy, but my parents were pretty liberal, so they didn't disown me or anything horrible like that. Occasionally my mom still says, "Are you sure you don't want to date boys? It would make life so much easier." I know she's thinking *her* life.

We were living in St. Louis, which is a pretty conservative city. I mean, where we lived, women still shopped at Talbots and the guys wore Dockers and polo shirts. Heinous. Even so, there were a few PFLAG groups in town, and shortly after I came out I gave my parents a pamphlet.

"I don't know," my mom said, crinkling her brow. "I mean, what do they talk about? How much could there be to discuss?"

"Come on, Mom. I'll go with you. It could be a mother-daughter bonding experience. You always say we don't spend enough time together."

"Yeah, but I never thought we'd be spending it like *this*."

"Life is full of surprises," I said, throwing my arm around her shoulder.

Eventually I wore my mom down, and we planned to go to next week's meeting, which was held at a community center. Still, I hadn't been totally honest with her: Part of the reason I wanted to go was to see if I could meet any lesbians my age. My dad decided it was best if just my mom and I went, especially since he didn't have as big a problem with me being gay as my mom did: His sister *and* his cousin are both gay. I was fine with him not going, especially since he has a tendency to embarrass me whenever possible; in fact, I think he *enjoys* it. To this day he jokes about how I'm the best son he's got.

The following Tuesday, we arrived at the community center a little before 8 P.M. About 20 people or so were there, chatting and milling about. I was a bit nervous, since I'd never really been around a group of gay people before. I scanned the room to see if I could pick out which of the women were lesbians. Most of the people there looked like mothers, but I saw a couple of middle-aged women with bad haircuts and immediately knew they were dykes. And one of them was wearing an Indigo Girls shirt, so that sort of pinned their sexuality down a little, if you know what I mean.

My mom and I went up to the refreshment table and got some cookies and coffee. "I'm coming around to the fact that you're gay," my mom said, "but don't you think you're a little young to be drinking coffee?"

"I'm 17!" I said. "Besides, you told me you started when you were 15."

"You don't have to follow my example with *everything,*" she laughed.

"Well, obviously I don't, since we're here!" I said.

At the podium, a large woman in her 50s tapped the mike. "Excuse me, I think we're just about ready to begin. If you all could just take a seat..."

My mom and I found chairs near the back. I looked down our row and spotted a boy around my age with someone who was probably his dad. I looked behind us and saw two elderly women. One of them was wearing a T-shirt that said, I LOVE MY GAY GRANDDAUGHTER. Where the hell were the cute young lesbians?!

"I'm Margaret Mohen, and I'd like to thank you all for coming to tonight's meeting. It looks like we have some new faces tonight, which is always wonderful," the woman at the podium said. "What I'd like to do now is have the newcomers introduce themselves. Why don't we start with you two in the front row." She pointed at a lumpy guy in his 30s and a gray-haired woman. They both stood up.

"I'm Betty Anderson," the woman said. "And this is my son Carl. Carl told me he was...umm...*that way* two months ago. We're just here trying to work things out, if you know what I mean."

It was Carl's turn to speak. "Yeah, things have been rough lately, especially since I still live at home and all, and I can't bring guys home or anything. But we'll get through it."

A round of applause erupted throughout the room.

My mom and I turned to each other and smirked. "You'd better not still be living with me when you're his age," she whispered.

"And you'd better not be telling people I'm 'that way!' " I whispered back.

"Who else is new?" Margaret asked. "You two in the back. Could you please stand and introduce yourselves?" She pointed at my mom and me.

We stood, and I looked at my mom, but clearly she wanted me to talk. So I did. "Hi, I'm Natasha. This is my mother, Sue. I came out to my parents a couple of months ago. Sue here has been pretty cool and all, but she could use some improvement." Everyone in the room laughed—except my mom!

When we sat down, she turned to me. "Very funny," she sneered.

"Thank you, Natasha and Sue," Margaret said. "Any other new faces tonight?"

I scanned the room: A girl and her mother were looking for a place to sit down. The girl was around my age and had dark brown spiky hair and pale skin. Even across the room I could see how blue her eyes were. She was wearing a jean jacket and brown-and-tan plaid pants, and she was pretty skinny. I could tell right away that she wasn't there because her *mom* was gay. She was there because *she* was a lesbian! A very, very cute lesbian! Or at least bisexual. I'd take bisexual.

"Come on in!" Margaret nearly sang to the mother and daughter. "And please, please, introduce yourselves."

"My name's Helen," the woman said, "and this is my

niece Jenna. It's nice to meet you all." They both sat down.

Her niece? I thought. *That's weird.* I couldn't help staring at her, and right when I was doing just that, she looked back at me—and smiled! I grinned back.

"Well, whaddya know," my mom whispered. "Do you know who that woman is?"

"Why would I?"

"It's your father's business partner's first wife! You know...Bob. Your dad told me she sued the pants off him after the divorce." My mom's the biggest busybody west of the Mississippi. But at least now I had a connection to the cute girl. Maybe I could work it to my advantage

After the meeting, which was kind of boring, people were standing up and gathering their coats. Some of them were chatting, and Margaret was working the room. Now it was time for me to put my plan into action. "Hey, Mom," I said, "why don't you go talk to that woman Helen and try to get the dirt?"

"A girl after my own heart," my mom giggled.

We both went over to Helen and her niece Jenna. "Helen, my goodness! It's been ages!" my mom said, laying it on thick.

Helen was a tall brunette and pretty attractive, but she looked tired. "Sue! I didn't even see you. What are you doing here?"

My mom pointed at me with this semi-sarcastic look on her face. Helen pointed at Jenna, and she and my mom both smiled. "So, Helen..." my mom said, and then steered her off toward a corner of the room, more than likely to drill her about her divorce from Bob.

That just left Jenna and me twiddling our thumbs. After a few seconds of silence I mustered up the courage to say something. "Hi, I'm Natasha," I said, extending my hand.

"I'm Jenna," she said, and her handshake was firm, her hand warm.

"My mom said your aunt is my dad's business partner's

ex-wife." We both laughed at my awkward phrasing.

"Yeah, Helen's my mom's sister. She's pretty cool. She's here because my mom is the biggest asshole in the world. When I told my parents I was a dyke, they freaked out on me. My mom even threw a lamp at me. Which was OK since I hated that lamp anyway. I even tried to sell it on eBay once, but it was so ugly nobody wanted it!" We both cracked up. "So I'm staying with Helen for a while until things cool off." Jenna smiled slightly, and it was the sweetest smile I'd ever seen, laced a little with what seemed like sadness.

"That sucks. My mom's pretty OK with me being gay. But it's kinda hard for me sometimes, especially since I don't know any gay kids at school. That place is so homophobic anyway. If anyone came out, they'd immediately be beaten to a pulp."

Jenna laughed. "Yeah, I know what you mean. There's this one out gay guy at my school who's trying to start a gay club, but they already have a drama club, so I figure, what's the point? It would be kind of redundant." She paused and looked at my—was she checking out my breasts? "Hey, I like your shirt," she said. *Phew.* I was so nervous my palms were sweating. "It's cool," she added.

I had on one of my many Radiohead T-shirts. "Thanks. I like your…uh…pants." Was this what was meant by the phrase "sexual tension"?

Jenna smiled, and then we saw my mom and Helen about to come over to us. "Hey, you got a pen and paper? Wanna hang out sometime?"

"Yeah…and yeah," I said, reaching into my backpack. Jenna and I quickly exchanged numbers before Helen and my mom could poke their noses into our business.

"Nice meeting you," Jenna said, and I just smiled.

As Helen and Jenna left, my mom turned to me. "So, Helen got the house and the car and $10,000 a month in alimony." My mom had been so caught up in her gossip mongering that she hadn't even noticed that I'd been talking to Jenna.

Which was good, because it would have embarrassed me to no end to have her leering as I tried feebly to "hit on" a girl.

Three days passed and I still hadn't called Jenna, mostly because I was scared to death. How did these things work? Was I supposed to call her? Would she call me? She was a little butcher than I was, so was it up to her to make the first move? By day two my fingers were itching so bad to call her I thought I had poison ivy. By day three I was a nervous wreck. But then the phone rang that night around 7. Luckily, I picked it up before my mom or dad did.

"Hello?"

"Hi...um...is this Natasha?"

"Yes."

"This is Jenna, from the...uh...meeting."

"Oh, hi," I said nonchalantly. "What's up?"

"I was wondering what you were doing tomorrow night. You know, if you wanted to go to a movie or something."

"Yeah, sure. That'd be great," I told her.

"Do you like old movies?" she asked. "They're playing *Breakfast at Tiffany's* at the revival house in U. City."

"That's my favorite movie," I practically squealed. How weird!

"Really? I've never seen it. But Audrey Hepburn is a babe. Did you see *Sabrina*?"

"Six times!" I said, and we both cracked up.

Jenna and I made plans to meet at the theater at 7:30 the following night—Saturday. I had 24 long, long hours to go until my first date with a girl. If I was a nervous wreck waiting for her to call, I was *ten times* that now.

The next night I put on some faded jeans, a long-sleeved black T-shirt, and my black Converse sneakers. To me, wearing something with long sleeves is dressing up. I put on a little lipstick, but that was it as far as makeup went. My curly brown hair fell just below my shoulders. I looked in the mirror and liked what I saw, so I hit the road in my orange VW bug to meet Jenna at the theater. I didn't want my mom giving me a hard time, so I just said I was meeting my friend Amy at the mall. During the entire 15-minute drive to the movie theater, my hands were shaking so bad I could hardly grip the steering wheel.

Jenna was right on time, and her sweet smile helped put me a little more at ease. We both went into the theater right away since the show was starting at 7:45. A couple of times during the movie our knees touched, and tiny bolts of electricity shot through my body. Then, all of a sudden, Jenna did that "yawn-stretch" thing you always see on sitcoms. You know, when the guy yawns, stretches his arms out, then places his arm around the girl. But Jenna was all obvious about it on purpose—I guess so I'd laugh and go along with it. And when she put her arm around me, going along with it was exactly what I did. I looked at her and smiled.

After the movie, Jenna asked me where I was parked. When I told her I'd parked four or five blocks away, she offered to drive me to my car. Once we were inside her car (a maroon Oldsmobile, which I guessed either belong to her aunt or her parents), Jenna turned to me before starting the engine. "That movie is the bomb, isn't it?"

"Yeah," I said. "My favorite part is when they go into the five-and-dime and steal the Halloween masks. It's so romantic."

"More romantic than this?" Just then she leaned over and kissed me. She kissed me on the mouth! I'd kissed a couple of guys before, but it was never like this. When they kissed me, I felt nothing. But right now with Jenna kissing me, I felt *everything.* Her lips were smooth, and she was very, very tender with me.

"Just a little more," I laughed when she pulled her lips from mine.

"Do you mean that scene is a little more romantic than this, or are you saying you want a little more?" Jenna asked.

"Both." And we laughed and then started kissing again.

When we finished, Jenna asked, "Is this the first time you've kissed a girl?"

"No," I told her. "I've kissed my mom." Jenna cracked up at that.

"Oh, and there was this other girl..."

"Really? Who?"

"My grandma!"

It turned out that this was also Jenna's first kiss with a girl. After that night we became girlfriends, but we didn't have sex with each other until we were both ready, which was about six months into our relationship. We did a bunch of other stuff, though, but didn't go "all the way" for a while. We both didn't even really know what "all the way" was with lesbians anyway! So we bought this book on lesbian sex, and she'd come over to my house when my parents weren't around and we'd read it out loud and try different stuff out on each other.

Eventually I told my mom about Jenna. She kind of freaked out a little; I guess having a daughter who's a "practicing" lesbian is a little different than having a daughter who's "theoretically" a lesbian. But over time my mom came to realize how sweet and caring Jenna is, and to this day they're very close. And I always laugh when my mother says, "At least I don't have to worry about you getting pregnant."

I met a few other gay and lesbian teenagers at subsequent PFLAG meetings, and Jenna and I would hang out with them on the weekends. It was great to finally meet other gay people my age and connect with them in ways I couldn't connect with kids at school.

Jenna and I are still together—even after two years! About a year ago, though, I got a huge crush on this girl Karen I'd met at a coffeehouse, and I broke up with Jenna for a little while to see if things could work with her. But I missed Jenna so much that we got back together a few weeks later and have been monogamous ever since. I don't think I'll ever find a more caring, tender, or beautiful lover than Jenna; she is truly beyond compare.

Oh, and by the way: Thank you, Mom. Without you none of this would have been possible!

So Began My Life as a Maltreated Lesbian Gigola

L. Dewlap

My mother warned me before I went off to college on a basketball scholarship. "You be careful 'round those lesbians on those sports teams, especially if you're drinking around 'em, because you're just the type, you know?"

"Just the type for what?"

"Just the type they'd jump on, that's *for what.* You just stay away and don't be drinking 'round no lesbians on no sports teams."

This led me to wholeheartedly embrace alcohol my freshman year. I beer-bonged Budweiser till I babbled nonsense and barfed down the front of my pajamas; guzzled Everclear punch till I passed out with my ear on some frat boy's speaker; chugalug-championed my way into being consistently the loudest and most off-putting ass ever. Still, no lesbians would take advantage of me.

What was the problem?

That summer I went home with a mild case of delirium tremens and nothing else. My hand quivered as I wrote in my journal: *Mom was wrong—lesbians do not molest all drunken freshmen.* It was a groundbreaking moment of insight. My life began to change.

The next year my university gave me a job as a tutor to the academically challenged athletes. Suddenly, I was popular in what had once been an impenetrable and intimidating clique: lesbian PE majors who were failing kinesiology. One of them, Patsy Genatos, was the loudest-mouthed dyke on the basketball team and a notorious lesbian lech, the female version of a 55-year-old balding male senator. I tutored her in anatomy, and she relished torturing me in my personal closeted hell. She was pale, with a great big ass, and a mauve mole right on her upper lip. In an underhanded and sleazy kind of way, Patsy wanted to nail me. I was so desperate to be with a woman that in a masochistic sort of way she totally turned me on.

One night as we were going over the female reproductive system, she boldly jiggled her thigh under the table and pressed it against mine while leaning her body into me. I pretended nothing was happening while I soaked my underwear and hated her for it. She had tits out to here that she puffily pushed out in front of her like a nice set of pecs. Copping feel after smarmy feel in the claustrophobic quarters of the library study lab, she lamented her relationship with her current girlfriend. "It's not even like we're together anymore," she sniffled, leaning over a diagram of the uterus as an excuse to mash her enormous breast into my elbow. "Kay sleeps on the air mattress. I sleep on the couch. We haven't had sex in months!"

A young woman entered the study room, and Patsy jerked her thigh away from mine. She leaned back like we'd been caught in the act of copulation. Once we were alone again, she patted my knee and, with that mole close to my ear, murmured, "It's OK. It's our little secret."

She wasn't the only lesbian I was attracted to. In fact, there wasn't a single one of them I wasn't. And it didn't stop there—no way. I was in tormented, closeted, Catholic-girl hell. For example, the teller at the bank was about 60, wore red lipstick and *lots* of face powder. But as I handed her my deposit slip, I imagined kissing her passionately and thought, *Oh my god, I'm going crazy, oh my god oh my god.*

Of course, I had a lot of emotional issues at the time (not like now, right?). Anticommunist white trash Catholic Republicans had raised me. I had acne, exercise bulimia, and low self-esteem. I was also a bit of a religion freak. At night I would say my rosary while my straight roommate Marcia worked on her crafts project—a sort of latch-hook-by-number kit for a welcome mat with the image of Princess Smurf. That Smurf thing really traumatized me—she had the whole collection of Smurf figurines and everything.

Smack-dab in the middle of basketball season, I tore my medial meniscus and received the lesbian athlete's badge of honor: knee surgery.

Patsy volunteered Kay to pick me up from the hospital. Kay was a hard femme—a real bitch, people said. Anyone who'd put up with Patsy would have to be. She was scary. At the lesbian beer parties I started getting invited to as Patsy's tutor, she'd bring beers to all the dykes with a tight-lipped face and stomp around with this funny gait that came from having one leg longer than the other. She always wore tank tops and was thin and sinewy with softly cut biceps. She had enormous green eyes, flashing and feline—dangerous eyes. They never looked directly at you. When she picked me up at the hospital she hardly spoke to me, but the next day there was a note from her, a folded-up piece of notebook paper in my campus mailbox. Her handwriting startled me. She dotted her *i*'s with circles, put smiley faces after certain sentences. How could someone so bitchy have such childish penmanship?

I wrote her back, and we began to correspond daily. Nothing serious, just gossip and stuff. No one knew—not Patsy, not my Smurf-collecting roommate, not anybody. This was the beginning of something, I was sure of it. But I had trouble believing any woman could ever like—much less love—an ugly girl like me.

Patsy continued her bizarre sidelong overtures during our tutoring sessions, vaguely brushing up against me while she explained what it was like to be the only out lesbian on campus. She taught me how maltreated lesbians were, and I soaked it all in.

About a month after the first note, I decided I had to tell Kay about my feelings for her. I marked February 8 on my calendar: D-Day. And on D-Day I forced myself to walk over to Kay and Patsy's apartment. Patsy was away at basketball practice.

It was a crisp February afternoon. I trudged through the frost-frozen grass in my best clothes: Levi 501s, high tops, and a Mr. Bill T-shirt. When I rang the doorbell my heart was pounding. When she opened the door she looked at me blandly, as if I were the housekeeper or something, and said, "Oh, hi, come in," and then turned around and left me there with the door slightly ajar. I went in. The heat was cranked up to about 72 degrees. Kay was wearing shorts and a tank top and bootee socks—the kind with balls on the heels. She still didn't seem surprised to see me, and she was watching *The Flintstones* on TV, sitting on the living room sofa with a crocheted lime-green afghan over her lap and her knees drawn up to her chest. She had those long lovely bare arms of hers wrapped around her knees, the biceps taut and ready. (This was a girl who did a lot of curls with five-pound dumbbells and took diet pills, but I didn't know that yet.) It was about 4 o'clock and still light outside, but the curtains were pulled and the room was dark. I watched her face as the glow of the cartoon swept across it.

We'll have a ga-a-ay old time.

I told her in the usual way that everyone tells, face flushed, agonized and stammering: the old "I like you more than a friend" routine. Except I think I phrased it even cornier by saying, "So, social worker (she was a social work major), I have a problem I need to ask your advice about..."

"Oh, really? What is it?"

"Well..."

I think I'll spare you that dialogue. But after it was out and it was really out, I sat there on the floor and stared ahead. I had no idea what would happen.

"Well," she said, "if that's how you feel…then why are you sitting way over there? You act like you don't even like me."

"Uh…what?"

"Why don't you come sit a little bit closer?"

I managed to get up and flop myself not onto the couch

with her, but on the floor, up against the couch, with my back to her. The blanket she was wrapped in was bunched against my left shoulder blade. On a bookshelf near the kitchen a tiny travel clock ticked. My knees were drawn up to my chest, and I was really scared and holding very still when I felt her finger trace its way down my neck, down my shoulder like a drop of water.

I started to cry; a quiet, stilted sort of cry.

"What's wrong?" she asked.

I said, "Nothing's wrong. It's just…so beautiful."

A couple of days later I showed up again at her apartment toting the essential items she'd requested: a gallon jug of Almaden chablis and a lavender-scented candle. The word "chablis" sounded so exotic to me, and I thought, *Finally, I'm going to learn about fine wine from someone older and more sophisticated.* OK, I lied about the candle—it wasn't lavender, but bayberry or some other such really tacky nonsense. We lit the candle and drank the wine out of Styrofoam cups and rolled around grinding at each other while we made out on the couch. It was heavenly. I remember thinking about how small a woman's mouth was compared to a man's, how delicate and subtle, and how much nicer-tasting.

Then Patsy walked in the front door.

She was holding a bright bouquet of yellow tulips.

This was very bad timing, of course. (Damned if I didn't lose my virginity to dyke drama before I even got to have dyke sex.) Patsy handed the tulips to Kay and said, "Here you are, slut." Then she turned to me. "I thought you were my friend." There was a huge fuss—lots of slamming and banging. I became very calm and pretended I was watching a movie on TV. Kay strode around the house with her angry rollicking gimp. She slammed the flowers down on the kitchen table and went to grab her coat. "Let's get out of here," she told me. She grabbed Patsy's flowers and chucked them at the ceiling. Broken-headed tulips rained down on the beige living room carpet. It was all so very white trash, so very *un*beautiful, and since my roommate was out of town, we grabbed our wine and our candle and headed for the dorms to finish up what we had started.

My messy dorm room was thick with the scent of hot bayberry wax, and my head spun some from the wine as we lay together on my little bed. Kay launched into an "ABCs of Lesbianism" tutorial. She rubbed her thigh between my legs like a piston and made me come. "That's the first way you can do it," she said savvily. She then jerked me off with her fingers. "That's the second way..." Finally, she went down on me. "And that's basically the third way you can do it."

Next it was my turn. I tried really hard to make Kay come, recycling her own techniques, plus those of one of the best lesbian lovers I'd ever had or would have—my high school boyfriend. But I knew I was home from the moment I first tasted her. And in my earnest desire to please, I entered a zone and added a fourth "way" of lovemaking to her repertoire: fucking a woman's brains out. But after I had proudly taken her there and back and then some, she suddenly shoved me out of bed. I was down on the floor again, just like when I had first proposed my love.

"You said you'd never been with a woman before," she said. "You must have lied to me. There's no way you could be that good."

You probably think I made up that last part, but it's true.

I really was that good.

And I've been a maltreated lesbian gigola ever since.

First and Last

Zonna

I ran my fingers through my straight, short, wet brown hair. I forced myself to look in the mirror: I was as flat as the prairie. I usually didn't mind, though, since I preferred not to wear a bra, and I liked the fact that the boys didn't bother with me. But sometimes I wished I had more than tiny handfuls. Would Helen care? Would we even get that far before she threw me out?

I'd been in love with Helen for about a year by then. We were 15, and we'd been best friends since we were seven. At first I hadn't known what it was that made me want to be around her all the time, but something about Helen made my heart beat faster. Sometimes when we were doing our homework and I looked at her across her kitchen table I could hardly catch my breath.

It was 1975. We lived in a quiet suburban neighborhood outside of New York City. I had never heard the word "lesbian," so I had no idea I was one. That worked to my advantage, though, because I had no shame about the way I felt. All I knew was that I wanted Helen to be my girlfriend. A part of me knew that didn't make sense, that girls didn't have girlfriends where I came from, but it was a small part, so I ignored it.

I pulled my T-shirt on, drew the string tighter on my sweatpants, and fixed my hair again. This was it, the sleepover where I'd find a way to win Helen's heart. All afternoon I'd been rehearsing what to say, how to say it, and how to look when I said it. Finally I'd given up. I knew I'd be so nervous I'd probably forget everything anyway. The general plan was to come out a little at a time, like a rabbit nibbling at the soft grass but ready to bolt at the first sign of danger.

I'd stalled in the shower long enough, so I exited the bathroom to find Helen lying on her double bed listening to a

Partridge Family album and peeking at my math book. She shut it quickly when she saw me enter the room. I thought of that stupid psychedelic bus and tried not to gag. I wondered for a moment if I could really be in love with someone who liked the Partridge Family.

"Finally! What took you so long?" Helen sat up. "I'm glad I went first. There's probably no hot water left in the entire neighborhood!"

"I wasn't that long."

"Yeah, you were. I was just about to call the Coast Guard! You must be squeaky-clean. Let's see."

Helen jumped up and threw me onto the bed, tickling me mercilessly. I was stronger than she was and could have escaped easily, but I liked the closeness. I pretended to be helpless, laughing and twisting as her fingers found my most sensitive areas.

"Listen! You *are* squeaking!" she gloated.

In one quick motion I switched our positions, pinning Helen to the bed, sitting on top of her and holding her arms above her head with one hand.

"What were you saying?"

Helen laughed, admitting defeat. "Uh...oh, nothing, I guess."

"I thought I heard you say something about somebody squeaking..." I took my free hand and started to lift Helen's pajama top to tickle her ribs—this was her weak spot.

"Please don't! I'll do anything. Please don't tickle me!" Helen gasped. She loved and hated the feeling of being tickled: loved the tension it created, hated the sensation of being out of control.

"Anything?" I questioned her promise. I was willing to barter, but there was only one thing I wanted.

"Your wish is my command," she said.

I remember thinking, *If only that were true...*

I let go of Helen's arms, freeing her. I sat next to my

former prisoner, my own fear making *me* a captive. My feelings rendered me silent for a moment.

"Is something wrong?" Helen sat up and fixed her shirt. I knew she was looking at me, but I couldn't face her.

"No."

"You let go. You had me, but you gave up without getting anything first. If I'd had you pinned, I would have made you promise me something, like giving me your cardigan—that gray one with the pockets."

"You can have it if you like it so much, but it'll never fit you." We had always been about the same height, but in the last year I had outgrown Helen by three inches.

"Really?" Helen loved that sweater. It was probably the nicest thing I owned.

"Sure."

"Well, why didn't you get something out of me? You could've asked for anything."

"I don't want anything." I was finding it more and more difficult to breathe as I came closer to telling Helen the truth. I studied the blue wallpaper, the shag rug, the stereo, the bookcase. My eyes traveled in a circle around the room until they landed back on Helen. Then they flitted away again.

"Nothing?"

"Well, maybe one thing."

"What? Why didn't you ask for it?"

I forced myself to look at her. "Because I didn't want it that way. I want you to give it to me because you want to, not because you have to."

"That depends on what it is," she laughed. "You can have practically anything of mine you want, except my blue jacket."

I sat up straighter. "It's not anything like that."

"Well, what then?"

I forced myself to say it. "Kiss me." The rabbit peeked out of the hole.

"What?" Helen stared at me, not believing she'd heard what she'd heard.

If I could only hold her in my arms, I knew I could make Helen understand what I felt.

"I said I wanna kiss you. That's all I want."

She didn't say a word.

"Well?" I was waiting. "You said *anything*."

"Why?"

"I don't know, I just do."

"Oh, all right." She gave me a hasty little peck. "There, happy?"

"Not like that, like this." I leaned over, placed my lips on hers, and gave her a long, lingering kiss like I'd done in my dreams a thousand times. I moved away, letting my hands drop from Helen's shoulders. I didn't want to stop, but I had to make sure she was OK with what we'd done.

Neither of us spoke for a long minute. I cleared my throat a few times, but what I wanted to say was still lost inside somewhere. I felt the ghost of Helen's lips haunting my own. Finally I managed to whisper, "Did you like it?"

"Did you?" She didn't want to answer first.

"Yeah. A lot."

"Me too. It's not the same as kissing a boy at all, is it?"

"I don't know—I've never kissed a boy. I've never really kissed anyone. Not like that."

"No one? Why not?" Helen had kissed her share of boys already—maybe my share too.

"Never wanted to." The words pressed against the roof of my mouth, against the back of my teeth. How much longer could I hold them in?

"Oh..." Helen looked confused. "Why did you want to kiss me then?"

"I think I love you." I felt the blood drain from my face then rise back up quickly, as I inadvertently quoted the background music. I knew my face was probably scarlet by now. I wanted to hide, but the room—the world—was too small.

"I love you too. You're my best friend." Helen messed my hair playfully.

"No, I mean I'm *in* love with you..."

Well, I'd said it. Now it was up to Helen. My heart floated in limbo as I waited for her to speak. The next few words could determine the direction of my entire life. I made myself glance over at her.

She wasn't looking at me. I took that as a bad sign and started to panic. What if she didn't even want to be friends anymore? Had I just made a big mistake?

"Do you hate me now?" I whispered.

"No, I just don't know what to say."

"Do you think I'm weird?"

"No."

"I can't help the way I feel." I was apologizing even though I didn't think I'd said anything wrong. I sensed Helen's resistance and wanted to salvage what I could. I was desperately trying to dig my way back into the rabbit hole, but the entrance was sealed.

But Helen moved without warning and pushed me down on the blue bed and wrapped her arms around me. We started kissing, and then it was like we couldn't stop. One kiss led to the next. Her arms pulled me closer.

We were making out—I was making out with another girl. I no longer thought about right or wrong. The sky-blue room was spinning, Helen's kisses making me dizzy. My heart felt as though it would explode, it was so full. I was kissing Helen, and Helen was kissing me back. I could tell it was real by the way she held on to me. I dared to slip my hands under her shirt and touch her skin, so smooth. Her normally tame hair fell wildly over both of us. I ran my fingers through it: silky. I'd always wanted to touch it, and now I was. I could smell her shampoo, a fruity, delicious scent.

I had an urge to switch places with her, so with a gentle

nudge I rolled us both over. As I smiled down at Helen, I felt the fear leave me. Something clicked as though falling into place.

"I really love you," I said.

She touched my face.

I lowered myself slowly, placing the full length of my slim body over Helen's, inch for inch. I kissed her neck and shoulders. I moved my hand to her pajama top again, suddenly wanting to touch her there.

"Take your shirt off."

Helen looked frightened. "Why?"

"I just want you to."

"I'm scared. What are we doing?"

"I don't know. Do you wanna stop?"

She bit her lip but didn't answer.

"I'll take mine off first." I sat up and yanked my T-shirt over my head. I felt the cool air on my bare chest. "Now you. I'll help."

I reached a trembling hand over to Helen's buttons, undoing them, one at a time. "OK?"

She nodded and allowed me to unveil her. I slid the shirt from her shoulders.

"Wow..." I traced Helen's breasts gently with my hands, almost afraid to touch her. "I have hardly anything."

Helen reached up to me. "I think yours are perfect."

I looked at her and smiled. Then I lowered my head and kissed Helen's left breast, shyly. It was so soft. Our nipples brushed against each other as we made out some more. It felt good—like being tickled, only better—tingly and warm. I was so glad I'd gotten up enough courage to tell her how I felt.

I figured my luck was going so well that I should go with it. I had just started masturbating a few months earlier, and I wanted to share that feeling with Helen. I wondered if she'd let me. I decided to give it a shot.

I put my lips around her nipple and sucked. She sighed.

"Does that feel good?"

"Yes."

"Wanna try something that feels even better?"

"Like what?" She sounded nervous.

"Do you ever touch yourself, you know, down there?" I gently cupped her through her pajamas.

"Sometimes."

"Let me touch you then."

I felt her body tense.

"I wanna make you feel really good. Trust me?"

She hesitated but then parted her legs a little. I couldn't believe she was really going to let me touch her. Then I got scared that I might not do it right. I was sweating and praying I'd remember everything I'd enjoyed, hoping Helen would like the same things.

She lifted her hips as I slid her pajama bottoms down. She wasn't wearing any underwear, and I recall how beautiful she looked lying there naked with the moonlight shining through her window. I slid closer and kissed her some more. When it felt right I moved one hand down to her pussy and put my finger just inside. She gasped when I touched her, and I figured I must be on the right track. I rubbed gently up and down until she started to get really excited. Then I pressed harder and rubbed faster, the way I had with myself. Suddenly she was panting and shaking and I knew she was coming. I remember feeling proud that I'd been able to make her feel that way.

I held her in my arms until her heartbeat slowed back to normal. We kissed for what seemed like hours. Then we fell asleep curled together, my chest to Helen's back.

When we awoke the next morning, we were suddenly shy, fumbling through the tangled sheets for our clothes and not speaking. I took Helen's hand in my own.

"What's wrong?"

"What we did last night..."

"What about it?"

"What if someone finds out?" she asked.

"So what?"

She looked scared.

I tried to hug her, but she pulled away.

"I don't ever want to do that again."

I felt my heart drop to my stomach.

"Why not?"

"I just don't. Let's just forget it and be friends like before. Please?"

I wanted to take her in my arms and shake her. Why was she shutting me out? Just the night before we'd been adventurers, pioneers. We'd gone exploring together, and we'd captured fierce emotions and unearthed buried pleasure. I'd thought we had discovered our sexuality together. I couldn't understand why she didn't want to hang hers on the wall next to mine, like a trophy.

And then it hit me: It was true enough, we both *had* discovered something about ourselves. It just wasn't the same thing.

Jennifer

Ren Bisson

The year was 1980, and I was in junior high—eighth grade, to be exact. I was a trumpet player in the band and a rather good one at that. I sat first chair, which was usually given to the best player. That school year, the first day back in band I met a seventh-grader named Jenny. She was tall for her age, wore huge glasses, and was clumsy. I'll never forget her entrance to the classroom that day. She tripped going up the steps to where the trumpet players sat, and everyone busted out laughing. But she handled the embarrassment gracefully, which immediately gained her my respect.

The year went by quickly, and our interactions were limited to the band room. I never really befriended Jenny outside of class, but during class I'd crack jokes and try to make her laugh. On a couple of occasions the band teacher threatened to kick us out if we didn't stop our horseplay. Once, Jenny asked me if I wanted to do something outside of school, but she wasn't in the clique I hung out with, so I made up some excuse as to why I couldn't, and she didn't ask again.

It wasn't until the summer before my sophomore year and her freshman year that our paths crossed again. If you played in band, you were required to be in the marching band that played at all the high school football games. We were forced to show up the first week of August for marching band practice and also for our performance in the Battle of Bennington parade, which usually happened the third week in August.

I'd had a mad crush on the first-chair trumpet player my freshman year. She was the daughter of the band teacher and was phenomenal. This led me to practice for two hours or more a day. As a result, my skill had improved immensely. I wasn't yet at a place where I was able to identify this crush as sexual. I just thought I wanted to be like her or with her constantly. Bennington, Vermont, was a small rural town where anyone who deviated from the norm was ostracized. I grew up Catholic as well, so even if I did have any idea that homosexuality existed, I certainly wouldn't have considered it an option.

After school started in the fall, Jenny asked me if I'd give her private trumpet lessons, for which her grandmother would pay me $10 a session. That was great money back then, so I grabbed at the chance to get some extra dough in my hands. I'd taken private lessons the year before, so I had a lot of lesson plans from which I could pull. A few days later Jenny came over to my house, and week after week her grandmother would pick her up later and later, until we just started hanging out and the lessons stopped.

I began to realize that Jenny felt about me how I'd felt about the lead trumpet player the year before. I felt a bit weird about it, but I liked it in a way because it was kind of a power trip. As our friendship developed I'd try to influence her to be cooler. She even let me cut her hair and go shopping with her and her grandmother to help her pick out more stylish outfits. I also convinced her to go by Jenn or Jennifer, since it sounded more mature.

By the end of my sophomore year I'd started a part-time job at Burger King and had gotten my driver's license. I was lucky, since my parents bought me a car so they wouldn't have to taxi me around anymore. After that, I had more money and more freedom to do the things I wanted.

Jennifer and I started to pal around regularly. She lived with her grandparents, and they were rather strict about her curfew and how often she could do things. Her mother and father had divorced when she was three, and her mother couldn't afford to raise her, so Jennifer's grandparents had gladly volunteered. They were very old-fashioned, and she found this difficult, often arguing with them and defying their wishes, which resulted in her being grounded a lot.

During this time I had a boyfriend, mostly for show, and

another best friend. Jennifer often got jealous about the amount of time I spent with them, but she'd always say she was angry because she wasn't allowed to do the things we did. It wasn't until later that she confessed her true feelings.

My parents were super lenient and let me do just about anything I wanted. I played guitar as well as trumpet and was in several rock bands throughout my teens, which made me a bit of a partyer. I influenced Jennifer, and I was with her the first time she got drunk, one night when she stayed overnight at my house. The corner store sold alcohol to anyone who looked close to 18, which was the drinking age in Vermont back then. I knew we would be intoxicated, so we walked to where we were going instead of driving. I bought two bottles of Boone's Farm wine, and we each drank one while sitting in an abandoned train car that sat on a railroad track that was no longer in use. Jennifer got so drunk that she threw up before I even got her back to my house and then a couple of more times in the bathroom across from my parents' bedroom. We were supposed to have gone to the movies, so we blamed her vomiting on spoiled popcorn butter. We had really gone to a house party and left right before the cops had shown up to bust it up.

I had a single bed, and because Jennifer and I were so drunk, I told her to sleep in it with me instead of on the floor. After her nausea passed, she began to rub my back, unsolicited. My whole body responded, and I found myself extremely confused. I was too afraid to ask the questions I wanted to and too afraid to do anything about my feelings, even if it had been an option. I pretended to fall asleep as if nothing was happening.

The next day, Jennifer claimed not to remember anything that happened after we left the party. I was relieved in away, but I felt kind of stupid about my emotional response to her touch. This began a new ritual of her staying at my house or me at hers every Friday night, unless she was grounded or I had to work till closing. We'd exchange back rubs and push the limits of where we touched, but we'd never go too far and we'd never discuss it.

About six months into this, Jennifer told me she had written about her feelings for me in her journal. Unfortunately, her grandmother read it, grounded her for a month, and forbade her to spend any time with me. She never did tell me what she wrote, but somehow she convinced her grandmother that it was nothing. As a ploy to be able to spend time with me again, Jennifer begged her grandmother not to say anything to me about it. Her grandmother was hesitant for about three months, but her attitude changed when I brought my boyfriend to her house with one of his friends to take Jennifer out on a mock double date. I say "mock" because Jennifer never showed any interest in the guy and pretended that he was jerk as an excuse not to see him again.

By my senior year and her junior year, Jennifer began working at Burger King too, and we were basically inseparable. She bought some contact lenses with some of the money she made, which made her so unbelievably gorgeous that often I lost myself in her stare. She'd been hiding these incredible green eyes behind her glasses. The denied sexual tension between us was getting worse, and every time we drank we'd push the envelope. I was thinking of her sexually, and I knew she was feeling the same way. I was the dominant one in the relationship, and I knew it was up to me to make the first move, but I wasn't ready. It was so obvious that my sister even asked me if Jennifer and I were lovers. I, of course, reacted as if the thought appalled me. I also did a better job of hiding my feelings in front of others than Jennifer did—meaning, I dated a lot of different guys. I had to do this to keep up appearances. It broke Jennifer's heart, but I think she knew why I was doing it.

I finally graduated and decided that I'd had enough of school, so I didn't plan on going to college right away. Jennifer convinced me to be a counselor at a summer camp she had attended as a kid. She'd been a counselor there for a couple of summers and would be working there this summer too. We finagled it so that we'd be co-counselors sharing a cabin.

The first day of camp was counselor orientation, and we spent the morning and afternoon preparing for the kids' arrival the next day. That night, though, a group of us snuck out to the horse ring, which was about half a mile from base camp. I brought along some whiskey I'd hid in the secret compartment of my Camaro. There were four of us, including Jennifer and me, and we all indulged in the whiskey and talked about senseless things. The two that were with us had been dating for a while and took off after about an hour, letting us know that they needed to spend some time alone.

Jennifer and I were lying on the floor of the viewing stand, looking up at all the stars. All we could hear were the crickets and peepers. I asked her if she loved me. She thought this was a silly question, laughing and saying, "Of course I love you, why?"

"Do you really love me?" I asked her. "You know...more than just as friends?"

With that, Jennifer rolled over next to me and put her hand on my stomach. I was trembling with fear, but mostly with excitement. She whispered, "Yes."

I rolled into her, embraced her, and kissed her like I'd never kissed anyone in my life. That fateful kiss lasted only about ten seconds, but it felt like an eternity. I knew right then and there that this was what I had longed for and that I was so incredibly in love with Jennifer that I didn't care what anyone else thought about it. We laughed after the kiss, and she joked that it was about time I'd done something. As we kissed again, our passion overtook us and I ached for more of her touch everywhere. I felt heat in places I didn't know existed. I let my kisses wander over her face and down her neck. My hands caressed her entire body, teasing her, then came close to touching her breast and rubbed the inside of her thigh, just skimming her sweet spot over her jeans. I was doing what I'd always rehearsed in my daydreams about making love to her. She moaned when I touched her and pulled me up for more of those priceless kisses. I was so hot for her that I felt myself getting wetter by the second. Jennifer pulled me on top of her and bent her knee so that her thigh was rubbing against my crotch and mine against hers. She moved her leg expertly, and before I knew it I rode the wave of orgasm for all it was worth.

I knew I wanted to return the favor of this unbelievable pleasure, so I went to work. I positioned myself between Jennifer's legs, pushing myself gently against her as I kissed her. I lifted her shirt and her bra and put my mouth to a breast for the first time. It was soft on my tongue, yet her nipple was hard. She grabbed my hair and pushed my head harder into her breast. As I undid her jeans and slid my hand down her pants, I felt her tremble and her grip on my hair grew tighter. I slid a finger into her and then two. Then she slid her pants down to allow me better access. She was so wet that I easily inserted three fingers, and she gasped in approval. She pushed my head down toward her sweet spot, and I took my time getting there. I kissed her stomach and the inside of her thighs. I put my mouth very close to her clit and let her feel the heat of my breath on her.

Her scent was so sweet and desirable that I could no longer resist putting my mouth on her. She tasted so good that I was salivating and finding myself gushing again. Her clit throbbed and swelled under my tongue, and when Jennifer came, I felt her tighten around my fingers and she squeezed my head between her legs as she pulsated. She reached down and held my hand inside her as she asked me to kiss her. I continued to move in and out of her with my hand against my crotch and found myself coming with her for the second time.

Eventually we got dressed and straightened ourselves up and then held each other under the stars, caressing and kissing each other tenderly between heartfelt conversation. What a memorable night that was on July 13, 1985.

We spent the rest of camp sneaking away to be alone for a moment or waiting for the kids to go to sleep so we could steal a moment of passion in our cabin.

Jennifer and I remained lovers, and I decided to attend the same college in the fall of 1986 in a town in East Puckafuck, Vermont, so that we could be together. We kept our affair secret from our families and didn't come out to anyone except a few friends at college. We began to plan our life together and talked of having children together someday. We were soul mates, and although our love didn't seem validated by the outside world, in ours we were the queens.

On our second anniversary of being lovers we decided to take a trip to visit a friend. He claimed to be very lonely, and the trip offered us an opportunity to get away from working and the apartment we were sharing on summer break with two other women.

Unfortunately, this trip would change our lives forever.

Our friend went to his job for the morning, and Jennifer and I spent it making love. It was always exciting to make love in different places. Upon his return we all decided to go for a swim in the local river. There had been an extraordinary amount of rain that summer, and the river was high. We managed to find a safe place to take a dip and then ventured up the river to view some nature and relax. We found this beautiful sight that was a natural rock bridge. The water that rushed into it was white and treacherous, but it came out into a lovely, calm pool. Jennifer ventured out with our friend onto the rock bridge while I sat on the side watching the breathtaking scenery.

At this moment my life changed. I saw Jennifer stand up and slip on the wet rock, falling into the treacherous water. I got up and looked over the other side of the bridge, figuring she'd come floating out and start laughing at how accident-prone she was. But she didn't. Under the rock I'd been sitting on, the undertow had sucked her in and she drowned. I remember looking at my watch and seeing that the time was 7:12. It occurred to me later that the date was also 7/12.

This is in memory of Jennifer Lee Puffer, 1968–1987. She was an incredible person with the biggest heart of anyone who has ever graced me with her presence. I learned so much about love and friendship from her. She taught me how to laugh and cry from the depths of my soul. Through her departure, I learned to savor every moment and not to take any day or person for granted. Every day I see them, I tell the people in my life that I love them. I've learned to forgive and not hold resentment and also ask for forgiveness, because after someone is gone, it's too late. Jennifer, I will always love you. Thank you for the time you shared with me in this lifetime.

Strawberry Woman

Jasmine Marah

She dipped her finger into the sour cream, reached around me—twisting over my body—and indicated that I should open my mouth. We were sitting back to back on her bed, each leaning on the other. I tried to hide my trembling, opened my mouth, and sucked her finger. Her face was so close to mine. Pale-blue eyes; icy at times, now hot, lilacs. Would there be a wet spot when I got up from the bed? I hadn't imagined that I could be so excited, sustain the longing for such a stretch of time. Julia was so cool, feeding me strawberries dipped in sour cream and brown sugar. Her Siamese cat, Thorn, was knocking her roommate's toiletries into the tub.

Montreal, 1973. I was the wife of an American draft dodger, William John. Julia, an American student. We'd met in a consciousness-raising group. The Woman's Liberation office, upstairs from the War Resisters' League, had caught my eye. I'd gone up to visit while my husband got some counseling from the compatriots in the office downstairs.

Black walls, black floors, black ceiling, a small wooden table, painted the same flat black with a hand-lettered notice in both French and English: MONTREAL WOMEN'S LIBERATION, ALL WOMEN WELCOME.

The only relief to the serious paint job was a canvas flag with a red woman's symbol encircling a raised fist. The room was so small that the flag curved around most of two walls. I was awestruck. *These must be powerful women indeed!* I thought. I left my name and telephone number on a pad to be notified of this new happening thing: consciousness-raising groups.

Having heard of women's liberation only from my husband, who characterized the movement as run by a bunch of dykes in overalls, I had no idea of their principles. In this new city, I knew only a few of the housewives around the Barclay

Avenue apartment complex. The street was block after block of tan brick four-story apartment buildings, off Côte-des-Neiges. They'd been built on a huge hog farm at the beginning of World War II to house immigrant families who came to work in the growing war industries. I once heard a woman on the Canadian Broadcasting Company say, "Not likely that women from Barclay Avenue, eh, listen to this program. I know I wouldn't want to live there."

Still, the apartments were cheap and spacious. William John and I and our two children lived in a basement apartment. Three bedrooms, living room, dining room, heat paid, door to the garden, windows looking onto the varied feet of passersby. One hundred dollars a month. So what if the green-and-red linoleum was worn in spots and I had to walk up two flights of stairs to hang laundry? Sometimes in the gathering 5 A.M. light, I stood and could feel the spacious past, the farmers, the wives, the vegetables, acres of corn bowing to the breeze off the St. Lawrence. It eased the loneliness, this farm feeling.

I had been excited to come to a foreign country. At 23, in 1970, I'd never been out of the United States. I loved Montreal; it glittered like a sunlit stream, rich with history, fragrant with many cultures. I had arrived pregnant with my second child, happy, looking forward to his birth.

But three years later, by 1973, several apartments up the economic scale and closer to the center of town, I could not escape the sure knowledge that my husband did not really like me. He had always had a struggle having sex with me. We were such opposites. Deeply involved with the all-night chats of intoxicated male chess players, college dropouts, political theorists, and would-be activists, he loved men and used almost any situation to dismiss women in general—there had been no women geniuses, no women artists, no women musicians; they could only dance because the men did all the work; all female world leaders had men to really run everything—including Golda Meir.

And if only I'd lose a few pounds here and here...and if I could cook an easy-over egg, and keep the house cleaner, and not pay so much attention to the kids (they should be just put into a play pen and I should clean), and why did I have to belong to that La Leche League anyhow? What made me read poetry, since I obviously didn't understand it? Why did I want to plant a garden? Didn't I know it would die in the winter? What difference did it make what colors the rooms were painted? It wasn't our place anyhow. Why was I so concerned about vegetables, cow food, rabbit food?

I had not one smidgen of an idea how to go out on my own, to leave him, to support my children—I, who modeled at the art classes to support us and had not even a high school diploma.

I wanted to try and "save" the marriage—or at least interest my husband in sex again. So I bought a sheer black shortie nightgown, with little panties, and red lipstick and black eyeliner. Getting dressed in the lingerie excited me; I flushed, I sparkled, I was fevered. It had been so long since we'd had sex. But nothing. He just couldn't get it up, and I had never heard of a clitoris.

It was after I'd found a very good private college that had all-day child care, and scholarships, and that had accepted me as a first-year student based upon my test scores, that I began to get a feel for being independent. My scores in the highly competitive science courses were the highest of any student with children, and I was the only mother at the college taking five classes.

I say, therefore, that I was ripe. Julia had been the only lesbian in the CR group. The other six of us were, oddly, married and Jewish. And expatriate Americans. Julia was single and a Catholic dyke but also an American. I wanted to get to know her yet didn't know how to approach her. She seemed so independent, while I couldn't imagine the future without a partner.

One day I came home for a while to the house my husband and I now rented, leaving the children in day care. It was late spring, and the trees had leafed out. I smelled hot pretzels, lilacs, and the salt from the St. Lawrence. My husband was dressed in my black negligee, eye shadow, and lipstick, his longish hair puffed around his face. He was excited, hard and huge, and took me quickly, with obvious delight. He asked me to repeat out loud to him what a beautiful girl he was. As he came inside me; I couldn't understand why I was so frustrated. I was empty. Bereft. He didn't notice. He then told me that he was in love with my friend Nancy's husband, Fredric.

Sharing this in the next CR group meeting didn't seem to be a good idea. I was certain no one else had ever had this happen. It was beyond the usual subjects: housework and education. We sat around Felice's brown, gold, and blue living room speaking of the female orgasm and clitoris. Someone had drawn a diagram, copied from *Our Bodies, Ourselves.* We were serious, but we giggled. No one would say if they'd ever had an orgasm. I was hot with embarrassment. I looked across at Julia, and she appeared amused.

As I was leaving that night to go home, Julia asked me if I'd like to get together for dinner some evening. I was so pleased. I had fantasized about asking her to come over sometime but wasn't sure she'd want to be around the kids and my husband. We planned to meet for dinner the following Saturday.

Dinner was exciting. Julia knew all the cheapest places, wonderful little hole-in-the-wall restaurants, where the cook was somebody from the old country, sharing favorite family recipes. That first evening, we went to a Hungarian place called Paprika's. It was down some basement steps, the floor shiny red concrete. There were six tiny tables, all full. The basement was cool, the fragrance of the food welcoming. A plate of noodles with beef, in a creamy sauce with peas and pearly onions, was $1.50. Hot tea with jam and lemon: 20 cents. A woman in her 50s, bright red hair showing gray at the roots, with two aprons and a worried expression until we paid, hovered over us, making sure everything was "OK? OK?"

Afterward, we walked, careful not to touch, and then I caught the bus back home. William wanted to know if I'd been out with another man. I assured him I had not. I'd just been out with Julia, I told him. He fought with me about it, and I finally agreed to invite Julia to the house.

I started a double life. Julia and I would meet for lunch or go up to the museum café on Sherbrooke Street. We talked about art, about what it was like for her to grow up Catholic, me Jewish. She studied theater and would be directing a student play about Virginia Woolf in a few months. I wondered if Woolf was a great writer. Didn't my husband know about her?

I was becoming disoriented. I stopped trying to seduce my husband, but instead of being relieved, he was suspicious. Julia came and had dinner with us. William didn't like or trust her—"damn dyke"—but the kids adored her. She played with them, pushed them on the swing, chased them around the park, laughed, told stories, and showed them tai chi. Then, at the end of the summer, the last week in August, Julia went home to Connecticut to help her mother who had a nervous condition. I didn't think I'd see her again. We were just friends, after all. I wrote to her twice, three times, no answer.

In October, three weeks before my son's third birthday, my husband left me. He went to Toronto to find a job, as he'd been unemployed for three years. He was living with the husband of a friend of mine, who was also job hunting. William found a job and stayed. He didn't send child support. I continued in school and working as a model. The kids got special low child-care rates, and my rent was cheap. I'd had independence thrust upon me, and I was enjoying it.

That last week in November, just before the first snow,

the temperature at about 35 degrees, I walked the brittle sidewalks to a bus stop on Sherbrooke Street, waiting to go up the hill to Marianopolis College. I was working through my second year, doing well and hoping to go to medical school. The woman next to me said hello, and I turned to her and saw Julia. I shocked her by hugging her, enfolding her in my thrift store raccoon coat. I wanted to show her that her lesbianism did not bother me. Little did I know of butches, their allure. I just knew that she seemed gorgeous to me.

Several weeks later, squirming on her bed, begging her to have sex with me. Touching her cheek, lifting her fine blond hair. I trace the line of her jaw. She sucks on my finger, holds it with her hand, pushing it into and out of her mouth. Julia's breasts are high, tight, and small. I tentatively put a hand above one breast. She leans hard against my hand and then reaches around me, bringing a sugared strawberry up to my mouth. I lick the sugar off but don't bite the berry. I don't think I can manage to chew or swallow. The room pulses, hums. The window looks out onto a brick air shaft. We are reflected pinkly back at ourselves. "We look like strawberries," she says. "Is that why you didn't bite?"

Wordless, I can only let her lead. Patient, she undresses me. I hope my underpants don't have holes. She wears no bra. Just a ribbed undershirt. She leaves it on. Lays me down, lays me back, kneads and pulls on my full breasts, sees the milk—a remnant of nursing my son—doesn't stop. I lift her undershirt off, circle her breasts with my tongue, and am surprised, in turn, by the thick blond hair that makes a furrow on the midline of her tummy from pubis to navel. I have never seen skin so milky, like a full vine of white roses. Puts her hand between my legs, unfolding my labia, coaxing the wet out farther, asking if I like it, asking what I want, telling me that everything is fine, that it is all good. Not wet enough, I say. She wets me with her finger dipped in her mouth and finally drops down to my clit with her tongue, and I am moaning, crying, confused, hungry, and rising to her. Another second and I will come, another second...I do, and she does, and indeed, there is a large wet spot on the bed.

I want to talk afterward, but Julia "isn't into processing." That's fine, as long as we continue to have sex. It is the beginning of a two-year journey together, and my lifelong lesbian self.

Strawberries become a mode of wordless speech for us. They were never again as good after Julia and I parted. Yet even now, nearly 30 years later, when I bend to open a lover's body, the scent of them envelops me.

Searching for Myself

Chenille Wilson

The first woman who loved me in a sexual way was Alicia, the controller for the company I worked for. She was the most beautiful woman in the world to me, perhaps because she was the first woman who did not see me as a rival for a man. She also had a mocha-and-cream-colored complexion and the softest, biggest brown eyes I'd ever seen. She looked like a human version of Bambi, all long lashes and delicate features. But fine in only the way a well-seasoned woman can look.

I knew Alicia was different my first day of work, when she graciously shook my hand and introduced me around the office as the new account manager. She didn't glare daggers at me as did most of the women I'd known all my life.

My mother told me when I was a little girl that I'd always have troubles in life "because you're God's own jewel. You gotta watch the men so they don't touch you where they shouldn't be, and you gotta watch the women so they don't pull out your pretty hair or scratch your face. Beauty is its own price, child," and my mother would sigh, because she knew what she was talking about. My mother was the most beautiful black woman in Charleston, or at least that's what I thought growing up. And she didn't have many close women friends until she was good and married at age 20. I inherited her features, which were like those of a proud Nubian queen and dark like a strong cup of coffee.

My mother was right, of course. Aren't they always right? When I was growing up, girls were always jealous of me, hanging onto their boyfriends in school when I passed, as if I were going to reach out in the hallways and just snatch their men away. Every time I dated a boy it seemed all the girls in school breathed a sigh of relief, and when I inevitably broke up with them because of a certain missing something, every girl seemed to hold her breath and her boyfriend more tightly than usual. It wasn't possible for me to tell anyone that I didn't really want men, that they didn't attract me or make me giggle and melt like the other girls. Who would admit that in a mostly black high school in the South in the early 1970s? Not me, for certain. So I pretended to like boys just like all the other girls, all the way to having a husband right when I graduated from college.

In 1990 my husband and I got divorced, mostly because I didn't love him, but also so I could search for that intangible something that had eluded me all my life. I knew it was somehow related to women, but I wasn't sure exactly how. Divorced, 36 years old, and very curious about who I was and what I wanted, I moved to the bright lights of New York to find the answers.

During my first year with the new company in New York, Alicia became a very close friend. She was also from the South—Mobile, Alabama—so we got along from the start.

"Girl," she often exclaimed, "people in New York just do not know how to cook good food!"

"Tell me about it," I'd agree, and we'd exchange recipes for our favorite deep-fried Southern meals. Alicia was a person with whom I felt very comfortable; this was the first time except for family I could count a woman as a friend. It was a good experience.

We'd known each other well for six months before she told me she was a lesbian. She told me over what had become our traditional Saturday brunch one April weekend, and I wasn't too surprised. I'd never seen the men at the office goggling over her the way they annoyingly did over me, and it was strange, considering how beautiful she was. This, combined with her ease around me, told me she was like no "usual" woman I'd ever met. I didn't think *lesbian* until she told me, however. But when she did, I was thrilled. It was like a light went on in my head, and I quietly said to her, "Alicia, I think I am too."

Alicia and I spent even more time together the next several months. She took me to gay and lesbian bookstores, lesbian coffeehouses, and to pride parades and festivals. I felt so at home in my own skin for the first time. Not only did lesbians exist, there were black lesbians. It was like I'd discovered a new world, a wonderful and comforting sisterhood, and I explored it as much as I could. Well, I explored everything except for the physical side. I wasn't sure I was ready for that.

"Don't worry," Alicia assured me. "When it's right, you'll know." Since Alicia had been in two serious lesbian relationships and had dated many women in her 40 years, I trusted her and accepted her advice. Well, I never would have guessed that she would appoint herself personally in charge of my education.

For my 38th birthday, Alicia arranged a fancy dinner for the two of us at our favorite Southern-style restaurant. There were beautiful tulips, my favorite, and good red wine. All the servers sang "Happy Birthday," and the chef even came out and placed my meal in front of me, wishing me a prosperous and fulfilling year. I felt like a princess in a fairytale.

We spent the evening on the town, watching a movie and going for a carriage ride in Central Park. Alicia came back to my house afterward, and I invited her up for coffee, as was our custom. But as it turned out, this evening was going to be anything but customary.

When I came out of the kitchen with the steaming cups of coffee, Alicia was seated on the couch, looking very nervous. I immediately sensed something was wrong, so I set the coffee on the end table nearest her and set myself down on the couch beside her.

"What's wrong?" I asked, gently stroking her arm in a manner that to me was not suggestive but merely supportive.

"Chenille," she said, and stopped with a tortured look on her beautiful face.

"What?" I asked again, slightly panicked. It must be something terrible, I thought.

"I want to ask you something. But I'm really scared to mess up everything we have."

"I don't understand," I said, watching her carefully. She was gazing at her hands, which were clenched in her lap over her dark blue silk pants she'd worn specially for my birthday.

"Chenille," she whispered, finally looking up at me with those gorgeous chocolate eyes, "I want to kiss you."

"Is that all?" I said, relief sweeping over me. "I thought you were going to tell me you fell in love with someone and were moving back to Mobile." I could joke because I was so happy at last to get closer to this fine woman whom I trusted with all my heart.

Smiling at me with her big brown eyes seemingly lit up from inside, Alicia moved toward me on the couch and took me in her arms. When her lips touched mine a spark went off in my heart, head, and body. I thought with satisfaction, *This is absolutely who I am. I have found that thing I was seeking.*

Alicia loved me most of the night. We made love, then drifted to sleep, then awoke and touched each other again until the fire was stoked good and high, then slept again, then awoke and started all over. It was blissful, and it changed me forever. No longer would I have to worry about women being petty and jealous over their men; men were no longer an issue in my life. From now on, women were to be my only interest. Realizing that I loved women, that I was a lesbian, made sense to me in a way that the first 38 years of my life had not. Luckily, I had at least another 38 to go!

Alicia and I stayed lovers for three years before we regretfully broke it off, realizing that we made better friends than partners. I have since returned to Charleston, the city of my soul and my family, and am now seeing a younger woman who daily brings me joy and laughter. But Alicia will always remain in my heart as the first woman to open the world to me and help me discover who I am.

The Tattooed Heart

Jessy Luanni Wolf

The year I was 17, I fell in love with a woman and I made love to a woman. Unfortunately, these were two different women. But my sexual experiences with women started much earlier. I didn't know I was a lesbian because I didn't know there was such a thing. I only knew that women were much more desirable than men.

When I was a little girl, my sister had a poster of Ricky Nelson on her wall, but I had a poster of a stripper on mine. Her name was Candy Barr, and she wore stars on her nipples, a G-string, a big hat, and boots. My stepfather, who owned a striptease bar in Hollywood, had brought the poster home. Candy was beautiful. I spent hours looking at her silver-star-decorated breasts, the curve of her tiny waist flowing into her temptingly rounded hips, and her perfect legs that rose from red cowboy boots up into a delicious triangle covered by a fringed little piece of leather.

Since I was only eight years old, I didn't really focus on my feelings and know what they were made of. I only knew I loved and wanted Candy Barr.

I was a very small, blond, pretty little girl. I never knew there was any other way than to be the beloved of a male, to be acted upon, to be controlled. I saw no way to escape this destiny. My feelings didn't seem to matter to anyone, especially to the boys who flirted with me. But I always had my sister, and she was my first love. I loved Susie more than any other person in the world, so she was my very first model for a beloved of my own. She and I were just a year apart, and most people actually thought we were twins. We learned to masturbate together. We lay side by side on the floor in our room and touched ourselves when she was seven and I was eight, the same year I worshiped Candy Barr.

As we explored our bodies, we told each other about our discoveries. "Move in circles around the little bump. It feels so good," Susie told me.

"Yes," I answered, "and if you put some spit on your finger, it moves better."

"Oh, I'm at the good part," Susie said, and this brought me to the good part too.

We didn't know the word for orgasm yet. But as we each moved toward our personal good parts, she looked into the sleepy eyes of Ricky Nelson while I gazed at Candy Barr. Just as I reached the good part, I'd focus on Candy's perfect breasts and long to see what was behind the stars covering her nipples.

One day we discovered the vibrator. Our parents had left it in the living room after using it for a body massage while watching television. We brought it into the bedroom we shared and massaged each other, on the back, the neck, the head, then moved to the front. Suddenly I wondered what it would feel like on my little bump.

"Susie, let's try it down there," I told her, and she grinned at me. She tried it first. Her smile got so much bigger, and she shut her eyes.

"That is so good," she told me. She lowered herself to the floor and started to shiver all over as she reached her good part. Then it was my turn. The feeling was just so wonderful, like nothing else. I was hooked a vibrator user for life.

I don't know whether seven years old, or even eight, was very young to masturbate or to have orgasms. Maybe mutual masturbation with a sister is incest, but it didn't seem wrong, and I still don't see that it hurt us in any way. Was it a lesbian experience? My sister grew up to be straight, and she never had any other lesbian experience. But I did.

When I was 13 I had a neighbor, a girl two years older than I was. Cheryl was unusual because both of her parents worked, so she was alone often at home.

"Come over to my house so we can be private," she told me after school one day.

When I came over, she sat me down in front of a mirror and painted my face.

"You're so lucky," Cheryl said. "You have perfect eyebrows and an oval face. You hardly need any makeup at all." She combed my hair, stroked my face, and talked to me about sex. "Do you ever wonder what it will feel like?" she asked. She led me to the living room, and we lay down together on the couch. "Have you ever done this?" she asked, as she touched herself. I told her I had. She kissed me and touched her tongue to mine. "This is practice," she told me, "so you'll know what to do when a man kisses you."

We practiced kissing and stroking each other for several minutes. Then Cheryl brought out a long skinny thing made of rubber that was shaped like a banana. She said, "This will teach us what a penis is like."

So I had my first experience with penetration. I liked the vibrator better, but it was nice having Cheryl there with me, so I pretended to like the rubber banana. She was a dancer, with a beautifully strong and lithe body. As we masturbated together, I watched her. She was too absorbed in her own experience—and masturbated with her eyes closed—but I watched her, and my pleasure grew from sharing hers. That made it almost as good as a vibrator.

That same year my mother started to hate me, and I had to run away. My stepfather discovered psychedelics and the hippie movement, and our life changed. My home became dangerous for me. For the next several years I was either running away or locked up in some institution. I gradually moved through all the juvenile facilities in Southern California until I ended up in California Youth Authority, at Ventura School for Girls. That's where I fell in love and had my first lesbian sexual experience, with two different girls.

The second time I went to Ventura, they put me in the

cottage for special girls, Las Cositas. The first time, they had put me in the cottage for the younger girls, but I was older now, 17. Before being placed in a cottage, we were tested in many ways—IQ tests, psychology tests, and assessment tests. All the girls in Las Cositas were smarter than average, and we had more counselors than the other cottages. And less arguing and fighting went on in our cottage. I don't know if this was because we were smarter or because we had a lot more therapy and staff involvement. Maybe some of it was due to the expectations of the staff—since we were smart girls, they expected us to act better.

On my first day I was scared. Here were 50 girls, all strange to me, in a place I couldn't escape from. The staff might be cruel or kind; I had yet to find out. A woman brought me into the cottage and led me to a desk in the dayroom. Everyone was smoking. (This was before all the bad publicity about smoking, so it wasn't frowned upon as much.) There was a lot of noise. Some girls were watching television. Others were sitting and talking on couches. Several sat at tables, playing cards. There were three women at the desk.

Suddenly, from the floor, a girl stood up. She was tall and thin; she seemed to go on forever as I looked up at her. I was only 5 foot 2 and she was at least 6 feet tall. She had huge green eyes, a mop of curly blond hair, and fair skin. Her fingers were long and elegant. She smiled at me, and in a slow Southern drawl said, "Hi, I'm Melva."

I was mesmerized. I was in love. I was speechless. I felt totally stupid, unable to say even one word, so the woman who had brought me told Melva and the women on staff who I was. Then Melva led me out to the dayroom to meet the others. She claimed, right from the start, that I was hers. "This is my sweetheart," she told everyone, "so nobody better mess with her."

I knew some of the girls there from other places, even a couple from my last time in the younger girls' cottage. But I spent all my time with Melva. My feelings were so strong that I couldn't deal with them at all; I was terrified. I never questioned my feelings for her or asked myself why I loved a woman so much or why men had left me feeling nothing at all. The feelings just existed as a reality of my being. Like many girls there, Melva pretended to be gay. It was the "in" thing to be in an all-girl institution. All the same intrigues that girls were prey to in a normal high school were worked out here without boys. Some girls, of course, really were gay—quite a few, in fact, since in the 1960s girls were actually arrested and locked up for being gay, even for cross-dressing. These were the real butches of the unit, the girls with the most status. Melva pretended to be one of these. But for her it was all an act, and I sensed that what for me was an earth-shattering reality was for her just a way to pass the time. She liked me for my feminine ways, my prettiness, my middle-class background. She wanted public kisses to build up her reputation. She wanted power over me; she wanted to work out her fantasies on me.

"Kiss me, why won't you kiss me?" she'd say to me, and I'd have no answer. Instead I'd run away.

Finally, in frustration at my unwillingness to play along, she gave up. "I found a new lover who likes to kiss me," she said as she embraced a big girl.

I was tormented; I was ashamed that I felt so much.

When Melva entered the room, even if my back were toward her, I felt her heat from across the room. I could smell her whenever she came near me. Once, as I lay in my room (all of us were assigned private rooms), she passed down the hallway on some errand. As I felt her approach, my body heated up. She looked into the small window set in my door, and our eyes met. She opened my door and tossed in an old shirt of hers. "To remind you of me," she smiled, then walked away.

My heart lurched, then pounded wildly. I pulled the shirt to my face and inhaled deeply. The scent of Melva filled me up. My heart burst with the pain of that smell. I had to do something. I searched for the small needle I had in my room to mend my clothes, and when I found it, I brought it and some liquid eyeliner to my bed. I opened my shirt and removed my bra. I stabbed the pin into my left breast until blood leaked out around it. I put the brush in the liquid eyeliner and stroked it over the bloody spot. Gradually, dot by dot, I tattooed Melva's name over my left breast, over my heart. As her name appeared, the pain in my heart lessened. The tattoo was my secret; it named my love and my pain. It helped me to gain control over what I felt, but it wasn't enough.

Girls' rooms occupied two long halls, and there were 25 rooms in each hall. At night I spoke through the cracks in the wall to my neighbors on either side. Sometimes we shared cigarettes, passing a match through the cracks, blowing the smoke out the windows. The girl on my left was named Pat. She was an Aleut Indian from Alaska, the only Aleut I'd ever met. She said she was sent to Ventura because there were no similar places in Alaska.

Pat had trouble sleeping at night. "Sing to me, please. Sing me to sleep," she asked me every night, and I sang old songs I remembered the words to, like "Lemon Tree" and "Patches" and "Angel Baby." One song I've forgotten the title of went like this: "Standing on a mountain looking down on the city / The way I feel is a dog-gone pity / We used to be so happy / When we were in love / High on the mountain of love..." Pat wanted to hear that song over and over.

On the other side, Edmona, an African-American girl from Los Angeles, would yell, "Stupid song! That is a dumb-ass stupid song! Don't you know any *good* songs?" So I'd try to sing something more popular, maybe "Our Day Will Come," for her.

We were pretty far down the hall from the main desk, so the staff mostly didn't bother us. At shower time we'd go in small groups from our rooms to the showers as the staff called out our room numbers. Coming back, some girls had the opportunity to slip into each other's rooms. The girl across from me, Linda, did this often, slipping into the room of the girl next to her, one of the real butches. I was the only one who knew this, because out on the unit they never even spoke to each other. They always looked so smug and happy later, after Linda had managed to slip out and back to her own room. When we were called to line up, Linda would quickly come out of her girlfriend's room first and just step over to her own room door, and then the other one would step out of hers. Linda must have kept some clothes in the other girl's room, as she came out dressed. I watched them do this over and over, as I nursed my own pain.

One day Pat told me she wanted to learn what women did together, what it felt like.

"I can show you," I said. "Let me come to your room after showers."

"Do you know what to do?" Pat asked.

"I know what feels good to me."

"I want someone to go down on me. I heard that feels really good."

"I think I can do that," I said. "I know which part feels good. I know where to rub and all that. I'll come to your room after showers."

I was surprised at myself. I didn't know why it would be easy to do with Pat what I could never do with Melva. I didn't feel much of anything for Pat. I liked her, she was cute, but that was it. No real feelings of passion, no longing or lust, stirred me. I was just curious and I knew I could do it. And Pat wasn't really a lesbian; she just wanted the experience. Still, I was looking forward to the time when I would be in her room and able to touch her.

That afternoon I gave Pat some of my clothes so I could get dressed in her room. She giggled as I handed them to her. Her eyes crinkled into half-moons, and I noticed one of her teeth was just enough crooked to make her smile charming. I let my eyes wander over her body and stop to rest on her nice plump breasts. She blushed and said, "See you later."

I smiled, feeling totally in control. It was a good feeling. Pat went to join her friends and I went to mine. We, like the couple across from my room, never socialized outside of our rooms.

That evening I showered especially well so I'd be nice and fresh for Pat. I walked down the hall toward my room, passed it, and entered Pat's. She was standing near the bed with just her towel covering her. She let it drop. Her breasts were round, full, and firm, and her hips were round too. She was very short, even smaller than I was, and slightly plump, but even so, she curved very nicely. I let my own towel drop. I was thinner than Pat, and my breasts were smaller. But I was proud of my figure, my flat tummy, my round bottom. I knew I was also beautiful—just as she was—but we were different. She was dark and I was fair. Her hair was thick and short, while mine was very long and fine. Her nipples were pink on a background of olive-colored skin.

I moved closer to her and put my arms around her. I leaned down into a kiss, tasting her full lips.

"Do you want to go first or should I?" she asked, a little breathless.

"I don't want you to touch me," I said. I hadn't until that moment realized this was what I would say; I hadn't known I felt that way. "I just want to touch you. I want to do everything, and you just enjoy it."

Pat looked a little uncertain. "Are you sure? You don't want to feel anything?"

"Oh, I'll be OK. This is exactly what I want."

I let my hands explore her body, stroke her skin, move up to cup her breasts. We moved to the bed. I kissed her neck, smelled her scent, and slid my hands down to her breasts; they were soft, so soft. I kissed them and licked her nipples. I heard her gasp. I sucked one, then the other. Pat lay back, abandoned to sensation, softly moaning. I squeezed her breasts as I licked and sucked one and the other, one and the other.

I moved up to kiss her lips again, and she opened her eyes and said, "Oh, you know just what to do. This is so good."

I kissed her again and felt some stir in my own body. My heart was beating a little faster, and my belly was starting to feel tight; my insides throbbed a little, which was all unexpected. I thought I'd just be observing. I had no idea I'd be feeling too.

I went back to her breasts, gave them a nice, long kiss, and buried my face between them. Just for me, this was just for me—this being smothered by her breasts, so wonderful, and so soft. I moved my face lower, licking her belly, kissing her belly button, kissing her nice, soft little belly. I worked my hand down between her legs, spreading them apart, feeling her fuzzy mound, the wetness below, stroking and stroking so that she parted her lips and her legs and let me inside. I moved my face lower and looked at her. This was the first time I'd ever looked at a woman's secret place. It was beautiful. I gathered my energy and looked to see where all the parts were.

Then I zeroed in on her little bump, spread her lips apart, and exposed it. I kissed it and started to lick. I'd never done this before, but I just imagined my own and what would feel the very best. Then I did exactly what I imagined would feel good. I licked and sucked. I moved my mouth around and inserted my tongue inside her and licked there too. It was salty, it was warm, it was delicious. I went back to her button, and as I sucked I inserted a finger into her vagina. I moved up and down, around, back and forth, as I licked and sucked.

Pat moaned and moved with me. She grabbed my hair and pulled, she cried out my name, and she begged me to go faster, then slower, then harder, then softer—and I did all of this. Finally, she shivered all over and became calm, and I softened my sucking, licked a bit more, and stopped with a gentle kiss on her vulva. I raised my head and looked at her. She was smiling at me, her eyes soft and unfocused. "You really do know just what to do," she said.

I smiled back. "I'd better get dressed. They'll call us out soon."

I left soon after and went to stand in front of the door to my room. Linda, across the hall, saw me leave Pat's room and gave me a surprised look, and then a slow, appraising smile. I smiled right back at her, feeling like I was on top of the world. I was very excited, but even though I hadn't reached orgasm, I still felt satisfied knowing I had satisfied Pat. My excitement flowed all through me, warming my body, making me feel as if I glowed.

I went to Pat's room many times and was never caught by the staff, though most of the other girls, including Melva, found out. One day she came to me in the laundry room, angry, and pulled me around to face her. My heart still jumped to her touch, my stomach flipped, and I couldn't breathe.

"I heard you've been fucking Pat," she said. She had two little red spots of color on her cheekbones. "Well, what about it?" she demanded.

Somehow I found my voice. "Yeah, well, so what?" I said.

We stared at each other. She narrowed her eyes, frowning as she stared. Suddenly she smiled. I kept my face stiff, not responding, as I wasn't sure how my face might betray me.

"Son of a bitch," Melva said. "You really are something." Then she laughed, and I risked a small smile. She walked out of the room, laughing, and went to play cards with her friends.

I let out the breath I'd been holding. I wasn't sure what I felt; too many feelings were swirling around inside me. Grief over not ever having Melva. Relief that she would never know how I felt. Triumph that she admired my guts. Love, hopeless love, for her and fear of the tremendous feelings she inspired in me.

Melva left soon after, released home. Pat also left around the same time. And then so did I, and in the crazy psychedelic world of the late 1960s I soon buried my feelings and experiences and went on with my life. I never saw Pat or Melva again. I got married, twice, and had children. I didn't come out until nearly 20 years later. But that's another story.

A PAIGE IN MY LIFE

Maria Morales

I had just been hired to work as ground personnel for Scandinavian Airlines System and was getting trained for my new job. She appeared at the entrance of the conference room wearing a black mid-length trench coat, black pumps, and very sheer hose. Her short, slicked-back hair framed patrician features coolly set off by a pair of dark Ray-Bans. I couldn't breathe, and I couldn't stop looking at her. She suddenly smiled, said hello to the audience, and took long strides toward the front of the room. I stared at her as she passed by, sure she could hear my heart pounding. Up at the front, she exchanged greetings with Lars and Ula, our trainers, and then removed her glasses to reveal warm eyes the color of jade.

She was about 5 foot 10 with a slender build. Her light golden skin radiated with a natural tan. Her pearly white teeth lit up the room when she smiled. She had a very charismatic personality that gained everyone's attention as well as envy. She reminded me of Princess Diana, and I think she knew it. Her hairstylist definitely knew it.

I wasn't sure what was happening to me; this was a totally new feeling. I only knew I had to speak to this woman. How would I get her attention? What would I say? I asked the person next to me if he knew who our visitor was.

"That's Paige. She's the new liaison between SAS and Continental."

Perfect, I thought. I could ask her about Continental's benefits plan. Confidently I stood up and walked over to where she was still chatting with Lars and Ula.

"Hi, my name's Maria," I said, offering my hand.

She just looked at me, her right eyebrow arching up.

"I just heard that you'll be the SAS/CO liaison," I went on. "I just wanted to ask what kind of benefits plan is being offered and when we'll get it. You see, my husband is an independent contractor, and we have to pay an arm and a leg for health insurance, but we need it since we have two small children."

Why was I going on and on?

Paige just stared at me, her clear gaze seeming to take me in all at once. "Don't know," she said and turned back to the trainers.

I felt heat rise up my neck and into my face. I'd blown it. *She hates me,* I thought. I mumbled thanks and went back to my seat, feeling like a puppy scolded by her master. I sat down and leaned my forehead against my fingers, still not believing what an ass I'd made of myself. Suddenly from behind I heard, "You said your name was Maria, right?"

"Yeah," I answered, before I even turned around to find her standing over me.

"You used to work for Eastern, right?"

"Yes, why?"

"I remember you. You sat at the end of the counter on the left side. You had pictures of a little boy all over your desk."

"My son. How'd you know that?" I was starting to get worried.

"I used to work for Eastern too."

"You did?"

"Yeah. I looked a lot different then. I was *fat*!" she grinned.

"Ah..." I didn't know what to say.

There was silence for a moment, then she said, "OK, bye." On her way out she looked back from the doorway and added, "Maria, if you'd like, come by the airport tomorrow around 3 and I'll get those benefits answers for you. Just ask for Paige. Everyone at the airport knows me."

All eyes in the room were on me.

"Uh...OK."

Paige had almost disappeared when I added, maybe a little too loudly, "Wait, where?"

She popped her head back in, smiled slowly, and said, "Terminal B."

The next day I was a nervous wreck. I didn't know what to wear. I wanted to look sexy, but not too much. I wanted to look smart but also alluring. *What the hell is going on?* I thought. *This is a woman!* I finally managed to dress in a short but respectable skirt and a billowy blouse. I dabbed my usual Musk behind my ears and took off for the airport.

When I spotted Paige at the terminal where she'd told me to meet her, my heart pounded. She saw me and waved me over. She'd been talking to some friends, and when I neared them she said, "This is Maria...the one I told you about."

Told them what? I wondered. *What exactly did she tell them?*

"I have your information," Paige said, smiling, her eyes seeming to send out little beams of light. She looked even taller than she had day before. "Have you eaten yet? I thought we'd grab something."

"Sure, OK," I told her.

We'd started walking toward the food court when she was paged over the PA system.

"I'm sorry, I have to take this," Paige said.

Shit, I thought. I consoled myself with some coffee and was just about to leave when I heard someone running toward me from behind.

"Maria, I'm so sorry. Could we have lunch another time?"

"Sure," I said, trying not to sound too disappointed.

That afternoon at the end of training class, Paige stopped by to drop off some papers for Lars. We walked outside together. It was raining, but I had an umbrella. I asked if I could walk her to her car. "Sure," Paige said, "but I need to leave right away." She explained that her parents were coming home from Florida and she wanted to see them.

"Oh, too bad. I was going to ask you to have coffee with me. I know this place that makes the best coffee in the world."

"I'm sorry, I really can't," she said.

"Are you sure? I wouldn't take long. It's a cold night and you have a long ride."

"Thanks, but I really want to see my folks. Maybe next time."

Disappointed again, I started to walk to my car.

"Maria, Maria, wait. How long will it take?" Suddenly, she was next to me again.

"An hour maybe."

"How good is the coffee? You know, coffee is my weakness." She ran her slim fingers through her hair, leaving dark streaks where the rain had fallen.

Paige got in my car, and we went to the diner. Amazingly, we talked until 3 A.M. Not only were Paige's parents waiting, but so was my husband. When I got home, my husband told me he had phoned the police and all the hospitals. I'd never done anything like this before. Little did I know this was just the beginning.

Soon Paige and I were seeing each other every day and speaking on the phone every night. We were always together. My training seminars went on for eight more weeks, and on graduation day, SAS threw us a party and served champagne. Paige and I both drank a little too much.

We went outside to her car to recuperate. We were sitting in the front seat when she turned to me and said, "You are coming dangerously close." This was the first time she had come on to me. Well, we both came on to each other. I grabbed her hand and told her I was a fortune-teller. She revealed to me that her family background was Hungarian, thus explaining her stunning looks. "A self-proclaimed queen of the gypsies," Paige said. "So, little girl," she smiled, "can you see a future with me?" I was titillated even though I wasn't sure what was happening; I was married and had two children. She knew my situation, but this thing between us had developed a life of its own. As I looked at her, all I wanted was to press my body next to hers and plant a big wet one on her. I wondered if she felt the same.

Nothing happened that night, but now the door had been opened. Still, I didn't know what kind of relationship this was.

I was in love with her, but how could this be? I wasn't *gay.* I liked being a girl. I wasn't one of those *dykes,* but I *was* in love with a woman. What would I do? Who would I tell? How would I tell *her*? What about my family? All these questions ran through my mind.

But I *was* in love with her, undeniably, and my days and nights grew unbearable. I was in love for the first time in my life but unable to say anything to anyone. I knew I had to pretend, but for how long?

On the first of May, SAS celebrated their inaugural flight to Scandinavia with a big party, where they served all kinds of food and drink. I got pretty drunk, and Paige was only a little tipsy. Outside it was raining very hard. "Let me drive you home. I can pick you up in the morning," she said, standing very close to me.

"Sounds good," I slurred out

We went to the parking lot. I watched her walk ahead of me to open the driver's side door. Her uniform skirt stretched and pulled across her ass to the rhythm of her walk. All I could think about was kissing her. I realized it was all I'd thought of from the moment I'd first seen her. Would it happen?

We got into her car. She looked at me a moment then made a move to lean over. *Oh, my god. She's going to kiss me,* I thought. In that split second it takes to decide these things, I closed my eyes, grabbed her, and kissed her first. I kissed her like it would be our last kiss ever, because it very well could have been. Then I pulled back to look at her.

"Wow, do you always kiss someone when they try to lock the car door?" she said.

I was mortified. She looked at me and laughed that deep, strong laugh she alone has, the kind that makes everyone want to join in. Then she grabbed me and kissed me back in a way I'd never been kissed before. For the first time in my life I knew the meaning of the expression "you make me wet." The rain began to pour even harder, creating a curtain of water to hide us while we kissed and kissed and kissed.

Up until then it had been enough to be like kids playing with each other, running on the tarmac, playing hide-and-seek on planes, always laughing at something. We both had this quirky sense of humor—so much so that people use to give us funny looks. We really enjoyed each other's company; everyone called us Heckle and Jeckle.

After our night of kissing in her car, I'd flirted with the idea of making love to Paige several times, though I'd never done anything about it. Sometimes I'd look at her and ache with the pain of not having her. She was the most incredibly beautiful woman I'd ever seen. To this day I think her beauty is incomparable. I even indulged in fantasies about making love to her. I'd go over and over every detail in my mind: the smell of her body, her breath on my neck, her licking and sucking my breasts, her hands going over and into my body. I knew how it would be, if only it could happen. I wanted to tell her how I felt. What would she say? Kissing was one thing but sex was another. The one time I had talked about lovemaking and desire with Paige, she had spoken very openly about a man named Anthony who had hurt her very much. She said he had left her for an Italian girl and moved to Italy to be with her. He had broken her heart, and she wasn't in any hurry to be hurt again.

How could I try something after that? What if she got insulted? She might never speak to me again. I couldn't bear the thought. Better to just keep quiet. Just dream…

I'd just about given up hope when Paige asked me one day, "How about going to Tampa with me? "

"What?"

"Tampa, Florida. It's beautiful there! Come on, say yes…my treat."

"Well, I'd love to, but what about my kids?"

"Well, think it over and let me know if you can go."

Oh, my god! Florida! I wanted to go, but how? What

would I tell my husband? Would he believe I had to attend a training seminar in Tampa? Well, he did, and now I was faced with the most difficult aspect of the trip: what to pack.

When the day finally arrived all I thought about was how much I wanted Paige and how much turmoil I was in because I was married and had two children. If she just looked my way, I trembled with desire. Sometimes when she walked near me, I'd smell her perfume and get dizzy. *Tonight I'll be with Paige in Tampa. Tonight,* I thought over and over and over.

Paige and I boarded our flight. We were flying first class on standby status like all good airline employees. We made the flight, but our seats weren't together. This was fine with me, since I was nervous and the excitement was leaving me speechless. Instead I sat next to a button salesman, a sweet guy who calmed me with boring tales of his adventures in fabric.

After we landed in Tampa, Paige rented a red Mustang convertible. I was impressed; she knew just where to go and what to do. We got directions to our hotel from the car rental place, but before we headed there, we decided to get a drink. We stopped at a local pub, outside of which stood a flower stand where Paige bought me a purple iris, my favorite flower. Before we had left for Tampa she'd given me a survey to find out my favorite foods, flowers, colors, scents, etc. Now I was curious what else she had in store.

I wasn't disappointed: The hotel room was a suite with an upstairs and a downstairs, a living room, a full kitchen, and a bath. Paige led me through the kitchen and opened cabinets and the fridge to reveal them stocked with all my favorite foods. "Wait here," she said, then went upstairs. A moment later she called, "Maria!"

"Yes?"

"Come upstairs, please."

As I walked up I saw she had placed candles all over the stairs, and when I turned I saw their glow in the bathroom as well. She stood there waiting, and when she took my hand in hers and kissed it, then looked at me with her beautiful green eyes, I was melting.

"Would you take a shower with me?" she asked.

"Yes!"

Paige's hands trembled as she undid my blouse. The entire time I looked at her, I saw the love and desire she had for me. She took off my bra and softly kissed my breasts, then unzipped my skirt and helped me take it off, gently pulling off my panty hose. As I stood naked and vulnerable I thought, *This is right because I feel no shame, only love for her.* Then Paige looked at me and said, "You are so beautiful. I've wanted you for so long. I'm in love with you." A tear rolled from her eye, and I kissed it, then helped her out of her clothes. The bathroom was steamy from the running shower. When we got in, she took the soap and lathered herself. Then she lathered me with her whole body. We made love in the shower, in the tub, on the floor, and finally on the bed until we were both exhausted and fell asleep tangled together.

The bedroom had large windows that looked out onto the ocean. We had left them open to see the sunrise. We'd also left the TV on, and when we awoke we heard some preacher talking. Paige kissed me and said, "Will you marry me in front of God, the sun, and the sea?"

It was September 15. I'll never forget that date. I said yes, I would marry her in front of God, the sun, and the sea. And in my heart, I did.

Since this experience, I left my husband. Paige and I are no longer together, but I remember her fondly. She introduced me to a wonderful world where I can really be me—I don't have to fake it. I'm now in a loving relationship with a beautiful woman. We've been together seven years, and I appreciate and love her more each passing day. *Thank you sweet P...*

One Night at Lizards

Brenda King

Wendy and I had known each other for two years, ever since ninth grade, when we both were trying out for the soccer team. I was trying out because I had a crush on a senior, Jim Branson, who was a big soccer jock. Wendy was trying out because her brother was a star on the football team and her parents were pressuring her to try out for a sport. But Wendy was clumsy and didn't care about athletics that much, she told me, so she picked the one sport that required the most coordination and that she knew she'd be terrible at. At least her parents would think she had tried to get on a team.

We met each other while we were both benched. It was hard to believe that you could get benched during a *tryout,* but every afternoon it would be just the two of us sitting in the hot sun, watching the other girls on the field. It didn't take long before we were best buds.

It was the mid '80s, and I had just moved from Minneapolis to Madison, Wisconsin, that fall of ninth grade and hadn't made that many friends. I was pretty shy back then, but over time Wendy helped me come out of my shell. We soon discovered we had a lot in common: not making the soccer team, not caring much about school, and listening to hard rock and heavy metal. By the time our junior year rolled around, we were both thinking about dropping out and getting an apartment together, but we knew our parents would never let us.

There were a few underage clubs (16 and over) in town where we could dance to our favorite music—Bon Jovi, Whitesnake, and Poison. (OK, you can laugh, I *told* you it was the '80s!) Wendy and I didn't really have many friends at school because we were what you might call "burnouts." Back when I was in high school they actually had a designated area in the back of the building where students could smoke: It was called the "smoking lounge," and we'd hang out there during lunch and free periods. Hard to believe now, I guess, but this was before it was illegal for minors to smoke. Wendy had blond, teased, shoulder-length hair and wore a lot of lip gloss. She also wore this black jean jacket that she had spray-painted the logo for the band Ratt on. We both thought it was pretty cool. But the other kids didn't. Most of them were either rich snobs, kids they bused in from the south side of town, or drama club geeks. I looked kind of like Wendy's twin, I guess, except I had dyed jet-black hair, and I mostly wore long plaid shirts with black stirrup pants. We were kind of like Romy and Michele from the movie, except with way worse fashion sense.

The other kids had a nickname for us—The Metal Twins (and sometimes The Headbangers)—and they teased us a lot and generally made life pretty miserable for us. But we didn't care that much, since we had each other. And we fit in at the underage clubs, where we made friends with a lot of kids from other schools in the area.

One Friday at school during lunch, Wendy and I were in the smoking lounge, sharing a Camel filter. She was wearing one of her dad's undershirts and some cutoff jean shorts.

"Hey, Brenda, I heard about this new underground club on Saturday nights. It's called Lizards. Wanna go tomorrow night?" Wendy asked, a curl of smoke escaping her lips.

"Man, I wish," I said. "But I'm still grounded for four more days."

"That sucks big time. I'm getting sick of Club 557. All the jocks and snobs are starting to take over. Pretty soon they're going to be playing Wham! or some other gay shit. You should just fuckin' sneak out!"

I took a long drag off the Camel and passed it to Wendy. "Yeah, right. You know how my mom is. Why do you think we call her The Hawk?"

Wendy smiled a devious smile. "I got an idea. Tammy, you know, that redhead chick we met at Hardee's a few weeks ago? She said Lizards doesn't really get hopping until 10 or so. So just tell your mom you're not feeling so hot and pretend like you're going to sleep around 9:30."

"But I'm never sick. She'll know I'm faking," I told her.

"Stop being a wuss. Haven't I taught you better?" Wendy laughed. "I'll grab the ladder from your dad's shed behind your house a little before 10, and you just climb out the window and down the ladder. OK?"

"I don't know..."

"I heard Lizards is doing a Poison tape giveaway."

"All right, all right, I'll do it. But if my mom finds out, I'm dead meat."

All day on Saturday I sat in my room, sick to my stomach because I was so nervous about sneaking out. In fact, I felt so sick that I probably wouldn't have to fake it for my mom that night. I'd gotten grounded a couple of weeks before for staying out too late with Wendy on a school night. At least my mom hadn't smelled the grape Mad Dog 20/20 on my breath when I stumbled in around midnight. If she had, I would have been grounded for the rest of my life. My mom was pretty cool, now that I look back upon that time, but when you're a teenage girl, your mom is *never* cool.

So even though I was scared as hell to sneak out, I still followed Wendy's instructions. I had even taken the screen out of the window in my room earlier that day and shoved it under my bed so I'd save time when Wendy came to get me that night. Luckily, my mom made Salisbury steak for dinner that evening, which to me was and is the nastiest entrée on the planet. So I could pretend I was sick from that. And she *knew* it grossed me out, but she would never let me leave the table until I'd eaten at least half of everything on my plate. I bitched and moaned the whole time, but when she wasn't looking I stuffed half of the steak into a baggie I'd hidden in my pocket. (I did that a lot.) After she excused me, I went into the bathroom and flushed the meat down the toilet, then went into the living room and watched TV for a while with my younger brother Mike.

Around 9 P.M. I started acting all sick, and by the time 9:30 rolled around I was in the bathroom pretending to barf. I even put a hot washcloth on my forehead just to pretend I was feverish from throwing up.

"You'd better go lie down, Brenda," my mom said when I came out of the bathroom. I guess my fake retching was pretty convincing. "Hold on a second..."

Oh, no, she knew I was lying!

"Here, take some of this Pepto-Bismol," she said, opening up the bottle and spooning some of the vile pink stuff into my mouth.

After Salisbury steak, to me Pepto-Bismol is the second nastiest entrée on the planet, but I downed the stuff anyway, since I'd promised Wendy I'd go with her and I truly wanted to convince my mom I wasn't feeling well.

"I think I'll just go to sleep for the night," I told my mom, clutching my stomach.

I went into my room and shut the door, then heard my mom, dad, and brother laughing over some lame-ass sitcom in the living room. They'd watch TV for hours at a time, so I knew my mom wouldn't bother me, especially if I had the light off in my bedroom. I turned out all the lights in my room, except for a small lamp on my dresser, and got ready to go out with Wendy. I had just finished putting on my black eyeliner when I heard a noise outside. I looked out and saw Wendy throwing pebbles at my window to get my attention. She had already propped my dad's ladder up against the house.

"Hey, cute thing!" Wendy half-whispered. "Come on down!"

I grabbed my wallet and shoved it into my back pocket, took a quick glance in the mirror, opened the window, and climbed down.

"Lizards, here we come!" I said, and hugged Wendy,

proud of my small feat but anxious about getting caught sneaking out.

Wendy and I walked around the corner to her beat-up Plymouth, then headed for Lizards, which was just a couple of miles away.

"Cover's 3 bucks," said the burly guy at the door of the club, which was a small converted warehouse.

Wendy pulled out a five and a one and handed it to him. "Tonight's on me," she said. "Since you snuck out and all." She grinned, and for some reason at that moment she'd never looked more beautiful.

Once we got inside the dark club, we immediately knew something was awry. The Smiths were blaring on the speakers, and the crowd wasn't your usual heavy metal bunch. I didn't recognize any of the usual kids from Club 557. Everyone looked pretty New Wave: guys with poufed-up hair and bolo ties, girls with hair dyed orange and pink and blue and wearing all black. There were so many chains and dog collars you'd think it was the city pound.

"I thought this was a heavy metal club," I said to Wendy.

"So did I," she said. "Maybe it's alternative night or something. Oh, well. Might as well stay for a while. It's not like there's anything else to do in this fuckin' town."

"All right. At least it'll be interesting."

Wendy went up to the "bar" (as I said, it was an underage club, so all they sold was soda and snacks) and got us two Diet Cokes and some corn chips. We grabbed a table near the dance floor and watched as kids undulated to Bauhaus and Siouxsie and the Banshees.

"Jesus Christ!" Wendy said. "Look at that guy! Like, could he have any more safety pins in his ears?"

"Yeah, we should go over and pin a note on his ear that says, 'You look retarded!' "

"And what's up with that girl in that scary old-timey

dress? Hel-lo! It's 1985! Go back to the prairie, Laura!"

Wendy and I were cracking up so bad, but when we both looked up, we were speechless. Three feet from our table two chicks were actually *making out.* Now, when you're 17 and living in a small town in the Midwest in 1985, this is a HUGE deal. The only time I had ever seen two girls kissing was in the movie *Personal Best* on Showtime one night when my parents were out and my brother was in the basement playing Atari. I must admit, it kind of turned me on a little, but I never told Wendy about it, since I thought she'd freak out. We always called gay guys "fruits" and lesbians "bulldykes," but I was always just joking around. I didn't know what Wendy's opinions about gay people were, but that's just because I never really thought about it. I knew I liked guys—at least I always had crushes on them; on Jim Branson, for sure—and I knew for a fact that Wendy did, since she was always gushing over this one stoner guy at school, Dan Rudin.

"Oh...my...god!" Wendy and I both said in unison, and right when we did, one of the girls, a tall, skinny chick with a shaved head and black bangs, looked straight at us.

"You got a problem?" she said, and she was all business. "Or did you want to join us?"

The girl she was with, a short redhead with Thompson Twin hair, piped in. "Why don't you go back to your trailer and leave us alone?"

"Um...we...uh...sorry," Wendy stammered. "It's cool, it's cool."

The two girls walked off, hand in hand, to the other side of the club. I was looking out of the corner of my eye at them, trying not to be conspicuous, but Wendy could tell I was watching them.

"What are they doing?" she asked me.

"The tall one has the short one pressed up against the wall," I told her. "They're *totally* going at it! Grinding and everything!"

"Jesus!" Wendy said. "I can't believe no one's hassling them."

"Yeah, except for us. That was pretty lame of us, you know."

"I know—it just took me by surprise, is all."

"You mean, it doesn't make you sick or anything?" I asked her.

"Sick? Hell, no. I mean, we're freaks, right?"

"Yeah, and...?"

"Well, how the hell can we judge them when *we're* judged and made fun of every day at school by the jocks and snobs? Plus, my Uncle Gordon is gay. It's no big deal."

After a few minutes I got up the courage to tell Wendy about how I'd seen *Personal Best* that one time and how it had kind of turned me on. "But no way does that make me like those girls," I said. "It was probably because I hadn't had a boyfriend in a while. You know, some kind of hormonal thing." I laughed to cover up my nervousness, but Wendy looked serious.

"Have you ever thought about kissing a girl?" she asked me.

I was looking down, a little embarrassed about where this was going, but I answered truthfully. "Once I had a dream where I kissed Brooke Shields," I said. "But then she turned into Mel Gibson. Does that count?"

"What do you think it would be like, you know, to make out with a girl? You think it'd be the same as with a guy?"

"I don't know...I mean, I've never really thought about it..." I stammered.

I don't remember exactly how it happened, but the next thing I knew, Wendy had her lips pressed to mine. And man, this wasn't like watching it on TV at all. I was tingling in places I didn't even know I had.

"Wendy!" I pulled away from her. "Someone's gonna see us!"

"And you think anyone would care? Look where we are!" she said.

I looked up and saw two skinny guys in fluorescent suits holding hands. Another glance revealed a rather masculine-looking woman wearing a T-shirt that read I SCREWED YOUR MOM. I'm *not* making this up!

"This place is crawling with gay people!" I said, then cracked up. After a moment I got up the courage to ask Wendy the all-important question: "So, did you like it? You know, the kiss?"

"Yeah…it was…nice." Her lips were turned up at the corners, and she had a really sweet, shy look on her face. "What about you?"

"It was much…softer, you know, than kissing a boy."

"Wanna do it again?" Wendy asked.

I just smiled.

"I've got an idea," she said. "Come on." She grabbed me by the hand and led me through the crowd to the bathroom.

"I don't have to go," I told her.

"That's not why we're here." She grinned and led me into an empty stall, locking the door behind us. "OK, kiss me like you'd kiss Mel Gibson—you know, kind of like a science experiment. Just to see..."

Wendy didn't need to make excuses—I was more than ready to do this. "OK, Road Warrior," I laughed, and placed my lips on Wendy's full mouth. But what began as rather tentative experimentation quickly became something more. The more Wendy and I kissed, the more turned on I got. For a full 15 minutes we made out in that bathroom stall, her tongue feverishly darting in and out of my mouth to travel down my neck and back up again. It felt so good that I didn't even stop to question what was going on. This was my friend, I loved her, and if I was going to make out with a girl, I couldn't think of a better choice than Wendy. Her slim body pressed against my more curvaceous one, and she rubbed her thigh up against my crotch. At one point she even started to put her hand down my pants, but I told her I wasn't ready for that.

"It's OK," she said. "It can wait."

When a couple of girls started screaming about needing to use the toilet, we got ourselves together and left the stall. We still looked disheveled, though, and Wendy's lipstick was smeared across her face.

Whaddya know: It was the two girls we'd seen making out.

"Heh, heh," the tall one said.

"Guess the trailer will be rockin' tonight," the short one laughed.

Needless to say, Wendy and I were totally embarrassed, but it was kind of funny too, and I felt proud for some reason—like having those girls see us like that kind of made up for how we'd reacted to them earlier.

"Thanks for the lesson," Wendy said to the tall one, and then we bolted out the door and out of the club, laughing the entire time.

When we got to Wendy's car and were heading home, I turned to her. "Hey, how the hell did you know where the bathroom was? You dragged me there like you'd been to that club a hundred times."

"I have," she smiled, and grabbed my hand.

So, yeah, my mom did find out that I'd snuck out that night (she came to check in on me around 11 and found me missing), and I did get grounded for another two weeks. But it was all worth it. Wendy opened up a whole new world for me. She later told me that she'd never really had crushes on guys, that she'd made up her crush on Dan Rudin just so I wouldn't suspect anything. She also told me she'd had a crush on me since ninth grade and that she'd actually gotten benched during soccer tryouts *on purpose* so she could get to know me. Wow.

I know it sounds weird—me not really having any lesbian tendencies and then all of a sudden making out with my best friend. But it happened. And what happened after that was even weirder: Wendy and I dated for the next year and a half, until we both started college. I ended up going to a two-year community college and then transferring to the University of Wisconsin in Madison, where I got a computer science degree, and Wendy got a soccer scholarship to a big school on the West Coast. She joined our high school team her senior year, and she was *incredible,* the league's highest scorer and the team's MVP. Our parting was sad, but we both knew it couldn't last forever, so we decided to cut our losses and move on with our lives. Today Wendy and I are still the best of friends, and we both live in Milwaukee. She works in telecommunications and has a partner, Julie, of eight years. They also have a three-year-old son, Jake. I'm bisexual and date fairly regularly, but I still haven't found "the one." But thanks to Wendy and that first night we kissed, I always keep my options open and I know enough to never, ever take anything or anyone at face value. Thank you, Wendy, for that one night at Lizards...and the lifelong friendship that followed.

My 25th Birthday
Carol Demech

Her touches took my breath away. Her softness gently caressing my hot, smooth skin made me delirious with pleasure. She slid her taut breasts across my aching body as she made her way to the heat between my legs. I arched my hips to be closer to her tongue as it slow-danced on my... The bedroom door flew open, and there stood Suzanne's senile grandmother, Nana.

She pointed her finger at Gerry and me and screamed, "Suzanne, wake up, wake up! There's a bear on the floor! There's a bear on the floor!"

I pushed at Gerry's shoulders, whispering for her to stop. She never did.

Suzanne sat up in bed and yelled, "Nana, close the door and go back to bed. That's not a bear on the floor. It's Carol and Gerry, and they are bare!"

Terry and Judy looked over at me and smiled. What else could I do? It was my 25th birthday and my first time with a woman. I closed my eyes and let Gerry's tongue take me to nirvana.

I suppose I should take you back to the beginning. A coworker had temporarily moved in with me to get away from an abusive boyfriend. One night he followed her to my home and began to threaten her. I called the police and he was taken to the station house. She refused to press charges, and the next day she moved into her parents' house. The boyfriend now began to harass me. I wanted to move someplace where he couldn't find me.

My friend Barbara and her husband, Joe, told me that three of their friends lived in a beautiful 14-room farmhouse and were looking for another roommate. The house was a mile from the main road, on 40 acres of land. Barbara said she would introduce me to her friends but that there was one other thing I should know: They were lesbians. No problem; I had no fear of lesbians. It was 1972, and I was a 24-year-old liberated woman on the pill. I had literally burned my bra.

The next evening I went to dinner at the farmhouse and met the three women, Judy, Terry, and Monica. The house was magnificent, and I had a wonderful time. Two weeks later I moved in. The farm was definitely a woman's world, where only certain men were allowed access. One of those men was John, their previous roommate. I met him a few days after I moved in, and we began sleeping together. He was a nice guy, and he tried, but he wasn't the world's greatest lover.

I had gone back to college part-time and was taking a women's studies course that put me more in touch with my womanhood. I stopped seeing John and began to spend more time with the farm women and their friends. The women showed a gentle, loving, caring intimacy toward each other. It didn't matter to them that I was straight. They shared their time and wonderful loving energy with me. The farm was a warm oasis, and each evening various women would come and hang out. We'd have wonderful discussions, get high, listen to music, and laugh. A frequent visitor was a woman named Gerry. I liked her right away; she was intelligent and a lot of fun.

I was surprised when Gerry asked if I would consider going out with her. I thought it might be interesting. After all, I was a free spirit, a veteran of Woodstock, and open to experimenting. Besides, she had a lover, so it would be just sex, no attachments. And anyway I was straight; how involved could I get? Gerry and I began to hang out a lot. The more time we spent together, the more I liked her. She was easy and comfortable to be around.

It was the time of sex, drugs, and rock 'n' roll, and there was a party every weekend at the farm. Everything and anything happened. I was mesmerized when I watched women kiss and slow-dance with each other. They moved in a sensuous, sexy rhythm—unlike the straight couples, where the men were groping and pawing. When the women's bodies touched there was no vulgarity in their movements—only subtle gestures, gentle motions; they were slow and dreamy and very erotic.

At one of the parties, Gerry asked me to slow-dance. I reminded her that I was straight. She just smiled, put her arms around me, and pressed her body against mine as she led me around the dance floor. She rubbed her breasts against mine, instantly making my nipples hard. A tremor of heat shot through me. I closed my eyes for a moment and moved with her body, forgetting that I was dancing with a woman. Opening my eyes, I pulled away and continued to slow-dance with her but with a space between us. When the dance ended, my nipples were still hard. I quickly sat down and crossed my legs, only to be made aware of the wetness between them.

Later that night, Gerry asked me to go for a walk in the fields. It was a clear, beautiful night with a full moon. We stopped to rest and lay next to each other in the tall grass as we gazed at the stars. We talked about our lives and laughed at each other's stories. We pretended we were on the beach and that the bright moon was the warm, soothing sun. We stroked the grass as if it were sand and listened to the sound of the ocean's waves. I was sure that the Big Dipper tipped slightly and sprinkled us with stardust. Gerry said it was pollen. We both rolled over on our sides, laughing.

There I was facing her. I was afraid to look into her eyes, sure she'd know I wanted to kiss her. She stroked my arm, causing a tremor of delicious sensations to run through my body. This time I didn't think about being straight; I just wanted to be close to her. We began to kiss passionately. Every cell in my body was awakened to intense currents of desire that urged me to move closer.

With each kiss, I melted into her, my heart pounding, my breath quickening, my moans asking for more. She pulled open the snaps on my denim shirt, exposing my breasts to the gentle touch of her hands. My nipples were standing up, waiting for her lips to satisfy their need.

Gerry whispered in my ear, "I want you."

Oh, how I wanted her. My body was taken over by hunger and desire. The wetness between my legs had soaked through my jeans. She stroked the inside of my thighs, and I gasped as a wave of pleasure swept over me.

My clit was erect and swollen, pushing against my tight jeans, desperately aching to welcome her. She moved her mouth to my breasts. Her lips and tongue captured my rock-hard nipples, and I surrendered. I wanted to make love to her in that field. I wanted us naked so that I could caress every inch of her with my body. I wanted her on top of me, under me, inside me. I wanted to be on top of her, under her, inside her.

I quickly unzipped her pants and began to pull her T-shirt over her head when we heard women talking. We pulled apart, and I snapped up my denim shirt. Then Gerry pulled her T-shirt down and we went back to the party. I was unsteady on my feet, still filled with desire. I wasn't sure what was happening. I wasn't a lesbian. Why was my body responding so powerfully to a woman? I convinced myself that it was just sex and that every woman would respond the same way. For the rest of the evening I avoided Gerry.

A few days later, Judy and Terry asked me to go with them to their friend Suzanne's house. Judy and I had birthdays that were a week apart, and we were going to plan a huge party. The night before my birthday, I drove the three of us to Suzanne's house. Gerry answered the door. It was the first time I'd seen her since the party. She smiled and gave me a hug, her chest lightly brushing across my breasts. Her erect nipples made my body shudder. I pulled away and walked into the kitchen to gain my composure, but I found it difficult to focus on the party preparations. Every time I looked at Gerry, my thoughts drifted to that night in the field.

Just after midnight, as we were preparing to leave, Gerry

asked if I could give her a ride home. When we neared the car, Judy noticed that the right rear tire was flat. I opened the trunk to find it completely empty, no spare and no jack. It was too late to call anyone for help, so we all stayed at Suzanne's. Judy, Terry, and Suzanne slept in Suzanne's bed. Gerry and I slept on the floor, facing the door, on the other side of the room.

I lay there, in only my panties, on my side, with my back to her. I couldn't sleep, but I was afraid that if I turned over, I'd lose all control as I had in the field. I felt the heat from her body and heard her breathing. I moved my foot slightly and brushed her leg. Her hands began a slow descent from my shoulders to the top of my ass, barely touching me. My body involuntarily moved to the graceful dance of her fingers. I rolled over on my back, and her fingers slid down to my stomach, fingertips under my panties, combing my damp hair. I turned my head toward her and was swept away by a flood of hot kisses.

I ripped off my panties and pulled her on top of me. Her cunt dripped its wetness over my body. The softness of her skin was intoxicating. I was drunk with desire. We rubbed, pushed, and ground our bodies into each other, trying to be as quiet as possible. I strained to be closer to her. As she slid one finger into me, my hips rose, inviting more of her hand to enter me. Four fingers easily slid into my hot, oozing cunt. Her fingers pushed farther into me.

"Are you sure you want to do this?" she whispered.

"Yes, yes."

My cunt gripped her fingers, wanting more.

Gerry whispered "Not yet" and withdrew her hand.

I groaned in protest. Her hand stroked my face. Still holding the scent of me, her wet fingers traced the outline of my lips. One by one she slid her fingers into my mouth, and I tasted myself for the first time. Instinctively, I wanted to give her pleasure. I rolled her on her back and climbed on top of her, covering her mouth with kisses. As my mouth cupped her breasts, my tongue glided around her nipples, teasing their hardness. Her wet, fiery cunt pressed against my leg.

Flames of desire overcame us, and for hours we explored each other's bodies. I was on the edge, ready to come, Gerry's tongue massaging my clit, when Nana flung open the bedroom door. That was 28 years ago. I've never had a birthday quite like that one, but a few have come close. Gerry and I tried to see each other as much as we could, but she had a girlfriend and I was bisexual—yes, I was now convinced I was bisexual. Gerry moved West with a new girlfriend, and I moved to New York and fell in love with a beautiful, charming Southerner who never made me doubt for a second that I was a lesbian.

RUMORS

C. Alex

A tropical island surrounded by beautiful white sand, coconut-laden palm trees swaying in the breeze, warm turquoise water, and a guarantee that the warm Caribbean sun will shine on you—this was how the travel brochures advertised many of the Virgin Islands when I was growing up. *A romantic getaway.* When I was a teenager living there, well, it was another story altogether. Walking down the street was an exercise in patience, particularly if you were fortunate enough to be a member of a prominent family. If anyone saw or heard anything unusual, you could bet your family would know about it almost instantly. Too much fun in the sun could lead to idleness, as it was called. Parents made sure they found constructive things for their kids to do.

My folks tried to get me into the ballet/musical instrument thing, but I was addicted to softball and no doubt a tomboy at heart. To me, playing the game was as necessary as breathing. Each game was a direct challenge to my athletic ability and put me in touch with my body. I couldn't wait for the ball to cross home plate so I could feel the satisfaction and power of hitting it into the outfield or out of the ballpark every so often. During my senior year, in addition to playing softball for my high school team, I also played fast-pitch and slow-pitch women's league softball.

If you were a rookie, the key to playing women's league softball was finding a team that wasn't the best; that way you wouldn't have to spend too much time keeping the bench warm and would get a chance to perfect your game.

My mother, a very refined woman, had her objections. She didn't want me in the company of butches, especially since I was 17, technically still a minor, and very impressionable. She never said this outright, being a good Christian woman and living by the words "If you don't have anything nice to say, don't say anything at all." But she gave me little hints, such as, "Those women are much older than you and have a lot more life experience." Now, what kind of reasoning was that? It only made me more curious.

Even though I thought I had a glimmer of an idea of what a butch or a dyke was, I never put the pieces together. Actually, I didn't have a clue, and none of the dictionaries or encyclopedias really clarified what a lesbian was, except that it involved two women. Besides, all I really wanted to do was play softball. My mother finally gave in when she realized I was very serious, and it didn't hurt when my softball coach told her I had enough potential to eventually play at a professional level.

At school, I'd heard whisperings on and off about one of my 10th-grade teammates, who supposedly had been caught behind the gymnasium with another girl who was in the mechanics shop program. After that, everyone at school treated them like outcasts, except me. I spoke to everybody.

My interaction with the women's team, the Rockets, was more than I could have hoped for. I saw these women lovers up close and found out that these women were just that—women. Unfortunately, the word around was that I was jailbait, so they stayed away from me even though my body made me appear more than legal.

Women between 16 and 50 of all occupations played in this league, but not all of them were lesbians. Some were married, a few played both sides of the fence, and more than a few were strictly into other women. This concept was new to me, but I took it in stride and had plenty of opportunities to observe all the goings-on.

By my second year playing grown-up softball, my game improved and I was no longer a minor, plus I'd started college. I'd come of age during the winter season, so I was officially on the market. First base was where I performed best. Sometimes I played second, but regardless of my position, I always warmed up with the third base player, Tommy. She was the best third basewoman in the league, and she wasn't bad-looking either. While we were warming up at our first practice of the season, she started talking to me. I was surprised because Tommy, who was 22, hadn't said more than a couple words to me during my first year, but now she was chatting me up. She intrigued me, especially since she was the kind of woman people in normal society considered ungodly. I could only imagine what lesbians did with each other behind closed doors, and I was very inquisitive.

From my first day with the team, I'd taken an interest in Tommy. She was the second woman I'd had a serious crush on. Diane, a drummer in my concert band class, was my first, but I shied away from her because I didn't know any girls who had crushes on other girls. Plus, at the time, she was a senior and I was a lowly freshman.

Tommy was a strong-looking woman whose skin was the color of dark butterscotch, and the shape of her eyes gave the impression that she had some Asian blood flowing through her veins. When a ball came her way she moved with the grace of a dancer, and her muscles rippled when she intercepted any ball that penetrated her area of the field. My hand stung from the force of her throw when she hurled the ball at me, and every time I looked at her my heart fluttered.

After two weeks of brief conversations and running warm-up laps together, Tommy and I learned that we had a friend in common, Callie, whom I'd known since junior high. She was one of those slim, dark-skinned, fine-featured girls all the boys wanted for their girlfriend, plus she was a pretty good artist. We were also in the same college trigonometry class that semester. One day Callie told me that Tommy had been talking about a woman she had a crush on, but Callie didn't have a clue that it was me, because Tommy always referred to me as the "young girl" on her team.

When I heard this, I freaked out. I couldn't believe another woman would like me like that and that Tommy had been scoping me out since I was in high school. From that point on, Tommy was always on my mind. I couldn't sleep, eat, or function. What was I going to do?

At the next softball practice I avoided Tommy like the plague, only because I didn't know what to say to her. I tried not to make any eye contact, but how could I avoid her? We were warm-up partners. It's one thing to like someone, but what happens when she likes you too? It makes for an extremely uncomfortable situation, and the fact that I'd had no sexual experience at all, much less with a woman, didn't help.

Another love of mine back then was video games, and the arcade was my favorite hangout. One day, shortly after my shocking discovery, I ventured into a new video arcade, and who do you think the manager was? Tommy. I couldn't believe it. Then I realized I needed to approach her to get tokens to play Millipede, my favorite game. I wondered if I should just run out the door instead. But before I could make a hasty exit, Tommy spotted me. I felt myself blushing, and I wasn't thinking clearly. All I knew was that this woman had the hots for me and I didn't know what to do and I didn't want to look like a wimp, so I boldly walked up to her and said in a shaky voice, "Five dollars worth of tokens, please."

Tommy smiled at me, and as she was about to hand me the tokens she said quietly, "Would you like go to the movies with me?"

"Like on a date?" I asked calmly, not believing my ears. I wanted to appear cool, like this happened to me every day, but deep down I was quivering with excitement.

Tommy nodded her head while her strong fingers gently touched mine as she gave me the tokens.

"Sure," I told her more confidently.

Now our infatuation was mutual, and we were going on a date. Tommy didn't even take my $5 bill for the tokens. Instead she wrote her phone number on the palm of my hand and told me to call her that night.

Later, while I was playing Ms. Pac-Man, Tommy brushed against me, making me shiver in anticipation. Every now and then while I manipulated the controls, I'd glance around to see where Tommy was. I was so nervous that each time I played the game, Ms. Pac-Man got gobbled up and I lost all my tokens. That had never happened to me before. When I left the arcade I had Tommy's number imprinted in my mind.

Ten-thirty couldn't come soon enough. That's when Tommy told me she'd be home. She lived with her grandmother, whom, I might add, did not approve of her granddaughter taking up with women, so Tommy wanted to make sure her grandmother didn't have a chance to answer the phone when I called.

I was anxious, because I didn't know what to talk about or how the conversation would go, yet I couldn't wait to talk to her. When I made the call, at 10:31, she picked up on the first ring. Our first real conversation off the softball field was sheer ecstasy. I'd never been so excited in all of my 18 years.

I asked Tommy how she knew she was a lesbian and what I'd done to attract her attention. I wanted to know everything she could tell me, because I'd always felt an attraction to other women but I'd never had anyone to talk to about it. I couldn't imagine going to my mother or grandmother and saying, "Hey, I like another girl. Do you have any advice?" Yeah, right.

"I've always liked women," she replied. "And to your second question, I like the way you move and carry yourself." Tommy also told me about her girlfriend, Sharky Connors, who had gone away to college, but she said they'd been incommunicado for some time. I was incredulous. Sharky had been in my concert band class and had a reputation for being easy—but with guys, lots of guys. Tommy then revealed to me other girls in my graduating class who were also lovers of women. My head was spinning from all this information. I couldn't believe it.

Through the night we spoke of all sorts of things, talking

until the sun peeked over the horizon. The realization that I had to go to class, and that she had to get ready for work, hit us. Tommy and I decided we'd go to the movies Saturday night.

"When we see each other from now on, we have to be careful," Tommy said. "I don't want anyone saying nasty things about you or hurting your feelings. People can be terrible, and this is your first experience with a woman."

"I'll try to remember that," I said hesitantly.

I recall sitting in trig class trying to resist the urge to give Tommy a call and futilely attempting to keep my mind on the lesson. Callie was in my class, and of course, being the young women we were, I had to tell her about the previous evening's happenings. So a few minutes after class began, I slipped out and went to the bathroom, where I met Callie. This was our regular place of gossip as well as our refuge from our boring math class. Seeing the crazy smile on my face, Callie asked slyly, "So what happened?"

I blushed as I related some of our conversation to her. I also asked her why she didn't tell me Tommy had a girlfriend. "I would have," Callie said. "but Tommy asked me not to. She wanted to tell you herself."

"I don't know what to do, Callie. I really like her."

"Just don't rush into anything. You know people are gossipmongers."

"Well, I'll have a lot to tell you, because we're going to the movies Saturday night," I said, bubbling over with excitement.

Callie and I both erupted into what my mother would describe as wanton laughing. That night I had softball practice, and the entire day everything moved in slow motion. Six-thirty took its time coming, and I couldn't wait to see Tommy. My walk to the softball field gave me a chance to put my feelings in check.

On the way to practice, I was deep in thought about my affections, so I didn't notice or speak to anyone. All I could think about was Tommy and what people would say—especially my family—when they found out I had a certain fondness for another woman. Perhaps they'd disinherit me, but that's the price you pay for living on a small island where everyone is related to everyone else or your mother or cousin is well-known. You get my drift.

When I got to the ball field, two other players were suiting up. I said "Hey," which got me a nod, but then I was ignored. After a while one of the coaches pulled up with a van full of my teammates. Tommy was the last to exit. As she approached the dugout, I watched her while pretending to tie the strings on my cleats. She walked with such practiced smoothness, her bronze skin reflecting the setting sun. Tommy was definitely, no denying it, an amazon.

Suddenly it dawned on me that I found the female shape attractive and I'd never even thought about it. All of Tommy's curves and imagined softness begged me to reach out and touch her. My mother had kept me and my brothers so busy that we didn't have time to ponder sex, much less sexuality. But being with women certainly had its advantages—like not having to worry about getting pregnant.

By the time Tommy was ready to run her lap, I'd already been around the field once, but since we were used to running together, I ran an extra lap. Between breaths we didn't say much, but her closeness felt good.

Practice was distracting, as it took my mind off Tommy for a few hours. Not one ball got past me. My coordination was shaping up, and I was on top of my game. We were getting ready for the start of the season, and diversions would not do.

Our team training continued, and Tommy and I had our nightly talks and got very little sleep. I had to concentrate on school, plus my game, and when I had free time, Tommy.

One night that week after practice—but before our date—Tommy and I were in my mother's car, and she leaned over and kissed me. Before we knew it we had our tongues in each other's mouths. I happened to glance up as two of our teammates passed by, catching us in a serious lip lock. Tommy was more embarrassed than I was. This was our first kiss, and all I could think about was being consumed by this 22-year-old woman, but all she could think about was how we'd be ostracized. Thus, the gossip began.

At home in bed that night, I all I thought about was Tommy's warm lips on mine, the wetness of my underwear after our kiss, and the way my nipples wanted to be touched; still, the intimacy hadn't been right. I had to show Tommy the way I wanted to be kissed. That was one thing I enjoyed doing with the boys I'd gone out with. I liked the way they got all excited after I French-kissed them. Of course, they got pissed when I wouldn't put out, but they were good practice for me.

That Saturday, in preparation for our date, I scrubbed my skin thoroughly with a loofah. I wanted to really impress this woman. You know, show her how good I looked outside of a softball uniform. After my bath, I rubbed myself with cocoa butter until my skin shone, then combed back my thick curly hair. Poison was my choice of perfume—a subtle fragrance with a powerful kick. The creases in my black jeans were starched straight. I threw on a white tank top, over which I wore a denim shirt. Black soft-sided loafers completed the look. I was ready for Tommy, but was she ready for me?

I drove my mother's car to the recently built four-screen theater. As I pulled into the parking lot, I saw Tommy dressed to the teeth, sitting on a low wall. She looked great in her tight blue jeans, which showed off her muscular thighs, and wore a coral short-sleeved polo that complemented the shape of her strong arms. I was elated just looking at her. She saw me and waved.

Before I got out of the car, I spotted a couple of people I knew from high school. I greeted them and tried to keep the conversation short before they could ask me who I was all dressed up for. I didn't tell them, but they watched as I walked over to Tommy. In my mind I could hear their tattling and could only imagine what they were saying. At that point I didn't really care what they said as long as it didn't get back to my family, but I knew that later, through the island grapevine, it would. I decided not to worry about what the future would bring.

Tommy had purchased the tickets before I arrived, so we just walked inside and were admitted. Her strong cologne wasted no time reaching my nose. It was very masculine, and whatever its creator hoped it would do, it was working. Polo, Tommy called it. I knew I'd go home with Polo absorbed into all my pores.

During the movie, Tommy held my hand and gently stroked it from time to time, but at no point did she let go. I couldn't watch the movie because all I could think about was Tommy and what she would possibly do to me and with me. After the movie we grabbed a pizza, and then in my mother's car we headed over to a popular necking spot. A beautiful moon illuminated the bay below, which Francis Drake had passed through 300 years before, but all I had eyes for that night was Tommy. I couldn't even tell you if other people were parked there.

Sitting in the dark, listening to Luther Vandross, we enjoyed small talk until I reached over, found Tommy's lips, and kissed her like she'd never been kissed. She put her hand on my left breast and caressed my nipple with her thumb.

Briefly I pulled back, at which point Tommy looked into my eyes and said, "For a virgin, you really know how to turn a girl on." My panties were soaked and I was Play-Doh in her hands. But suddenly she decided it was time for me to take her home because she didn't want my first time to be in a car. Needless to say, I was a bit disappointed, but I realized she was an honorable woman who wouldn't take advantage of my excited state.

The drive to her home was very quiet; we just listened to the radio. When we arrived at the parking lot of her apartment complex, she said good night, gave me a brief kiss, and told me to call her when I got home.

Driving home, I contemplated what had happened and whether I'd continue on my way to hell by becoming involved with this woman, but I knew I couldn't stay away from her. I knew if I hung in there, better things were to come.

I didn't see Tommy again until our first game the following Tuesday, but we were in constant communication. Neither of us could get enough of the other, and since we couldn't physically be together, the phone had to do.

Our team was scheduled to play in the first game of the season, and we were ready. Two games were played a night, one at 7:30 and the other at 9. The stadium was packed, the lights were bright as day, and vendors were doing brisk business with hot dogs and drinks. The freshly mowed grass tickled the nose, and the diamond was newly chalked and ready for action.

As we took to the field in our maroon-and-yellow polyester uniforms, the noise level grew to a thunder. Our team was pumped up with excitement; we were up against last year's champs, and they were good. Personal rivalries existed between players on both teams. This became clear in the third inning of our first game, when Tommy ran at top speed to third base, slid, and slammed into the third basewoman.

According to the murmurs, the third base player had had an affair with one of Tommy's ex-girlfriends. Obviously, bad feelings still lingered, because a few punches were exchanged before the umpires could intervene. Both players received warnings.

By the sixth inning, the tension in the stadium was solid as concrete. The score was 4–4, and a lot of shoving and pushing went on between the ballplayers. I even got away with whamming into the second base player after I'd hit a line drive between shortstop and third base. If I hadn't bumped her, I would have been called out, since she had the ball in her glove and was standing on the base waiting for me. Not a smart move. When I ran into her, she dropped the ball, and the umpire called "Safe!" The fans in the stands were going wild—some for me, some against—and she was really ticked off.

After I stood up from my dirt bath, the second basewoman shoved me hard, making my head snap backward, but I knew I was wrong, so I didn't push back. The pressure was too great and the score too close to risk being thrown out of the game. Had it been under different circumstances, there would have been a fight.

At the bottom of the last inning, we were up to bat. Tommy was first up, and we needed only one run to win. The score was 7–7. Our coaches were giving all kinds of last-minute advice and signals—not that anyone was really listening. But we had to settle down or our enthusiasm could very easily lose us the game.

In the dugout, I used the very close quarters to my advantage by slightly brushing my breasts across Tommy's back as I passed her on my way to the bench. My nipples were so hard that I had no doubt she felt them through our polyester uniforms. She turned around slightly and gave me half a smile. The environment was so edgy that no one noticed our intimate exchange.

The other team took their positions and threw the ball around the infield until Tommy stepped up to the plate. As she check-swung her bat, I yelled, "Hit it out of the park!" But the first pitch was a ball, and Tommy held her ground and didn't swing.

Everyone in the dugout anxiously awaited the next pitch. On the next throw, Tommy swung. Her form was good, but she didn't follow through with the bat, so the ball hit the foul line. The next pitch, however, signaled the end of the game, as Tommy hit it into the parking lot. Our team ran onto the field, surrounded Tommy, and shouted at the top of our lungs. We had beaten last year's champs in the first game of the season! This was a good omen. We were flying high.

After the game, our team—along with about half the stadium—headed to the beach to celebrate. The calm glass-like black sea reflected the many stars above. While everyone was distracted with our team's win and busy eating and drinking, Tommy and I slipped off hand in hand to the other side of the beach. A gentle trade wind caressed our bodies as we stripped out of our hot and dirty uniforms and ran into the warm Caribbean Sea, where we hugged and touched each other.

The tropical water encircled and aroused us as Tommy's expert hands slowly probed and roamed my fully awakened body. Her fingers slid between my thighs and gently stroked my clitoris. I was lost in her embrace and the feel of the warm water and her body touching mine. Distantly, I heard the waves lapping gently at the seashore, but I didn't interrupt her passionate exploration.

The salt air mingled with Tommy' s scent and stirred new emotions in me. My mind couldn't keep up with all the sensations running wildly through my body, so I just gave into the feelings. Under the cover of darkness, I held onto Tommy and forgot where I was—but not who I was with.

Tommy's tongue teased my erect nipples as she licked them slowly. With tenderness and patience, Tommy loved me all over and took me into womanhood. For the next few days all I thought about was her, the huge hickey on my neck was a reminder of my first night of desire.

The few months we stayed together were difficult sometimes, because we could only show our true feelings in private and I was still learning the nuances of living two lives. Our team went on to win the championship that year, but Tommy left me at the end of the season. Talk was that she had heard from her ex-girlfriend. Who says rumors are groundless? People usually know when something's going on.

I dropped out of college to join the U.S. Coast Guard and left island living behind. My mother and family eventually found out about my wayward activities, but not from me. They chose to put another skeleton in the family closet and pretend that someday I'd grow up and marry a guy. Yeah, right.

Coming Out at 58

Ruth Malcolm

I guess 58 is a little old to be coming out. I mean, I should know better, right? Why rock the boat? I'd had a good life as well as a long, happy marriage—until my husband, Will, had died of prostate cancer two years before, at the age of 61. I'd never imagined he would die so young. For some reason I always thought I'd go first—probably because I was a smoker. Yeah, I should have known better about that too, but I was down to four cigarettes a day, so I figured that wouldn't kill me. But loneliness might.

I had retired from the nursing profession when I was 55, and I tried to keep myself busy. I have a beautiful home in upstate New York, and I worked in my yard every day during the spring and summer. My grown daughters, Jamie and Laura, would come over and visit a couple of times a week, and I had a few good friends, so I wasn't terribly lonely—except at night; nights could get pretty bad sometimes. It'd just be me and the TV almost every night for two years. Is this what my entire life had culminated to?

My coming out didn't exactly take me by surprise. As far back as I could remember, I'd look at a beautiful woman sometimes and my insides would turn to goo. But I'd never acted on it. How could I? I was raised to be a proper young woman and was afraid of living my life outside the box. Times were different back then, I suppose. I remember having the most painful crush on a girl on the track team in high school. I know if I'd just had the courage to tell her I loved her, it would have been reciprocated. Her name was Eileen, and she was tall, blond, and athletic; a little rough around the edges—I guess what you'd call a tomboy. But I was too nervous to say anything; it was the 1950s, and I'd always let the boy do all the work. What did I know about courting a girl? And I had a nagging thought in the back of my head that I'd go to hell if I did anything anyway. We weren't raised in a very religious home, but that huge Bible in the bookcase in the den seemed to glare at me every time I went in there. So dating girls was *not* an option for me.

Flash ahead 40-some-odd years later to June 1997. I was in the front yard doing some weeding, and all of a sudden I heard a voice: "Your roses are spectacular."

I looked up and saw a stunning woman around my age, maybe a few years younger. She had golden brown hair pulled away from her face and was wearing tan slacks and a crisp white long-sleeved shirt. At her side was a frisky cocker spaniel.

"Thanks," I said, getting up and wiping my hands on my old blue sweats. I went over to introduce myself. "Do you live in the neighborhood? I haven't seen you around."

"I just moved in a few weeks ago, over on Larrabee, and every day I walk by your yard because it's the most beautiful one in the entire neighborhood. I'm Liza Amos," she said, extending her hand. "And this little guy is Henry." She pointed to her dog, who was sniffing my pant leg.

"I'm Ruth Malcolm," I told her. "Nice to meet you."

Liza and I chatted for a while, and I learned that she was from Chicago, but she'd just moved to New York after retiring from a 25-year career in advertising. She was single, but she had some family here and wanted to get away from life in the big city.

Liza asked to see the rest of my yard, and I led her and Henry into the backyard to show her my vegetable garden. When she saw it, her eyes practically jumped out of her head. I had about 400 square feet of fenced-off land filled with zucchini, cucumbers, okra, lettuce, spinach, green and red peppers, herbs, and four kinds of tomatoes. I guess it was a bit much, but I love gardening, and I always give whatever I grow to my neighbors and daughters.

"This is incredible," she smiled, and when she did, I saw

that her teeth were perfectly white and straight. She must have come from a good family—or paid through the nose for some high-quality dental work. Whatever the case, her smile was lovely.

"Would you like to take some of these vegetables home with you?" I asked.

"Oh, that's all right," Liza said. "I don't want to be a bother."

"It's no problem. I've got more here than I could ever eat myself. Let me go inside and get you a grocery sack."

I was about to head for the house when Liza gently grabbed my arm. "Tell you what," she said, "I'll only take some of it if you'll come over for dinner tonight. That way we'll be even. And you can sample the exquisite fare I'll make from your homegrown goodies."

"It's a deal," I smiled, and went inside to get the bag.

What the hell has come over me? I thought that evening as I was getting ready to go over to Liza's. I was acting like a giddy teenager. I put on a black rayon blouse, a pair of taupe slacks, and some dressy loafers. My short dark brown hair, which I'd been dyeing for the past six or seven years, had a significant amount of gray in it, but it was too late to get the Clairol out; besides, it would be pretty obvious if I came over that night with hair two shades darker. I've always kept in shape by working in my yard and jogging a few times a week; still, I was no spring chicken. Would she even be interested in me? Is that what I wanted? *Stop, it, Ruth,* I told myself. *It's just dinner. Nothing more.* Even so, I dabbed a few drops of my favorite perfume, Trésor by Lancôme, behind my ears and on my wrists, and made myself up perfectly. I looked in my full-length mirror in my bedroom: For a 58-year-old woman, I was pretty hot stuff!

Liza lived about five blocks away, and it was a nice summer evening, so a little before 7 o'clock I walked over there. That afternoon I'd picked up a good bottle of chardonnay to bring along. As I approached the address she'd given me, I admired her well-manicured lawn and the two magnolia trees in the front yard. The house was a fairly large brick two-story with a curving path that led to the front door. Nervously I rang the bell.

"Right on time," Liza said when she opened the door and let me in.

"This is for you. To thank you for your hospitality." I handed her the bottle of wine.

"Well, that's what neighbors are for, right?" Liza smiled.

She led me into the living room, taking my purse as she did, and immediately upon entering I was flabbergasted by the number of gorgeous watercolors that hung on her walls.

"These paintings are magnificent," I said. "Are they all by the same artist?"

"You're looking at her," Liza grinned. "I've been painting since I was a teenager."

"Do you sell any of them?"

"I've had a few shows, but I was so busy in Chicago with my career that I gave that up years ago."

"That's a shame," I said.

"Oh, I still paint. But more for myself than anything else."

That evening we enjoyed a magnificent dinner of linguini with roasted red pepper sauce, sautéed zucchini, a spinach salad, and olivata crostini. Her adorable dog Henry sat at her feet patiently the entire time; it was clear he loved Liza dearly. Liza and I had an instant rapport, and our conversation was amazing: She told me about how she had lived in Paris for five years when she was in her 20s (she mentioned she was 53 now) and studied art. I told her about my marriage to Will and all the crazy adventures he used to take me on. He and I had done everything from cave exploration to searching for diamonds in Arkansas. I told her that now that he was gone, I really missed doing those kinds of things; my friends weren't that adventurous. After dinner we went into the living room for coffee and dessert.

"Well, I'm game," she said as she handed me a cup of delicious-smelling coffee and a slice of chocolate mocha cheesecake. "I'd love to go on an adventure with you."

"Really? I've always wanted to jump out of a plane," I laughed.

"I did that a few years ago," Liza said. "On my 50th birthday. It was absolutely incredible. It made me feel really alive."

"Would you ever do it again?" I asked. "Maybe with me?"

"I'd love to. Oh, I forgot the cream. I'll be back in a minute."

Liza went into the kitchen, and I got up to peruse her bookshelves. She had an eclectic mix of art, literature, history, and science books. She also had what looked like a small romance collection. I pulled out a copy of a book called *Curious Wine.* The front read "The Best Selling Lesbian Novel of All Time." So my instincts *had* been correct—which both frightened and excited me.

Just then, Liza came back with the cream for our coffee and caught me red-handed. "Oh, have you read that?" she asked. "It's wonderful."

"Um, no...I haven't," I said. "I mostly read mysteries."

"Well, I have a sizable mystery collection. Maybe you'd like to borrow something." She came over to the bookcases where I stood and pulled out a copy of book with two women embracing on the cover. "Oh, this isn't the one I was thinking of." She put it back on the shelf and pulled out another book. "Here. Claire McNab. She's terrific."

I read the jacket copy: a lesbian mystery. Did Liza know more about me than even I did? I wasn't ready to label myself anything. But I did know that I was painfully, overwhelmingly attracted to her.

"Listen, Liza," I said, "I don't know what you're thinking about me, but I'm still coming to terms with what I'm feeling—you know, about women... I mean, how could you tell, anyway?"

Liza smiled and looked me in the eyes for a moment before she spoke. "Honey, when you've been gay your whole life, you can just tell. You knew about me right away, didn't you?"

"Well, yes, I guess so," I told her.

"So there you go," Liza laughed. "It's obvious there's some kind of attraction between us, right?"

I gulped, but then answered, "Yes."

"So why don't we just go slow and play it by ear?"

"Or we could just kiss right now and get the hard part out of the way," I said. I'd only had two glasses of wine that night, but maybe it had gone straight to my head. Even so, I've always been a fairly direct person, so I usually just said what came to mind.

"That can be arranged." Liza led me by the hand to the couch. "Now, we want to do this right, yes? So I suggest *you* lead. I don't want to be the vulture attacking the prey," she laughed. "Here, kiss me." She tapped her bottom lip with her index finger.

Well, my days of waiting for the other person to make the first move were over, because I planted the biggest, longest, sexiest kiss on Liza I could muster. It was slow and sweet but filled with passion—and it sent the blood flowing through my whole body. I hadn't been with anyone since Will had died, and this feeling was like a friend coming back after a long vacation—except it was more thrilling than kissing any man had been. Just like jumping out of a plane had made Liza feel alive, this was making me feel more alive than I'd felt my entire life.

"That was the hard part?" Liza smiled.

"I guess I was wrong," I laughed. "It was actually very easy, especially with someone as beautiful as you."

That night Liza and I stayed up talking until 3 in the morning. I couldn't remember staying up that late since I was in my 20s. We talked about how I'd had crushes on women my whole life, we talked about my marriage and how hard it had been sometimes to suppress who I really was, we talked about how difficult it was being single when all your friends are married or coupled up.

Over the next few months, Liza and I grew very close, eventually entering a sexual relationship—which was beyond anything I'd imagined possible; she certainly showed me there's more than one way to make love. She's tender, caring, funny, smart—just plain amazing—and has helped me to feel proud of who I am. She even got me to finally quit smoking *and* helped me come out to my daughters. I had sweated about it for weeks, even though they'd never expressed any negative feelings about lesbians or gay men; I'd raised them better than that. But finally I sat them both down at my kitchen table and told them. I didn't get the reaction I'd expected.

"All right!" Jamie said. "Mom's a lesbian!"

Laura looked at me with a mischievous smile. "Yeah, how cool is that? I guess this is one adventure Dad *couldn't* take you on!"

About a year into our relationship, Liza sold her home, and she and her dog Henry moved in with me; she stayed over almost every night anyway. On our second anniversary, she surprised me by taking me on a plane ride—one that we both jumped out of! As Liza said, it really does make you feel more alive—but not more alive than *she* makes me feel. Nothing could do that.

So, it took me 58 years to come out. I just wish I had another 58 to spend with Liza. She is my heart and soul, and has helped me finally be the woman I was destined to be.

Shivers

Donna Rhodes

I didn't marry right out of high school. I waited. I wasn't pregnant, and I had no fear of being alone. I married Phil because I loved him—his sense of humor, his unusual sense of style, the little poems he'd leave taped to the milk carton in the morning, his foot rubs. We were both 25 years old, two years out of graduate school with matching master's degrees (his in philosophy, mine in literature), and we decided we loved each other enough to spend the rest of our lives together. At that time in my life I valued domestic compatibility over the "shivers" of immature infatuation and lust.

Our mutual friend Jay was one of the two readers during our wedding ceremony. He was "out" to us but didn't feel comfortable bringing his boyfriend to our Catholic service. This was 1983, after all, dead-smack in the dry center of the Reagan years. So instead he brought his friend Ally.

Every now and again you meet someone who changes your life with the subtlest of movements. A touch, a look, a word. When Ally shook my hand in the receiving line, I felt like leaving the reception and going for coffee with her. Leaving my husband for coffee with this intense-looking woman. She gave me shivers. It was such a strange and sudden feeling that I shook it off, grabbed my husband's hand, and immediately addressed the next person in line.

Throughout the reception I caught glimpses of her, but whenever I tried to walk over and start up a conversation, I was intercepted—relatives, pictures, congratulations, bouquet-throwing. Finally, just before the party broke up, I found a few minutes to sit at the table where she and Jay were chatting.

Ally stood just over 5 foot 6 and had short brown hair that was curly on top. Tan and athletic-looking. Strong cheekbones and soft lips. She was brilliant, articulate, witty, and unassuming. I, of course, didn't attribute my attraction to her as a *lesbian* thing, just an odd feeling. An urgent friendship.

A month after my husband and I were married, Jay called to say he'd found the perfect job, building computer programs for a new start-up company in Boston. He was leaving in three weeks, he said. Would we come to his going-away party?

"Sure!" I told him, guilty that the first thing that popped into my mind was not sadness about Jay's move but excitement about seeing Ally again. I quickly began planning the engaging topics I could bring up to show off my intellect—contemporary fiction or French film?

Two days later I found myself knee-deep in a pile of clothes dubbed either too boring or too flashy or too typical. "Honey, you look fine. Now come on." My husband had been waiting for 30 minutes while I rummaged through my closet. "It's just a Mexican restaurant. No need for dress-code concerns. Jay and tacos—that's it."

"Yeah…yeah, I know. But what about the scarf? Does this green match my eyes? If it doesn't, I could look jaundiced."

"It's just the boys," Phil said. "Come on."

"There'll be some ladies there—Ally, for one."

"No, she can't come. She's visiting her mother in Baltimore. And Jane's sick. So it's just the boys in their T-shirts and my wife in her silk scarves."

Thankfully, Phil didn't notice my sudden mood change as we trudged off to the party. I was now sporting the face of a girl whose friend was moving away.

Three years passed until Jay came back to town to visit. He called and invited us out for drinks. "It'll be a small group so I can talk to all my close friends—just you two, Johnson, Bill, and Ally."

Then I felt it again, those same shivers.

I loved my husband. I did. He was my best friend. But he didn't give me shivers. Never had. But should you base a relationship on shivers?

After another wardrobe drama, Phil and I finally left. We

spotted Jay right after we walked in the bar; he was the one with the big straw hat and a T-shirt that said JULIE, YOUR CRUISING DIRECTOR.

"I've missed you guys so much!" Jay hugged us both until I was nearly bruised.

"Hey, big guy! Watch the grip!" I laughed.

Jay backed away. "I don't know my own strength since I've become a gym boy." He flexed his biceps, then shuffled us over to the table with its glorious pitcher of margaritas. "I got the Monster Margaritas. I didn't think you'd mind."

He poured while I breathed deeply, grateful we'd arrived before Ally had so I could pull myself together. I sucked half my margarita down before Jay had finished pouring for the rest of the crew. "Thirsty, sister?"

Ally was late. I wasn't relaxing; I was just getting more nervous and drunk—a potentially fatal combination.

Finally, an hour later, she showed up...looking fabulous. Faded blue jeans, baseball cap, black sunglasses. "Ally!" Jay nearly jumped across the bar.

"Do you guys remember Ally?" he asked. "She was my wedding date back when I took the ladies where I should have taken the boys. Back in my *cowardly* days."

"Oh, stop." Ally swatted him. "Remember, that was also back in the days when I took boys where I should have taken the ladies. And I don't like people calling me a coward, even if it's true."

Where I should have taken the ladies... My heart did a mambo.

"Yes, I remember you. Hi," Phil said. "Sit down."

"Hi, Ally." I smiled as she took a seat next to mine.

Not five minutes passed before we were deep in a conversation about politics and card games and magic and recipes. The boys went off to play pool, leaving us to the pitcher and each other.

I cringed every time she referred to Phil as my husband

and finally asked her to call him by his name. "Did I offend you? Are you having some sort of trouble?" she asked.

"Oh, no, no. We're just more *open* than 'husband and wife,' " I lied. The tequila was definitely going to my head.

"Hmm..."

About two hours later Ally and I walked off to the store across the street for cigarettes and gum, leaving the boys to finish, as they called it, their Foosball Death Match. Ally grabbed my hand and pulled me across the street. We were both sloppy drunk, laughing and bumping into parked cars, lighting the filters of our cigarettes, acting like high school girls.

"I like you," she said, a little too loud. "I haven't done this in years!"

"Done what?"

"Drink like a fish, smoke like a criminal, and think the thoughts of—"

"Of what?" I stopped her near the Metro bench outside the store.

"Of a...teenager."

"It's been so long," I teased her. "What do teenagers think of?"

"Hopefully not married women!" Ally blurted. Her faced flushed red. "Oh shit, I am so sorry. That was so inappropriate. I'm so sorry..."

Then I did what I'd never done before. I pulled her shoulders toward me and kissed her. It was fast at first, then it melted into us. We slowly came together in the middle of the sidewalk, oblivious to the pedestrians and the buses and the boys in the bar across the street.

Ally felt warm and inviting. Real and imagined. She felt like the present, past, and future all rolled into one.

Then I thought, *Why shouldn't a relationship be based on shivers?*

In Bed

Angela Brown

Tonight we are wrapped together
like hair ribbons, tangling like pieces
of tether, our bodies so close
they are strangling all light in the room
and I breathe what air you give.

Tonight I know I could never die,
covering you like bees, loving to live.

Tonight is a lovers' dance: You seduce
and I reach out and you move away
and this wild goose chase is like a smile
of love, our toes playing like children
in the street, and you are saying
only nonsense, a victim of this heat wave.

Now is when I need to say I love you,
to tell you your skin is what matters.
Filled with greed, I want to eat you up,
eat your grin and your laughter and your
kisses. Your hair dances like a family of snakes,
snakes that smirk beneath their hisses.

Now the sun finally rises on you and me.